Readers love A

Artistic Appeal
"Mr. Grey's amazing storytelling ability captured this reader's attention from the first word and kept me enthralled with the story and the characters within the book until the very last word."
—Night Owl Reviews

Artistic Pursuits
"…settle in for one entertaining ride."
—Love Romances and More

A Troubled Range
"This is one book that I won't forget and you shouldn't miss it."
—Fallen Angels Reviews

Helping of Love
"This story, like the others in the series, is a well-written, feel-good story that I will be reading again."
—Literary Nymphs Reviews

Legal Tender
"Buy the book and have an engaging, enjoyable day of reading."
—Randy's Book Bag Reviews

Legal Artistry
"…a mix of old-fashioned romance and European flavour."
—Elisa Rolle Reviews and Ramblings

A Foreign Range
"If you are looking for a quick romantic read about some emotionally guarded but hunky cowboys then saddle up and take a ride on the Range series."
—Guilty Indulgences

Kathleen
Love is a fight.
win!!

Andrew Grey

THE
FIGHT
WITHIN

ANDREW GREY

Dreamspinner Press

Published by
Dreamspinner Press
5032 Capital Circle SW
Ste 2, PMB# 279
Tallahassee, FL 32305-7886
USA
http://www.dreamspinnerpress.com/

The Fight Within
Copyright © 2013 by Andrew Grey

Cover Art by Anne Cain
annecain.art@gmail.com

ISBN: 978-1-62380-400-8
Digital ISBN: 978-1-62380-401-5

Printed in the United States of America
First Edition
March 2013

To all of America's native peoples

CHAPTER

ONE

"SO, BRYCE, are you excited about this weekend?" Jerry, Bryce's boss, asked with a knowing grin that turned into a warm laugh. Jerry owned the small consulting firm where Bryce worked, and was a close friend. Bryce often thought his friends were as excited about the upcoming event as he was.

Bryce could hardly sit still. "Yes. I'm all set. The caterers are ready. The florist has been contacted four times and they finally understand what I want." Bryce looked up from his computer screen, temporarily giving up on trying to debug the program he was working on. It wasn't going to happen until he could concentrate, and he couldn't do that as long as he was thinking about Percy and his wedding. "Will you and John still help decorate the hall Saturday morning?" Bryce asked, and he saw Jerry roll his eyes.

"You've asked us eight times. Just relax. Everything will be just fine. You and Percy have done a great job organizing everything," John, Jerry's stunning Native American partner, said from the desk next to his. Thankfully they weren't on a particular deadline, or Jerry would crack the proverbial whip and get them all back to work. "Even the weather seems to be cooperating. The television said that it was supposed to be seventy-five and sunny on Saturday. The flowers are all blooming right now, so it should be a perfect day for an outdoor ceremony."

"Yeah," Bryce said with a grin. "It's going to be perfect." Everyone had told him he was crazy for planning an outdoor wedding in May. The weather was too changeable and uncertain, but Bryce had insisted, and he'd been prepared to order a tent if necessary, but the gardens they were using should be perfect. He had compromised and agreed to hold the reception inside, but it was important to him to hold the ceremony outside. His parents had held their wedding outside, as had his grandparents, so he very much wanted to carry on the tradition.

"You and Percy deserve it," Jerry said before his head disappeared behind his monitor and the clicking of the keyboard replaced the sound of his voice. John did the same, and Bryce forced his mind away from his wedding and onto the program.

"Got you, ya bugger," Bryce murmured as he spotted the error and corrected it, then ran the program to make sure it worked properly. Jerry was a stickler for details, so Bryce went through the specifications in detail, checking off each requirement before flagging the program as completed and moving on to the next one.

The work slowly consumed Bryce's thoughts and attention the way it always did. Code and numbers—they spoke to him. When Jerry had hired both John and him three years earlier, Bryce had been fresh out of college and very green. Jerry had taken them both under his wing, and now he could see the improvement and felt complete confidence in his work. Bryce worked straight on until lunch, and then they all broke and went inside.

Jerry had converted an old workshop into an office, which worked great for all of them. Jerry had been talking lately about hiring another associate, but there wasn't room, and Bryce was beginning to wonder where he was planning to seat them. At lunch, they went into Jerry's house and ate at his kitchen table. Bryce had asked him once why they didn't eat at their desks. "We all need a break and a change of scenery," Jerry had said, so this had become their routine. "I'm going to close the office tomorrow," Jerry told them once they'd sat at the table. "It'll give you an extra day for last-minute preparations, and I have a feeling that none of us will be up to working, anyway."

"You don't have to, Jerry," Bryce said.

"Think of it as an additional wedding present. The kids are home from school, too, some sort of in-service day, so they'll be able to help. Mato and Ichante are going to love helping their Uncle Bryce."

He couldn't stop smiling whenever he heard that. John and Jerry had adopted John's niece Ichante and his nephew Mato. Those two were incredibly special kids, and Bryce loved that they called both Percy and him uncle. It made them feel like part of the family. "Thanks. I was trying to figure out how I was going to get all the last-minute stuff done without working until midnight."

"Don't worry—we're all here for you," John said, and Bryce saw Jerry nod his agreement. "When does Percy get home?"

Bryce humphed softly. "I have to pick him up at six." Bryce took a bite of his sandwich and then set it back on the plate. "I can't believe he had to go to New York the week before our wedding."

"It was training for work, you know that," Jerry soothed.

"I know, and he couldn't help it, but that doesn't mean I have to like it," Bryce groused lightly before returning to his lunch, running over all the things he had yet to get done. The list seemed to grow longer every day, and Bryce had no idea how he was going to get everything done.

"Stop worrying. Everything will be great. You've got everything under control, so relax and enjoy it," John said, patting Bryce's hand lightly. "If you don't take it easy, the entire day will fly by and you won't even remember it. So what if the flowers aren't perfect and the chairs aren't in the exact position you want? You're sharing your love with Percy, and that's what's important." Bryce agreed with him, but the nerves didn't settle and that damned list kept running through his head.

They finished lunch and Bryce went back to work, the coding the one thing that seemed to soothe him. Late in the afternoon, Mato and Ichante got home from school, and they hurried into the office to say hello. They hugged Jerry and John before giving Bryce hugs too. Then they told John about their day. Or that's what Bryce thought they were doing, since they were speaking the Lakota language. John felt it important that both children have as close a link to their heritage as they could. Bryce had seen everything John and Jerry had gone through to get Mato and Ichante out of the state childcare system, and it was amazing how normal and well-adjusted the kids were now, considering how hurt and scared they'd been when John first brought them home.

"The office is going to be closed tomorrow, so would you two like to help get the guest favors ready?" Bryce asked.

"*Ai*," they both said happily. Bryce knew that was the Lakota word for "yes."

A short while later, the workday ended, and Bryce got ready to leave. He had errands to run, so after saying good-bye, he got in his car and drove to the tuxedo shop to pick up the clothes he and Percy would wear. Then he stopped by the printer and picked up the programs for the ceremony. After checking the time as he left the shop, Bryce placed the programs in the trunk and was about to head to the airport when his phone rang. It was Jerry.

"Can you come back to the house?"

"I need to get to the airport to pick up Percy," Bryce explained as he unlocked the car and slid into the seat.

"You'll have plenty of time to stop by here. It's right on your way," Jerry said insistently.

"Okay, I'm on my way," Bryce said and closed the phone, setting it on the seat next to him. He and Percy had made a mix CD of all their favorite songs. They were going to put a copy at each place at dinner. Bryce slid one of the CDs into the player and drove to Jerry's as "I'll Have To Say I Love You In A Song" played through the car speakers. This had been one of Percy's choices, and it always made him smile because Percy had sung that song to him when he'd told Bryce he loved him. Percy was nearly tone-deaf, but his rendition of this song was the most beautiful one Bryce had ever heard.

Thankfully, Sioux Falls was not very large, and Bryce pulled onto Jerry's street a few minutes later. He kept checking the dashboard clock and knew he could only spend a few minutes at Jerry's before he had to dash out to the airport.

Bryce parked out front and raced up the door before going right inside. In the living room, he saw John and Jerry each holding one of

4

the kids, who had obviously been crying. "What happened? Is there something wrong with the kids?" Jerry shook his head, and Bryce saw tears running down his friend's face.

"You're Bryce Morton?"

He turned and saw the police officer for the first time. Bryce nodded, his mouth going dry, and he instantly began to shake. Mato slid off Jerry's lap, and Jerry guided Bryce toward a chair. Bryce sat and looked up at the officer who said, "I'm very sorry to have to tell you this, but Percival Howland was involved in an accident at Midway Airport."

Jerry hugged him and so did Mato. "Is he okay? Do I need to get there to be with him?"

The police officer's expression changed, becoming even graver. "I'm sorry, but Mr. Howland didn't survive."

Bryce shook his head. "It can't be. Percy... my Percy is dead?" The officer nodded once. Bryce swallowed and tried to get ahold of himself. This was surreal, and suddenly he felt as though he were floating outside his body. "How did he die?"

"The investigation is still underway, but from the information we were given, a driver lost control of a loaded luggage cart and barreled into people who were walking onto the tarmac to board the commuter flight to Sioux Falls. I don't know if it was a mechanical issue or not, but two other people were injured."

Bryce nodded and looked down at the floor. Percy was gone. Bryce's head throbbed and the room began to spin. He grabbed the arm of the chair, but that didn't do any good. The room continued moving. Bryce clamped his eyes closed, and the last thing he remembered was falling forward.

He didn't know how long he was out, but when he came to, he was on the sofa with paramedics hovering over him. At first he couldn't figure out why they were there, but then everything came back to him. Bryce opened his mouth, but nothing came. He gasped for breath and then heard a banshee from hell scream at the top of its lungs. It took him a few seconds to realize he'd made that sound.

"Please try to calm down, sir," one of the paramedics said, but Bryce couldn't. Tears welled in his eyes and he opened his mouth to breathe, only to whimper. As Ichante took his hand, the last of Bryce's control burst like Hoover Dam, and he wailed and cried. A lamentation went up from somewhere else in the room, followed by another and then another.

"What are they doing?" the paramedic asked.

"Guiding Percy's soul to the afterlife," Bryce heard Jerry say, and then he too joined in the howling.

Then the room became quiet except for Bryce's tears and those of the children. Ichante curled next to him on the sofa, hugging him, and Bryce continued crying. "Should we take him in?" one of the paramedics asked, and Bryce rolled his head on the sofa cushion. He didn't want to go anywhere, except maybe someplace where he could die like Percy. With every breath he took, his heart broke a little more. The tears continued coming, and he couldn't stop them even when he did try.

"We're here for you," John said softly, but the words barely registered for Bryce. Everything from outside his head seemed muffled and distant.

"I'm very sorry for your loss," the police officer said, and Bryce watched as he walked over to him. He pressed a card into Bryce's hand. "If there's anything we can do, please give us a call."

Bryce mumbled something, but for the life of him he didn't know what it was. Through watery eyes, he saw the officer leave as well as the paramedics. Then, slowly, he began sitting up. Mato and Ichante sat on either side of him. "What do I do?" His mind was barely functioning, and he was supposed to get married in two days. "Oh God," Bryce wailed, putting his hands over his face.

Eventually the tears stopped, but the shocked and bewildered feelings continued, like his mind refused to work at all. "It's going to be okay," Ichante said from next to him, and Bryce smiled at the twelve-year-old, trying to make her feel better.

"I have to call everyone and let them know…," Bryce said before breaking into quiet sobs. He had no idea how he was going to be able to call everyone and tell them that Percy had been killed. He couldn't. There was no way. He'd never make it through all those calls.

"Don't worry," Jerry told him. "I'll go over to your place and get your computer. John and I can make the calls. You stay where you are and don't worry about anything." Jerry seemed to spring into action, and he was soon gone. John and the kids sat with him, but no one said anything, which was fine with Bryce. He couldn't deal with talking.

"Why did the police come here?" Bryce asked quietly.

"The number they had for you was wrong and they called your work and I said you were on your way," John explained, and Bryce nodded blankly, only half hearing what was being said.

"Percy was really cool," Ichante eventually offered. "At school last year, he came into my class and told everyone what it was like to be a guy nurse."

"He got me a stefoscope so I could listen to my heart," Mato said and slipped off the sofa. Bryce heard him run upstairs and then he came back down with the stethoscope around his neck. "I wanna be a nurse like Uncle Percy when I grow up."

Bryce tugged Mato to him and began crying again as he held the boy. How could his Percy be gone? He was too kind and caring and certainly didn't deserve to die alone out on some airport tarmac. "I'm going to miss him so much," Bryce said. Percy had loved him deeply, Bryce knew that, and now it seemed part of the light had gone from his life. "How can I keep going without him?"

No one answered, not that Bryce expected anyone to. There was nothing anyone could do. His phone rang, and he fished it out of his pocket and handed it to John without looking at who was calling. He couldn't bear to start the phone chain that would let everyone know that Percy was gone. Maybe if they didn't know, then he'd be around for just a little bit longer.

"Bryce, it's your mother," John said as he gave him the phone. "I don't think she knows," he added in a whisper.

"What happened?" his mother asked.

"Percy's dead," was all he could say before breaking into sobs once again. John took the phone, and Bryce heard him talking briefly to his mother before hanging up.

"They're on their way over," John told him, and Bryce got himself under control. Jerry returned, and Bryce's parents showed up a short while later. There were more tears and hugs, and then tears again, before everyone else sat down and began making calls. He heard Jerry, John, and his mother and dad tell people that Percy was dead. They cried, and Bryce was sure he heard every platitude people said when they didn't know what to say. After a while, Bryce couldn't take it any longer and blankly left the house. He wandered up and down the sidewalk, wondering what his sweet Percy could have done to deserve this. He sat on the curb, watching as the sun set.

"Come inside," he heard his mother say from behind him, but Bryce shook his head. "There's nothing you can do out here."

"There's nothing I can do at all. We were supposed to get married in two days. Percy loved me enough to put up with all my arrangements and plans." Bryce turned as his mother sat down next to him.

"I can't tell you I know how you feel right now, because I don't and I never can. You've lost someone very dear to you, and the only way I could feel what you are right now would be if I lost your father or you." She took his hand, and Bryce squeezed lightly. "I do know that the next few days are going to be very difficult." Bryce nodded slowly. He had no doubt about that. "Your father and I want you to come home with us for a few days."

Bryce shook his head. "No, Mom, I'm going to go home." He needed to be where he could feel Percy close to him, and their small house was just the place he needed to be. They'd bought it together a year ago. "I need to." She nodded and didn't argue with him. Bryce leaned against her and closed his eyes, letting his mother comfort him. "I already miss him, Mom, and he's only been dead a few hours."

"I know, honey, I know," his mother said and just sat next to him.

As darkness began to surround them, they walked back to the house. The chill of the evening air worked through Bryce's clothes, but he barely noticed it. Inside, he quickly warmed, and John helped him into a chair. "We called everyone and got in touch with the caterer, florist, and photographer. They all send their condolences," John said.

"I called the gardens and the reception hall, so I think we have that covered," Jerry said, and Bryce nodded as blankly as he felt.

"Thank you."

"Do you want to stay here tonight?" Jerry asked.

Bryce shook his head. "I'm going home."

"At least let one of us take you," Jerry said, and Bryce agreed. He said good-bye to his mother and father, who promised they'd be over to see him in the morning. After hugs and more tears, they left and Jerry drove him across town. "Do you want me to go in with you?"

Bryce stared at the dark house and shook his head. "I'll call tomorrow," Bryce said, closing the car door. He saw Jerry nod, but the car didn't move. Bryce slowly walked to the front door and let himself inside. After closing the door behind him, Bryce turned on the light. Nothing was physically different, yet nothing felt the same. Bryce wandered from room to room, remembering. Eventually, unable to take anymore, Bryce ended up on the sofa, curled into a ball as he cried his eyes out.

Bryce lost all track of time, but eventually he got up off the sofa and climbed the stairs. In their room, he stood staring at the bed. Percy's pillow lay in its place, and Bryce lifted it to his nose, inhaling his scent. Unable to actually lie down, not in their bed, anyway, Bryce carried the pillow back down the stairs. He lay on the sofa, pulled the throw over him, and hugged Percy's pillow to his chest. Eventually he cried himself to sleep, wondering how his life was ever going to be the same.

CHAPTER
TWO

BRYCE woke and rolled over toward the nightstand. Percy smiled back at him from a picture frame. Over the past year, Bryce had found he coped better if he saw Percy first thing in the morning. "I love you," Bryce said, the way he always did before getting out of bed. He knew it was probably a little odd to still be telling a picture of his dead lover that he loved him, and maybe it was, but it was how Bryce felt. Even after a year, he still needed to feel close to Percy. After shuffling to the bathroom, Bryce cleaned up and did his business before returning to his bedroom to get dressed.

The doorbell rang as he was pulling on his shoes. After tying them, he hurried down the stairs and opened the door. John, Jerry, and the two kids smiled at him from the front porch. "I thought you were leaving for the reservation this morning," Bryce said, motioning them inside.

"We are and we want you to come with us," John said in a calming tone.

Bryce shook his head. He didn't want to go anywhere. For the past year, he'd spent much of his time when he wasn't working alone at home. "Maybe next time."

"That's what you said last time, Uncle Bryce," Mato told him, his arms crossed over his chest. The kid was the spitting image of his uncle and even acted like him sometimes. "Grandma's going to cook, and she asked that you come for a visit."

"Please tell your grandma that I'll think about coming next time," Bryce said, knowing he probably wouldn't then, either. He wasn't ready to see a lot of people.

"Why don't you two go out back and see if Bryce has any new little fish in his pond?" Jerry told the kids, and they nodded, hurrying through the house and then out the back door. Percy had raised koi, and consequently he'd added a pond to the backyard and landscaped around it. Bryce kept the backyard just the way Percy had planted it. "Bryce, we're worried about you," Jerry said once the kids were gone. "You rarely leave the house except when you're working."

"Do you have any complaints about my work?" Bryce snapped, more harshly than he meant.

"No. This isn't about work. This is about you." Jerry sighed and looked around the room. "Your house is like a shrine to Percy. You haven't changed anything. If I go upstairs I bet I'll find his clothes still in his closet."

Bryce knew Jerry was right. He'd been able to get rid of very little. He'd known for a while that it was past time, but he couldn't bring himself to do it.

"We know you've had a rough time of it, and we care about you." Jerry moved closer, touching his shoulder lightly. "You need some time around people, and at the reservation you can help others."

"I don't know if I can," Bryce said, the grief welling up once again. That was the hard part. The grief and loss seemed to come back to him when he least expected it. There were times when he expected to feel it, like on the anniversary of when they met or on Percy's birthday. But once, he'd gone to the pet store to get some food for the fish, and as he passed the large pool where they kept the koi for sale, he'd stopped and stood there, crying. He remembered Percy standing in the same place, telling the salesperson exactly which fish he wanted and then waiting for him to catch that particular fish. Bryce had watched all this, and when they finally had the fish in the bag, Percy had given it to Bryce.

"I know it's hard, but you need to try to get on with your life," Jerry said. "We know you've been through more than anyone should have to go through, but isn't it time to move on?"

"But...."

"I'm not saying you should find someone to replace Percy, but it's time you got out of the house, and a change of scenery will do you good. We could really use your help. We're teaching a couple of computer classes this weekend, and one of John's relatives needs help with a new roof. You'll be busy."

Bryce found himself nodding slowly, unable to fight them any longer. Besides, maybe they were right and he did need to get away. It certainly couldn't hurt. "Okay," Bryce agreed. "Let me pack some things."

Both Jerry and John smiled, and Bryce turned to climb the stairs. Bryce went to his room and pulled a suitcase from under the bed. He did his best not to think about it, because he knew it was Percy's. He packed underwear, socks, shirts, jeans, and an extra pair of shoes. Before closing the suitcase, he placed the framed photograph of Percy between two pairs of jeans and then closed the suitcase. Last, he grabbed a jacket, then descended the stairs.

"I'll put this in the van," John said, taking the suitcase. "The kids have fed the fish for you."

Bryce nodded and began locking up the house. Once the house was secure, Bryce climbed in the backseat next to Mato, and they were off.

"I'm glad you're coming with us," Mato said, looking up at him from the center of the seat, an open book on his lap.

Bryce smiled at him. "What are you reading?"

"It's a bunch of Native American legends," Mato said with a grin before turning his attention back to the book.

Bryce wasn't really in the mood to talk much, so he simply stared out the window as Jerry guided the van through the city and then onto the freeway. They picked up speed and began their trek across the state.

"Have you heard anything from Percy's family lately?" John asked, and Bryce shook his head. "I'm sorry." John turned back toward the front and spoke with Jerry, but Bryce didn't listen.

"It hurts. The people who have the closest connection to Percy other than myself don't want anything to do with me."

"Why?" Mato asked, looking up from his book.

Bryce sighed. "Because people are strange when it comes to money, and Percy left his to me," he explained before turning to look out the window again. He'd made this trip many times over the past three years, just not since Percy's death. The land was beautiful—flat, but so very green, and full of spring. Bryce took a deep breath, then released it slowly, trying his best to let go of some of the hurt and pain.

"It's okay to be sad because Uncle Percy's gone," Mato told him. "And it's okay to be happy too. Uncle Percy knows we love him and he wants us to be happy." Mato looked so serious.

"Who told you that?"

"Uncle Jerry, right after Uncle Percy died. He said that it was okay to cry if I wanted to, but that it was okay to smile too, because Uncle Percy always made us laugh and he'd want us to remember him that way."

"He was right," Bryce admitted and smiled, hugging Mato lightly. He'd sort of forgotten that, and now he could see in his mind Percy playing with the kids, giving them pony rides on his back, everyone squealing and giggling with happiness. "Sometimes I wish the grief would just go away. I sort of figured it would pass by now," Bryce said.

"It takes time; everyone heals at their own pace," John explained from the front seat. "It took time for all of us to heal after their mother's death," John said, indicating the children, "and the ordeal we all went through, but we did, and we're all stronger because of it." John turned back to face forward. "Some time spent communing with nature and helping others will take your mind off your own cares."

Bryce nodded and then stiffened. "What do you mean communing with nature?"

"We're going camping," Ichante said with a grin. "The tents are in the back, and you're going to stay with Mato and me."

Bryce glared at Jerry in the rearview mirror. No one had said a word about camping. "We'll only be about five miles from my mother's," John told him. "We aren't disappearing into the wilderness."

"Aren't there wild animals?" Bryce asked.

"Nothing to worry about. Mato will protect you," John said, and Bryce felt so much better, protected by a preteen bodyguard. "Seriously, it's a place where others camp, so we won't be all alone. Trust us, you'll enjoy it."

Bryce didn't have the heart to tell them that what he'd really enjoy was a bed in a real house with running water and flush toilets. He humphed and said nothing, figuring he could always try it for one night, and after that, he'd see if anyone would be willing to take pity on him. He'd met John's large family—someone had to have a place he could sleep.

"Can we stop at the Corn Palace?" Mato asked when he saw the signs for Mitchell.

"Not this time," John said, and Mato went back to his book.

They continued driving for hours, only stopping for a picnic lunch and then continuing on. In Rapid City, they turned south and spent some time on main roads until they reached the reservation. Then the roads became narrower. Jerry, of course, knew where he was going, and Bryce watched out the window. Whenever he came here, he was always surprised by the poverty. In some places, homes looked almost cobbled together from scrounged building materials. Old travel trailers and mobile homes sometimes sat clumped together in the middle of open fields. Needless to say, the view didn't do much to improve Bryce's mood.

Finally, they pulled into the yard of John's parents' home. Bryce had never been so happy to step out of a vehicle in his life. It hadn't been a bad ride, but his legs and butt ached something fierce. While Bryce wandered around to get the blood flowing again, the kids raced inside. Soon John's mother, Kiya, came out to greet them.

"They convinced you to come," she said, pulling Bryce into a hug. "You'll feel better now that you're here." Bryce had quickly learned that no one argued with Kiya, so he nodded and let her lead him inside, where a table full of food had been laid out. Bryce wasn't hungry, but it appeared that half the reservation had been awaiting their arrival, so they sat down, and Bryce listened as the conversation became a din of overlapping excited voices. Everyone seemed to be sharing news and bringing everyone else up to date on gossip and happenings. "You aren't eating," Kiya said, and Bryce took a bite to appease her, smiling as he chewed. "You're way too thin."

"Mom, leave him alone," John told her with a hint of humor. "We got him to come this time, but he'll stay away if we nag."

Kiya sat back in her chair and laughed loud and full. "We only nag the ones we love," she retorted, and everyone else laughed as well. Bryce looked around the table, wondering what the joke was.

"Then we're the most loved people on earth," John countered, looking all around the table. The meal continued, and thankfully Bryce was able to just listen. He spoke up a few times, but mostly he sat. It was nice to be around a family again. After Percy died, some of those he'd thought of as his family had fought with him and then cut him off, and for all intents and purposes had disappeared from his life.

"How's your mother?" one of John's sisters asked. He couldn't remember her name, but she was always surrounded by a passel of children.

"Okay. The cancer is in remission, and they're continuing medication for now. Eventually they'll wean her off it and then we'll see what happens." For a while, the bad news had come in tsunamis. Thankfully it had stopped, because for a few months Bryce hadn't known where to turn.

"Dang," Jerry said from next to him, turning toward John. "I forgot to pick up hot dog buns for the campout."

"I can run to the trading post in a few minutes," John said, tapping Jerry's hand. "They'll probably have some, and if not, I brought a loaf of bread." Both Mato and Ichante groaned together. Obviously eating hot dogs on bread was not popular.

Bryce pushed back his chair. "I'll go in to pick them up if someone can give me directions," he offered. He was anxious to get away for a little while.

"I can go," John said, but Bryce was already asking for the keys, and Jerry handed them to him.

"Turn right out of the driveway and go to the end of the road. Turn left, and just before you reach the reservation center, the trading post is on the left," Jerry told him, and John pressed some bills into his hand. Bryce tried to give them back, but a stern look from his friend stopped him.

"I'll be back soon," Bryce said, shoving the bills into his pocket. He heard the kids ask to come with him, but Jerry quietly hushed them as Bryce left the house. He walked to the van and climbed into the driver's seat.

The directions Jerry had given him were easy to follow, and soon he was parked in front of what looked like a small, rustic grocery store. There was no one else in the lot, which Bryce thought a bit strange, but he slammed the van door, then walked to the front door and pulled it open.

Inside, the first thing he noticed was a complete lack of air-conditioning, though a number of ceiling fans stirred the air. Bryce looked around and realized this was much more than just a grocery store. It also appeared to act as post office, lending library, tackle and bait shop, as well as hardware store. And judging by the scent, a bakery.

The man behind the counter with long black hair and a stern expression that made him initially appear much older looked up from the magazine he was reading and met Bryce's gaze. Bryce shivered in response. Never in his life had he seen such a hard look from a complete stranger. "Afternoon," Bryce said, his mouth a little dry.

The man nodded but said nothing. However, his gaze never left Bryce. Figuring the best course of action was to get what he needed and get out, Bryce walked up and down the aisles, picking up hot dog buns, a case of the soda he liked, and some fruit snacks for the kids. He also couldn't help following his nose to the cinnamon-sugar doughnuts he'd been smelling since he entered. "What do you want?" the man said, the look in his eyes not softening one bit. "You some tourist here to see the injuns?" he asked mockingly.

"No. I'm a guest of the Black Ravens," Bryce said, and the man's look softened slightly. "I'm also helping to teach computer classes this weekend at the community center." Bryce forced a smile, because, after all, there was no need to meet rudeness with rudeness. He placed his purchases on the counter. "I'd also like a dozen of the cinnamon-sugar doughnuts."

The man got out a bag and counted out twelve doughnuts for him before ringing everything up. "That'll be $19.90," he said.

Bryce pulled out his wallet and handed the man a twenty. He didn't make any move to take it, and Bryce moved the bill closer. "Is something wrong?" Bryce asked, looking at the bill to make sure it was okay.

"We don't take those here," the man said.

"Take what?" Bryce asked in complete confusion.

"Bills with the Indian Hater on them. If you don't have something else, you can go." He actually sat down, so Bryce fished around in his wallet, but all he had were twenties. Then he remembered the money John had given him and pulled two tens from his pocket and placed them on the counter.

"Is that better?" Bryce asked, and the man took the bills and handed Bryce a dime without touching his hand. He bagged up the groceries and gave them to Bryce without a word. Then he sat back down and started reading his magazine again.

"You're welcome," Bryce said, turning away from the counter, as pissed off as he could ever remember being.

Bryce carried his purchases out of the store. As he opened the door, he turned back to the man and saw him staring at him. Bryce met his gaze as sort of a challenge, and then stepped outside. After placing the bag on the seat, Bryce retraced his route and drove back to Kiya's. Leaving the bag in the van for later, he went inside. It appeared that no one had moved in the time he'd been gone. Though more food had been devoured, the din of overlapping conversations hadn't lessened one bit.

"How did it go?" Jerry asked, and Bryce shrugged and rolled his eyes.

"You met Paytah Stillwater, didn't you?" John asked.

"If you mean the surliest, crankiest person on earth, then yeah," Bryce said sitting back down. "He made me pay with tens," Bryce said.

"That's why I gave them to you," John said as he shifted his gaze to his mother.

"There are many in the Native American communities who hate Andrew Jackson. They consider him the devil and a killer of our people. He stole land from native groups, including the ones that had helped him win his famous battles, and he was also responsible for the Trail of Tears, so many of our people avoid using twenty-dollar bills. The ATMs on the reservation generally only dispense tens."

"I didn't know. He looked at me like I'd killed his relatives," Bryce said, still a bit shaken up.

Kiya shook her head. "Paytah is a different sort of man. He's fiercely protective of our heritage and he tends to be a little militant about it."

"He relented a little when I told him I was your guest and was going to be helping with the computer classes."

Kiya sighed softly as she pushed back her chair. The other women seemed to take that as a signal and they got up as well, filling their hands with dishes and then taking them to the kitchen. The guys helped as well and then filtered outside. Bryce was about to follow them when Kiya spoke again.

"Life on the reservation is hard," she began. "Our family is lucky. My husband is a good man who works hard far from home in the oil fields in North Dakota. Others from the reservation do the same, but very often, little of the money they make gets back to their families. Instead, it's spent on alcohol and other things. It's sad but that's the way it is." She stopped rinsing the dishes and turned to Bryce. "Paytah has not had an easy life, and the blame for most of that he places at the feet of white men. I don't think that's fair, because people are people, but that's how Paytah sees it. He wouldn't harm anyone." She transferred the rinsed dishes to the dishwasher. "John should have insisted on going."

"It was okay. I know there are people here who are suspicious of white people. It doesn't really bother me." Bryce thought for a few moments. "I guess I just wasn't expecting it," he said.

Kiya chuckled softly. "Honey, you never expect it."

Ichante hurried into the kitchen. "Uncle Jerry says we're ready to go set up camp," she told him, taking him by the hand.

"Oh, goody," Bryce said softly, and he heard Kiya laugh again as Ichante lead him outside to the van. Mato was already inside and waiting. John and Jerry were talking to a few of the men, but their group broke up when they saw him coming.

"Ready for camping!" Jerry cried enthusiastically. The kids voiced their excitement, but Bryce was much less enthused. All the van doors were closed, and with everyone in their seats, they headed off with excited waves from the kids.

As promised, the camping place wasn't far from Kiya's, and it was beautiful, with a small stream running through a shallow but lush valley. They unloaded the stuff, and the guys put up the tents. Bryce wasn't sure what he was supposed to do, so he mainly carried things from the van in what seemed like a never-ending caravan of equipment. "That's the last of it," Bryce said as he set down the cooler on the grass. They had tents, chairs, a small fire pit, and not much else, but they all seemed pleased. The kids almost immediately took off their shoes and socks to wade in the shallows of the stream while John and Jerry took a moment to sit quietly. They offered Bryce a chair as well.

"This isn't so bad, is it?" Jerry asked, and Bryce grudgingly admitted that the view and quiet were a balm that his spirit needed.

"But at the first clap of thunder or weird sound outside the tent, I'm making for the van," Bryce quipped with a sarcastic smile.

"It's supposed to be nice all weekend, and the bears will leave us alone if we leave them alone," John said, and Bryce jumped to his feet, ready to head to the van.

"You said there weren't any bears," Bryce cried, knowing then he'd been had. "Fine, but I'm still keeping the van on reserve."

The kids joined them, keeping their shoes off, while John built a small fire. As darkness fell, they roasted hot dogs, told stories, and simply talked. A coyote howled in the distance, and Bryce looked all around, but didn't immediately race to the van. "It's okay, Uncle Bryce," Mato said. "They don't like people and they won't come near the fire."

Bryce nodded and listened as the haunting call was picked up by another and then another. "The land has its own music. If you close your eyes and let go, you'll really hear it," John explained.

Bryce wasn't so sure, but he closed his eyes anyway and listened. At first, he heard the coyotes, then the crackle of the fire, followed by the overlapping chirp of grasshoppers. The stream joined with its soothing gurgle, with tiny animals scurrying through the grasses. A bullfrog croaked loudly, and Bryce jumped, nearly toppling his chair, and the children added their laughter to the chorus. He closed his eyes again, leaning back in his chair and listening. The sounds, no longer scary or confusing, worked their way into his mind. As he listened, he heard a rock tumble down from a nearby bluff. No one said anything, and Bryce breathed deeply and calmly.

"It's beautiful," Bryce said as he felt tears well in his eyes. He made no move to wipe them away. Percy would have loved it out here, and Bryce had never been interested in camping. *I'm sorry*, Bryce thought, and a tiny breeze came up, caressing his cheek. The tears started in earnest as he swore he heard Percy's voice on the wind telling him it was all right and time for him to move on. *I'll always love you, but there's another out there who will love you too*, it seemed to say. The breeze caressed his cheek once more and then it was gone.

Bryce opened his eyes and saw Jerry and John staring back at him. "You fell asleep," John said as he poked the fire.

"So it was a dream," Bryce whispered as he looked around. He saw the kids through the screen of the tent, already asleep. "How long?"

"About an hour," John answered in a whisper before lifting his gaze to meet his. "What did you see?"

"I didn't see anything, but I heard Percy on the wind," Bryce said and then waited, but there was no wind, the air still and rapidly cooling. "He told me he'd always love me, but it was time for me to move on." Bryce swallowed back tears. "But it was just a dream."

John shook his head slowly. "No. You were given a blessing. The spirits allowed him to come to you and give you a message. Don't dismiss it or think it didn't happen." John placed his stick on the fire, stood up, and stretched his back in varying directions. Then he sat back down again, and no one talked for a while as Bryce sank deep into his own thoughts. Maybe it was time for him to stop grieving.

Bryce stood up and walked toward the van. He pulled out his suitcase and in the darkness changed into a pair of shorts and T-shirt before making his way to the tent he was sharing with the kids. They had insisted he sleep with them, so Bryce climbed into his sleeping bag on the air mattress and closed his eyes.

IN THE morning, Bryce woke to an empty tent and voices outside. Obviously he was the only one not up yet. Reluctantly, he got out of the sleeping bag and stepped into the morning air. Looking at his watch, he groaned. What was everyone doing up at this ungodly hour? Thankfully, John had made coffee and pressed a mug into his hand. "Sorry, I should have warned you that the kids get up at the crack of dawn out here." Even John yawned, and Bryce considered finishing his coffee and going back to bed, caffeine or not.

Bryce yawned again and sipped from his mug. After setting it on the ground, he grabbed his sleeping bag, unzipped it, and wrapped it around him in the morning chill before sitting in one of the chairs. Wrapped in his cocoon of warmth, he sipped coffee and closed his eyes. He felt happier and more content than he had in a very long time. He'd spent a long time asking the universe why Percy had been taken from him, and then he'd had to fight the airline responsible for the driver who'd killed Percy as well as Percy's family, after which he'd simply spent months being angry at everyone. It was a miracle he had any friends left after that. Now he felt quiet inside, a bit empty, but the shouting and rage were gone and it was okay. He could go on with his life. How he was going to do that, he wasn't sure, but he knew it was okay to try.

"You okay?" Jerry asked quietly, and Bryce smiled. Not one of those forced smiles so people would leave him alone, but a genuine smile that reached to his eyes. "I haven't seen that in a while," Jerry told him, patting him on the shoulder. "Who's ready for breakfast?"

A cry went up, and Bryce added his own voice as his stomach rumbled. Jerry made a basic breakfast of eggs and bacon over the fire, and Bryce added the doughnuts he'd bought the day before. But what surprised Bryce was that everything tasted different. It was only eggs and bacon, things he'd had a million times before, but they were the best he'd ever eaten. "Everything tastes better when you cook it over an open fire," Jerry explained, like he'd been reading his mind. "I found that out the first time John took me camping."

Bryce saw Jerry gaze contentedly at his lover, and soon John moved next to him. No words were said, but Bryce could almost feel them pull together. That was what he'd thought he had with Percy. No, he wasn't going there again. Percy was gone. Bryce had loved him very much and Percy would always be with him, but he had to let go. "So what sort of class are we teaching today?" Bryce asked.

"The last time we were here, a number of the business owners asked for help with business software," Jerry said. "Most of them are still doing their books by hand. So we're going to teach them to use a small-business accounting and management software package. I got the software company to donate it. I think there will be six students, and because this will be a little more complex class, we're going to have to give them some extra attention. So I thought we'd each work with two students during the exercises to make sure they really understand what they're doing." Jerry finished his breakfast and threw the paper plate in the fire before carefully placing the other trash in a bag.

"Leave nothing but footprints," John said, and Bryce nodded his understanding. He finished his breakfast and then burrowed back into his cocoon, closing his eyes for a nap. He listened to the kids playing, smiling at their happiness as his mind sort of floated.

"We need to leave soon so we can get things set up," Jerry said, and Bryce reluctantly stood up and placed the sleeping bag in the tent before quickly changing his clothes behind the van. Then he got his kit, shaved, and cleaned up with water John had heated for him. He was ready and waiting by the time Jerry and John got the kids ready to go. All the food was placed in the van, along with the cooler, and they left the campsite. Jerry dropped the kids at their grandmother's, and then they headed to the tribal community center.

It appeared that some of their students were already waiting for them. They got people set up as the other students filtered in. The class was about to start when the last person arrived.

Paytah still wore his hard expression when he looked at him, and Bryce wondered if he always looked like that, but then he turned to John and smiled, his face lighting up. Well, that answered that question.

"Please take a seat," Jerry said. "Bryce will get the software installed for you while we start the class."

Jerry handed him the CD, and Bryce sat in the chair next to Paytah and began working on his computer. He tried not to look at him as he worked, but he couldn't help it. That smile had been luminous. A few times he noticed Paytah glancing at him too, but his expression didn't seem to change. Jerry ran down an overview of the software, and Bryce finished the installation as Jerry was wrapping up. "You should be all set," Bryce explained in a whisper. "Just be sure to password-protect the files."

"Thank you," Paytah said in a gruff voice, and Bryce wondered how anyone could make a pleasantry sound so unpleasant.

"It's no problem," Bryce said and sat back in his chair. Jerry guided them through setting up their business profile and then actually using the software. After each section, he gave them exercises to do. It quickly became obvious to Bryce that Paytah wasn't picking up the concepts as quickly as the others. "Don't let the computer intimidate you."

Paytah turned toward him, and at least some of the hardness was gone from his expression. "You're doing all of this today by hand," Bryce said. "The computer is just a tool to hopefully allow you to get more done in less time."

"But…," Paytah began, but his face hardened again before he turned back to the computer. He picked his way through the rest of the exercise, but it was painful to watch. Bryce knew he could help if Paytah would let him.

"Let's take a break," Jerry said. "We'll start again in ten minutes."

Paytah got up and left the room with most of the other students, and John slid into the chair next to his. "What's going on?"

"He's not keeping up, and I tried to help, but he wouldn't let me."

"It's part of the warrior's attitude. He'll persevere through just about anything, but he won't actually ask or accept help. I can work with him if you like."

"It's okay," Bryce said. John returned to his place and the students returned. Paytah sat back in his seat, and Jerry began the class again. This time, when he saw him struggling, Bryce asked Jerry a question that led to a discussion of the issue Paytah was having. There was definitely more than one way to skin a cat. If he wouldn't accept help directly, then Bryce would do it in a sneakier way.

The class continued for much of the morning, and as noon approached, Jerry wrapped things up. "I hope this was helpful for you." Everyone clapped, including Paytah.

"Who's watching the store?" Bryce asked as Paytah packed up his computer.

"Alowa," he answered.

Bryce wanted to ask what he'd ever done to him, but then John sidled over and he didn't think it was a good idea, so he excused himself and said good-bye to the other students as they filed out.

"I don't understand why white people are teaching us like this," Paytah told John in a whisper.

"You need to let that go," John told him, and Paytah shook his head. "Jerry set up this program and has helped a lot of people here, including the kids. He loves Mato and Ichante." Bryce saw John glance at him and he turned away so it wouldn't look like he was listening.

"Jerry, I understand, but what about him?" Paytah said softly, and Bryce smiled as he folded the chairs to put them away.

"Bryce is a good guy," he heard John say. "And I think the two of you might have more in common than you think." Bryce figured their little conversation was over, but John continued. "You feel Native American rights are very important, I get that—so do I. But we've been persecuted because of invalid prejudices for centuries. Don't you think the way you treated Bryce was a little like the way you don't want people acting around you?"

Bryce turned around and saw Paytah's expression heat up, and he left the room to get out of the line of fire. In the hall, he sat down next to Jerry to wait. "John wasn't happy with the way you were being treated," Jerry explained.

"I got that," Bryce said. "But I can take care of myself, and Paytah was only hurting himself, not me." Bryce relaxed until John came out of the room.

"Let's go get the kids and have fun for the rest of the weekend," John said to Jerry before kissing him and then heading for the door. John said nothing about what they'd talked about, and Bryce didn't let on that he'd heard anything at all. Jerry followed John outside, and Bryce looked at the closed door to the room they'd been using. Slowly he opened it and peered inside. Paytah sat at the place he'd occupied without moving, looking lost and maybe a bit confused, supporting his head with one hand. Bryce wondered if he was all right, but any help from him probably wouldn't be welcomed, so he silently closed the door before Paytah saw him, and then he left the building.

The van ride back to Kiya's was quiet, but that changed as soon as the kids piled in. They were obviously ready for the rest of the outdoor time, and if Bryce were honest with himself, he was too. He'd slept well, and right now nothing seemed to bother him, not even a surly Native American with an attitude problem and a killer smile.

25

"Is everyone ready to go?" Jerry asked rhetorically, not waiting for an answer. "Wave good-bye to Grandma," he added as he backed down the drive. The kids waved, and their grandmother waved in return.

The drive to the campsite went fast. Everyone got out and unloaded the supplies they'd brought with them. Nothing had disturbed their camp. The kids had eaten at their grandmother's, so Bryce made sandwiches for the three adults before sitting for a while in the late spring sun. "I love how this spot changes through the year," John said as he sat down. "Right now everything is fresh from the spring rains, but in another month or so, the grasses on the slopes will start to brown, and then a month after that, the dryness will get closer and closer to the stream as it loses much of its water, but then fall comes and the heat breaks. Rain often returns and there's another burst of green before winter covers everything."

"I take it you camped here when you were a kid?"

John nodded. "I used to come with my dad sometimes." John turned to Jerry. "Mom said he should be home for a few weeks next month. We should make a point to come while he's here."

"Of course," Jerry said after swallowing the last of his sandwich. "See if you can arrange some workspace for us, and we'll work here for a few weeks."

"That I can probably do," John said before pulling Jerry into a deep kiss.

"Ewwww, kissing," Mato teased, but he quickly turned his attention to wading in the stream, and Bryce watched the kids to give John and Jerry a moment of privacy.

"You're welcome to come with us if you want, Bryce," Jerry said, "or you can stay and use the office at home if you want."

"We won't have to camp for two weeks, will we?" he asked, and both Jerry and John laughed.

"We'll stay in a cabin that one of John's friend's owns. It's a bit rustic, but there's electricity and running water."

The thought of going back to being alone again was not particularly palatable any longer. "I think I can do that," Bryce said with a smile.

The rest of the day was peaceful, quiet, and passed like wildfire. How sitting, talking, and really doing nothing but eating could make the time pass so quickly was beyond Bryce, but before he knew it, they were having dinner as the sun slid behind the valley walls.

John once again built a small fire, and as the evening wore on, the night sounds started. This time Bryce knew what they were and he was ready for them. Closing his eyes, he listened and relaxed. The stream and the crickets played, with bullfrogs joining in. There was definitely a breeze—he could feel it on his skin. *Percy, are you there?*

Bryce continued to listen as small animals skittered through the grass or blurped into the water. Again he felt a breeze, but there was no voice on it, just the wind adding its own tempo to the melody. Bryce's first thought was to be sad, but then he realized the coyotes were missing; they weren't calling. Bryce kept his eyes closed and strained to hear them, but they weren't singing.

Then, piercing the night, a single howl cut the air, mournful and long, ending for a few seconds before beginning again. Sadness gripped Bryce's heart, not for himself, but for the animal. What could have hurt it so badly it would make that sound?

"Wolf," John said softly, breaking Bryce's illusion. Slowly, he opened his eyes to see the two men get up to put the kids to bed. Jerry returned a few minutes later, sitting back in his chair.

"John is telling the kids stories about wolves," Jerry said. "They love to hear his stories, and it's good for them to know their heritage." Jerry got back up and returned with a couple of blankets, handing one to Bryce. "It's going to be cold tonight."

Bryce took the blanket and wrapped it around his shoulders before returning his gaze to the dancing flames. "I was hoping Percy would come back," Bryce admitted.

"I know," Jerry said softly. "But I think whatever you got to experience was a onetime deal."

"I wish I understood it," Bryce said.

27

"No, just accept it for the gift that it was." The wolf howled again, and Bryce sat back, warm now with the blanket and the fire. Closing his eyes, he just listened. The loneliness in the wolf's cry tugged at Bryce's heart. He didn't know how he knew that wolves mated for life, maybe John had told him once, but this wolf had lost its mate. Bryce knew that in his heart. The mournfully gut-wrenching sound echoed off the canyon walls, drowning out everything else. *I understand how you feel, but you have to move on,* Bryce silently told the wolf.

Another cry split the air, louder and closer. Bryce started and opened his eyes, but he didn't see the fire or Jerry. Instead, he saw Paytah's brilliant smile.

Bryce nearly fell over backward. Only Jerry catching him prevented him from falling flat on his back. "Are you okay? Did you stand up too fast?"

"Yeah," Bryce said breathily, looking all around, but he saw nothing out of place. Breathing deeply, Bryce wondered why he'd seen Paytah.

"Sit back down." Jerry guided him to the chair, and Bryce sat. John joined them a little while later, and the three of them talked quietly. But Bryce couldn't get the image of Paytah's smile out of his mind, and even after he went to bed, he could still see it whenever he closed his eyes.

CHAPTER
THREE

"CAN we have ice cream?" Ichante asked as she closed the door to the freezer in the cabin. They'd arrived the day before, and to Bryce's surprise, the cabin was much nicer than he'd expected. Yes, it was rustic-looking and wasn't big on modern appliances, but it had the basics, and that included running water, a real bathroom, and walls between him and the coyotes, wolves, and potential bears. Everything else he could deal with.

"If you like," Bryce answered before the other two adults could say anything. "What kind would you like?"

"They'll be happy with whatever's at the trading post," Jerry said with a wink as he moved the laptop from his lap to the log table in front of the sofa.

"I'll go," Bryce said, closing his laptop and getting up. He was going a bit stir-crazy and could use a chance to stretch his legs. Bryce noticed the expressions that both Jerry and John sent his way. "I'll be fine. I made sure I have plenty of tens before embarking on this little adventure."

Jerry pulled his laptop back onto his lap, and John turned in his chair. "Do you know the way?"

"I paid attention as we came in, so I should be able to find my way," Bryce said, telling John how to get back to the reservation center. John nodded and went back to work while Bryce got ready to leave.

"By the way, Jerry, I have those programs done and checked in for the West Houghton change," Bryce said, and he saw Jerry smile and nod. He'd been working on that account for weeks and they'd kept changing their specifications. Bryce had finally gotten them to make up their minds and he hoped it was done. He was tired of working on those programs.

"Great, thanks. I'll check them out and bundle them up," Jerry said, flashing him a smile. "Good job getting them reined in."

Bryce snorted slightly as he pushed open the door and stepped out into the near wilderness just outside the door. Trees and shrubs were a short distance from the building, and the drive seemed like a long tunnel of green out to the main road. According to John, there had been more rain than normal, and the plants seemed to be taking advantage of it. Bryce walked down the steps to the van and got inside, started the engine, and then pulled down the tunnel of green, being careful to stay on the narrow drive. A few branches lightly brushed the sides of the van as he moved forward. When he reached the road, barely more than a two-track, he slowly turned and carefully drove until he reached the main road and headed to "town."

Of course, he got lost and had to stop to ask for directions, but he made it without too much backtracking and parked outside the store. He got out of the truck and made another check that he didn't have any of the "offensive" money before going inside.

Paytah sat behind the counter, hunched over his computer, two fingers slowly typing at the keyboard. "Heeyah," he said softly, grumbling under his breath as he worked. Bryce coughed softly to get his attention.

"I can help you if you'll let me," Bryce said from across the counter. Paytah looked as though he were about to refuse, but then sighed. "I know you don't like me because I'm white, but I can help."

Paytah grumbled again and returned to his typing. Bryce gave up and turned away to begin finding what he'd come for. "This was supposed to save time, but I've spent a month on this and it still isn't working," Paytah groused with frustration. He stopped what he was doing, stood up, and stepped away from the desk. Bryce took that as an invitation and moved around the counter, settling in the chair. He made sure to save all the work before looking through the program. It didn't take him long to see what was happening.

"I think you're doing things a little backwards," Bryce explained gently as he turned around. "I'm Bryce, in case you don't remember."

"I remember," Paytah said, and Bryce felt himself smile for some strange reason. "Paytah."

"I remember too," Bryce said, and for a second he forgot what he was doing as he sort of lost himself in Paytah's eyes. Realizing what he was doing, Bryce blinked and returned his mind to the task at hand. "What I think you're doing is entering the numbers in the wrong place first and the program is fighting you." Bryce pointed to the screen. "You're entering the numbers you think are correct here, right?"

Paytah nodded. "It takes a long time to add everything up."

"Yes. But if you'd enter the individual values here, the system would record them and add them, filling in this entire screen for you, and you wouldn't have to add the invoices, or have the system fight you. They really should make this screen noneditable, because lots of people make this error." Bryce shifted the program to another screen. "Go ahead and enter your invoices on this screen one at a time, and when you're done, we'll check the other screen." Bryce got up and let Paytah sit down.

"Does this look familiar from class?" Bryce asked.

"I couldn't find it again," Paytah said.

"I bookmarked it for you," Bryce explained as he leaned over Paytah, reaching to the mouse. "Just look here and you'll see the Bookkeeping tab. In there is the link; just click on it and the computer will bring you right to it." Bryce demonstrated. Paytah turned to watch Bryce, his long, silky hair trailed over Bryce's arm, and Bryce nearly groaned. "Give it a try while I do the shopping I came in for."

Bryce walked down the aisles, grabbing a few things. He wasn't going to get the ice cream until the last minute, and he wanted to make sure Paytah understood what he needed to do. Bryce watched him a few times, and though he seemed to be working slowly, some of the frustrated rigidness left his body. Once he had everything except the frozen stuff, Bryce walked up to the counter.

"It's better, thank you," Paytah said with an actual smile on his face. "And the numbers match on the other screen."

Bryce nodded. "It's no problem. John's dad is home for a few weeks, so we've moved the entire office to the reservation so John and the kids can be closer to his dad while he's home. If you have questions, you can call," Bryce said. Paytah was about to start ringing up his purchases when a man rushed into the store. He almost skidded to a halt when he saw Bryce.

"Who are you? Oh yeah, you're one of those guys who teaches the computer classes, aren't you?" the man asked.

"Yes," Bryce answered.

"Paytah, it's Chay. I think you need to come," the man said urgently. "He's on the top of Rainbow Bluff and won't come down."

Bryce saw Paytah grow pale and become nervous. "Okay," he finally said. "I'll close the store once I'm done here."

"I can watch things for you if you want," Bryce volunteered and almost instantly wished he hadn't, based on the looks he got from both men. "I worked in a store when I was in college and I know how to run a register." Bryce turned to Paytah. "This way you won't have to close the store." Bryce had originally offered to help, but now his pride was up and he was tempted to tell them both where they could stick it.

"Okay," Paytah said, quickly showing Bryce where everything was.

"Come on, we have to get to Chay," the other man said.

"My brother can wait two seconds, Coyote," Paytah groused back.

"I'll be okay," Bryce told him. "Go help your brother." Bryce shot Paytah a smile, and Paytah looked longingly toward the door. "I'll be fine," Bryce told him, and Paytah rushed out of the store. Bryce turned, and within seconds the truck that had been parked next to the van pulled away from the building and took off down the road in a cloud of dust. Bryce turned back to the store and shook his head. He'd volunteered to do this on a whim, and now he wondered just what in hell he was doing.

The store was completely quiet, so he pulled out his phone and looked at a picture of him and Percy—the wallpaper image. Reminding himself for the millionth time to change it, he called Jerry. "I got a little delayed," Bryce said when Jerry answered. "Tell the kids I'll bring their ice cream as soon as I can."

"Where are you?" Jerry asked, sounding a bit concerned.

"I'm at the store," Bryce answered, and he could hear Jerry repeating things to John. "I got sort of roped into watching it because Paytah was called away to help his brother. It sounded like an emergency or something." Once again he heard Jerry talking to John, and this time John said something back, but Jerry didn't repeat it. "I'll be back as soon as I can," Bryce said and hung up. Shoving the phone in his pocket, he looked around and picked up a magazine off the rack. There was absolutely nothing he wanted to read, so he sat behind the counter with a copy of *Field & Stream*, reading about big-mouth bass before tossing the magazine aside, crossing his arms over his chest, and waiting for his first customers.

He had to wait a while. Eventually a woman came in, and at first she looked at him like he was from outer space. "What are you doing here?" she asked.

"I'm watching the store for Paytah," Bryce answered her. "I'm a friend of John, I mean Akecheta Black Raven. Paytah got pulled away, so I'm helping." Bryce needed to remember that here John was referred to mostly by his Lakota name, Akecheta.

Her expression changed almost instantly, the suspicion turning to a smile, her plain, middle-aged features brightening and instantly making her look younger. "You're one of the men teaching computers," she said as she placed her purchases on the counter. "My son and daughter took one of your classes at the school." She emptied her basket, and Bryce began to ring her up.

"I'm glad we could help," Bryce told her.

"You've done more than help. You've begun bringing our children into this century," she told him, and Bryce grinned as he finished ringing her up. He told her the amount, and she paid for the groceries, all in tens. Bryce thanked her, and she left the store. Bryce reminded himself to tell Jerry about her. It would make his day that people really thought that much of the program he and John had put together. Unfortunately, once she left, the store was quiet again and Bryce had nothing to do but wait.

Bored, Bryce pulled a few pieces of paper out of the printer to fan himself in the warm store. The fans were on at least, moving the warm air. A few times, Bryce wandered over to the frozen foods and pulled open the door to cool off. It worked until he closed the door again and a few seconds later he was just as warm as he'd been before.

The door opened and a kid entered. He must have been nine or ten, with eyes that widened, big-time, when he saw Bryce. "Hello," he said, and then he continued on. Bryce saw him pick up a basket that appeared nearly as big as he was. Bryce had seen a few kids like this on his visits, hands and face dirty, clothes in need of a good washing and a size or two too big. He was definitely in need of someone to take care of him. Bryce settled behind the counter, expecting the kid to go for the candy. Instead, he walked directly to the aisle that held the few baby items Paytah carried. A can of formula went into the basket, as did a small package of diapers and wipes. The kid continued on and seemed to deliberate over the diaper cream until he put the smallest tube into the basket.

The kid set down the basket and pulled a small piece of paper out of his pocket, checking it before folding it up again. He shoved it back into his pocket, picked up the basket again, and continued on, disappearing for a few seconds off to the side. Bryce craned his neck and could barely see the top of the kid's head by the refrigerator case. He heard the door open and close, and a few minutes later the kid carried the now full hand basket toward the counter. He'd added milk and a small loaf of bread.

As he got closer, Bryce saw how thin he was, with almost hollow eyes and straggly hair. Bryce leaned over the counter and helped him lift the basket. Bryce saw a round protrusion in one of the kid's pants pockets, the corner of a package of lunchmeat poking out through a tear in the pants, and a square one in the other pocket that Bryce figured was a package of cheese slices. His throat constricted as he rang up the kid's purchases. "That'll be $24.79," Bryce said when he saw the total, and the kid held out a handful of wadded fives and ones that he'd carefully fished out of his pockets while trying not to give away what was in them. Bryce completed the sale and closed the register drawer. "May I ask you a question?"

"Yes, sir," the kid said in a small voice, shifting nervously from foot to foot.

"I bought a doughnut earlier and couldn't eat it. Would you like it?" Bryce asked, and the kid widened his eyes in total surprise. Bryce lifted the dome and handed the kid a cinnamon-sugar doughnut. He took it and licked his lips. Bryce put the lid back on the doughnuts and began bagging up the kid's purchases, watching as he downed the doughnut in less than ten seconds. Bryce knew from personal experience just how good Paytah's doughnuts were, but a kid that small eating that fast…. "Here you go," Bryce said, handing the kid the bag.

The kid wiped his lips on the back of his hand. "Thanks, mister," he said as he took the bag. Then he walked quickly toward the door, pushed it open, and hurried outside. Bryce watched him through the window as he set the bag on the ground, then pulled the lunchmeat and cheese out of his pocket. He added them to the bag and then walked across the open area before disappearing down the road.

"Jesus Christ," Bryce said, nearly falling back into Paytah's desk chair. Yes, the kid had stolen from the store, but lunchmeat and cheese? Bryce shook his head wondering just how many kids were waiting at home for that small bit of food. Obviously there was a baby, and Bryce had the suspicion that the kid who'd just left was the primary caregiver. He seemed so careful to get what the baby needed first.

Bryce walked from behind the counter to the refrigerator case and saw where he thought the lunchmeat and cheese had been. He picked up identical packages and brought them to the register, ringing them up along with a doughnut. He paid for them with a ten from his pocket and then took them back. He was just returning to the front when he saw a truck pull up outside. Paytah got out of the passenger seat, helping another man get out. Coyote hurried around from the driver's side and took the man, who looked drunk, and helped him shuffle away from the truck. Paytah opened the door to the store.

"I'll take care of Chay," Bryce heard Coyote say, and then Paytah entered. He closed the door and looked all around, like he'd expected to come back to a pile of rubble, or bare shelves. The store wasn't large, by any means, and he wandered up and down the aisles before returning to the counter.

"A young kid came in here, about so big," Paytah said, indicating the kid's height with his hands.

"Yes," Bryce answered, wondering how he knew.

"Can of his brother's formula is missing," Paytah said as an explanation. He continued wandering but didn't seem to see anything amiss. "Did he take anything?" Paytah knew about the kid and that he stole. *Jesus, could I have been any dumber?*

Bryce felt completely foolish. He'd felt sorry for the kid, but apparently he did this all the time. Bryce nodded and walked around the counter. "Don't worry—I paid for what he took. He—" Bryce cut himself off and picked up the basket of things he'd filled. He hurried to the freezer to get ice cream, making sure it was frozen solid before taking everything to the register. So he'd been played by a kid with huge eyes and a needy expression. Fuck, he'd even given the kid a doughnut. What a sap he must have looked like.

Paytah rang up his purchases, staring at him like he was trying to figure Bryce out. "Thank you for helping me out," Paytah said when Bryce handed over the money.

Bryce nodded, unable to look the man in the eye. "I can't believe I fell for that…," Bryce said as an apology. "I'll see you." He grabbed his bags, hurrying to the van before he somehow made a bigger fool of himself. He opened the side door and placed the ice cream in the cooler he'd brought, rearranging the ice packs before closing the lid and climbing inside. He started the van and backed away, getting out of there.

Bryce filled his head with recriminations the entire drive back to the cabin. Once he got through the tunnel of vegetation, he parked the van and carried everything inside. The house was quiet, with Jerry and

John still working. The kids were playing a game on the floor, and after putting everything away, Bryce sat down on the sofa and lifted the laptop so he could get to work. "What happened?" John asked.

"Don't want to talk about it," Bryce said, looking at both John and Jerry before opening his laptop and going to work.

"Can we have ice cream?" Ichante asked, and Jerry turned to him. Bryce nodded, indicating he'd bought some, and Jerry put his work aside to help the kids while Bryce continued sulking behind his screen. When Jerry returned, he brought a bowl of ice cream to John and set one down for Bryce as well. Not wanting it to melt, Bryce set the laptop aside and let the frozen minty goodness soothe his ego.

"Thank you, Uncle Bryce," both kids said, and he smiled at them. It was a bit hard to sulk when those two were around. They were happy kids who played and laughed. They didn't have to worry about where their next meal came from. And so what if that kid had played him— Bryce had acted on what he'd thought was right and the way he felt.

"You're welcome," Bryce said, and Ichante climbed onto the sofa to sit next to him. She grinned up at him before taking another bite. Mato climbed up as well, sitting on his other side. The kids were exactly the cure he needed. "Is there a place we can go swimming?" Bryce asked John, who shook his head.

"There aren't any lakes, just streams like the one we camped against last time," John explained.

"There's a water park in Rapid City," Jerry offered. "If we got our work done, we could see if Grandma and Grandpa want to join us on a short road trip tomorrow." The kids cheered, and Bryce nodded and smiled.

They finished their ice cream, and the kids returned to their game. Bryce went back to work. His little jaunt into town had cost him enough work time, so he knuckled down and continued working until it was nearly time for dinner. Only then did he close his computer and emerge from the concentrative cocoon of his work. Wandering through the cabin, he realized he was alone, but heard voices outside. Following them, he found John and a man he didn't immediately recognize talking quietly in what sounded like Lakota.

"Bryce, we didn't mean to disturb you," John said, and Paytah turned around. Bryce wasn't sure if he should approach or leave them alone, but then John excused himself.

"After you left, I realized you might misunderstand what happened," Paytah said, stepping closer. "I was not accusing you of anything wrong."

"Little Wamblee, the child that came in the store, he bought formula, diapers, and baby things, right?" Paytah asked, and Bryce nodded. "His mother… well, she gives him money, and sometimes it's not enough. He always buys what his baby brother needs, but there isn't always money left over." Paytah's expression was very serious. "What did he take?"

"Lunchmeat and cheese," Bryce answered, the lump in his throat he'd felt in the store returning.

"He didn't have enough money left to buy food for himself," Paytah told him. "He does that sometimes, and I pay for it." Paytah sighed. "There is much poverty here."

Bryce nodded slowly. He'd seen it many times. "I gave him a doughnut, and he wolfed it down."

"It was probably the first he'd eaten all day, and the lunchmeat and cheese will probably feed him lunch for the entire week," Paytah said, and Bryce turned away, blinking hard as he remembered the skinny body and his hollow eyes.

"Damn it," Bryce swore, his throat rough. "No kid should have to live like that." He rubbed his eyes before turning back to Paytah.

"There are many here who sometimes do not get enough to eat, young and old," Paytah said as if it were a fact of life. The injustice made Bryce's blood boil. He clenched his fists in frustration, but didn't know what to do about it.

"That doesn't make it right," Bryce said.

"No," Paytah said softly. "I need to get back to the store, but I didn't want you to think you had done anything wrong. You helped him, and that was kind." Paytah turned and walked toward the front of the cabin.

"Why doesn't the council do something?" Bryce asked, and Paytah stopped.

"With what?" Paytah asked with a shrug. "They have no resources. There is no money and very little chance of getting any." Anger seared behind Paytah's eyes. Bryce could see the frustration and maybe hatred burning inside him. Bryce stared back, meeting Paytah's steely gaze with his own. "You really do care," Paytah said.

"You're fucking damned right I care," Bryce spat, not meaning to yell at Paytah, but everything that had been building all day seemed to come to the surface all at once. "I don't know where this distrust of people just because they're white comes from with you. Others I've met here don't have it. But, yes, I care that a kid has to steal to get enough food, and that a ten-year-old is at home taking care of the baby. Of course I fucking care!" Bryce's voice seemed to echo through the land. "But I don't know what to do about it."

"Do?" Paytah said quietly. "There isn't anything to do. Things are the way they are, and most people wouldn't cross the street to help someone who doesn't look like them." Paytah turned and walked away. Soon Bryce heard a truck engine. Turning his head to the sky, he seethed and simply voiced his frustration with a scream that left him shaking from head to foot.

"What's going on?" Jerry asked, running around the building with the two kids right behind him.

"Sorry," Bryce said. "Nothing." He was still shaking. "Paytah is just the most frustrating man I have ever met."

"Is that all?" John said, joining them. "You know, if every person who felt that way yelled at the sky, we'd never be able to hear the coyotes or wolves." John chuckled. "He has that effect on people."

"How can he take things like this lying down?" Bryce asked, turning to John and Jerry, who both gave him blank looks.

"You didn't want to talk about it, remember?" John said, and Bryce nodded.

"Well, I want to talk about it now," Bryce said, marching toward the cabin door, leaving the others to follow in his wake. Bryce stopped before going inside, whirling around. "How can anyone so... so...

gorgeous be such a pain in the—" He saw the kids. "—backside!" John smirked, and Bryce realized what he'd said. "Not that it matters what he looks like, because it doesn't matter."

John walked past him and pulled open the door. "So what did Paytah do to ruffle your feathers so much? He told me he came here because he felt bad about earlier and he wanted to thank you for helping him out."

"He did that," Bryce said as he flopped down onto the sofa. "There was this kid at the store who stole some food. I felt sorry for him and paid for it myself once he'd left. When Paytah returned, he didn't seem surprised, and I thought I'd been conned. Turns out, according to Paytah, he does this sometimes when he's hungry." Bryce told himself he wouldn't sniffle.

"Did Paytah say the kid's name?"

"Little Wamblee," Bryce said, and John nodded. "Anyway, when I told him something had to be done, he just shrugged and said there was nothing anyone could do." Bryce clenched his fists tight. "He practically made fun of me."

John sat on the edge of the chair across from him. "Bryce, Paytah may be right. There is only so much the tribe can do. Resources are very tight. They do try, but there isn't enough to help everyone."

John," Bryce pleaded, "this kid spends money to take care of the baby. He was so thin, and his eyes… God, his eyes looked hollow and so tired. I gave him a doughnut and he ate it faster than you could imagine. I barely saw it go into his mouth, he ate it so fast." Bryce wanted badly to make John understand. Lifting his eyes from the floor, his gaze met John's, and he realized John did understand. "God…."

"I know, Bryce. We have it really good. Mato and Ichante will never wonder where their next meal will come from. Little Wamblee will probably always wonder if he'll get enough to eat, and most of the time that answer will be no." John sighed. "Little Wamblee was named after my dad and it hurts to see him hungry. When the kids are in school, it's better, because most of them get free lunch and many get breakfast as well. They're guaranteed to get at least one and sometimes two good meals a day."

"But in the summer, there are children making a week's worth of lunches out of a package of pilfered lunchmeat, cheese, a loaf of bread, and a doughnut." Bryce could see Little Wamblee's face in his mind, and he realized he'd been stupid to think the kid had been playing him. That kid was probably hungry all the time. The only thing that made him feel better about this whole thing was that he'd bought the kid's food.

"Hey, because of you, whether he knows it or not, he and his sister will have something to eat this week," John told him, and Bryce held his head in his hands.

"There're two of them?" Bryce said. "What in hell can we do?" John didn't answer, and Bryce let his head fall back against the cushions. "Aren't there any organizations that can help?"

"There are a few groups that have a presence on the reservation, and they do what they can, but the need is greater than they have the resources for," John explained, and Jerry joined them, sitting next to Bryce on the sofa. "We do what we can, Bryce. Jerry and I have tried to give the kids here a better future. Teach them so they have skills that will hopefully open doors for them."

"But what good does that do when they don't have enough to eat now?" Bryce asked. Both Jerry and John nodded, but neither offered a suggestion, not that Bryce had any bright ideas either. But he knew one thing—he definitely owed Paytah an apology. He'd let his frustration get the best of him. After all, Paytah helped when he could, as well, and Bryce had taken his feelings of helplessness out on him.

"I know how you feel," Jerry said as Mato and Ichante hurried into the room.

"Uncle Bryce was yelling and he said naughty words," Mato said as he jumped up on the sofa.

"I know, and I'm sorry," Bryce said.

"Come on," Jerry announced. "It's time to start dinner, and you two are going to help." Jerry ushered the kids toward the kitchen. Bryce stayed where he was. John didn't move either, and once the others were gone, John's serious expression shifted to a wry smile.

"So you think Paytah is gorgeous," John said, and Bryce groaned. He knew he was going to pay for that single word. John chuckled softly. "Freudian slip," he teased. "You know there's nothing wrong with liking someone, and yes, Paytah is a good-looking guy." John smiled, and Bryce tried to smile as well. "I know you still miss and love Percy—you probably always will—but isn't it time to think about letting him go?"

"What's this got to do with him?" Bryce asked defensively.

"Come on," John said, lowering his gaze slightly. "You still carry a picture of him everywhere you go. There's one on your phone still, and I know if I went into your room, there would be one on the nightstand right now. You love him, I know that, but Percy is gone, and he'd want you to move on."

Bryce lowered his gaze. "I know. Percy would hate me for not moving on, but I…. It's not fair that I had him for so short a time. He and I deserved what you and Jerry have."

"I know you did. But if you let yourself move on, you could have that with someone else. Percy is gone, and carrying a torch for him the way you are isn't helping yourself." John settled back in his chair. "I'm not asking you to forget him or to stop loving him, but maybe make room in your heart for someone else too."

"And you think it's Paytah?" Bryce asked, even though he was teasing. There was no way, gorgeous or not, that he was going to let himself fall for the cantankerous man.

"I didn't say that, but may I remind you that you were the one who said he was gorgeous? And you're also the one who lets him get under your skin." John winked at him, and Bryce growled softly, grinding his teeth together. The man was way too observant sometimes.

"He's so exasperating," Bryce said.

John sighed softly. "He hasn't had an easy life, I know that. He and I were never particularly close, because Paytah never let anyone close. His brother Chayton was the only person I ever saw him really close with, and Chay has his own problems."

"They said something about getting him from Rainbow Bluff, whatever that is," Bryce said, and he watched John nod slowly.

"Chay has a problem with alcohol. A lot of people on the reservation do. When Chay drinks, he gets maudlin at first, and then thinks he's invincible. I heard that a few times he thought he could fly and had to be pulled back from the edge. Rainbow Bluff would be a place where Chay might go if he was feeling that way. There are sheer walls with many different layers of rock. It's very beautiful up there. If you were out of your head and thought you could fly, that place would be a very enticing location to give it a try." John looked away, like he was contemplating something. "Poor Paytah. He always seems to have the weight of the world on his shoulders." Then John seemed to shake off what he was thinking. "There are worse people you could like than Paytah, but I really don't know what his deal is."

"Deal?" Bryce asked.

"Yeah. I have never seen him go out with anyone, boy or girl, other than his brother and Coyote. I somehow doubt if Paytah has ever given any thought to who he might like, either."

"How can you say that?" Bryce asked, figuring John must be using some figure of speech.

"Paytah was a year ahead of me in school, and I always remember him being one of those guys who laughed a lot and had a ton of friends. Up until he turned fourteen or fifteen, he was the center of attention. You've seen how he looks. Well, imagine him at fourteen with those eyes and lips, skin that glowed, and a smile that lit up a room. He was gorgeous, and everyone seemed to want to be around him. Then, within a year, something changed. I don't know what, none of us did, but he withdrew. The friends sort of fell away, and he kept to himself. I have no idea what caused it, but a lot of people remarked on it when we were in school, mostly because no one could figure out why." John stood up and wandered to the blackened stone fireplace, cold because there was no need for a fire in this heat. "Paytah and Chay were raised mostly by their father, who ran the store before Paytah. He was an okay man, but he was one of those people who never seemed happy with whatever his kids did." John shook his head slightly. "Anyway, he died a year or so after Paytah got out of high school, and he took over the trading post. Chay helped sometimes at first, but he wanted more, so he left the reservation. Didn't stay away long, though. When Chay came back, he crawled into a bottle and seems to have pretty much stayed there."

"Good God," Bryce said softly. No wonder he seemed so dour. Bryce stared down at his shoes. Now he felt even worse for how he'd treated Paytah. "No wonder he feels like he can't do anything—he's just been trying to hold things together for so long." Bryce lifted his gaze with a soft sigh hopefully only he could hear. "Do you know what happened to him? Did he withdraw when his mother…." He wasn't sure what word to use. "Left?" he said, going for something safe.

John shook his head and wandered back to the chair, flopping back down into it. "No. His mother died when Paytah and Chay were little. They may remember her, but they would be old memories, and I doubt whatever happened to him had anything to do with her." John looked like he was searching his memory. "No, nothing comes to mind. But something definitely happened, and the only person who knows what it is would be Paytah."

Bryce was intrigued, and not just by what John had said. Like it or not, something about Paytah pulled at him and roused his curiosity. He wished he knew why. "Did you ever ask him?"

John widened his eyes. "Are you kidding? I heard that someone tried to talk with him about it once and he yelled at them and didn't allow them into the trading post for a month, and that was after telling them to mind their own business and threatening to get his gun. After that, I doubt anyone ever tried to bring the subject up again, and Paytah continued on the way he was." John became quiet for a while. "He's always been very Native-American-centric, even as a kid. He was exceedingly proud of the tribe and where he came from. But he got more and more vocal about it when he spoke, which wasn't much, and even before his father died, when he was working in the store, he refused to accept twenties. Once his dad died, it became the rule that everyone lived by if you wanted to do business with him, and since it's the only place on the reservation to get the basics, everyone does."

"I see," Bryce said, even though he really didn't.

"Actually, it's a good thing. It started off as quirky, but now every kid in school learns about Andrew Jackson and what he did to our people. There isn't a person here who doesn't know why Paytah doesn't take twenties, and many other people don't either now. It started off as a bit of weirdness on one person's part, but it's spread now and even raised awareness. So it's been a good thing."

"What do you think about it?" Bryce asked John.

"When I'm here I don't use twenties, but at home I do because I live in the real world. But I know plenty about Andrew Jackson and will tell people what he did. And that's all because of Paytah." John smiled, and Bryce did the same. "So you see, it isn't because he doesn't care. Like many of us, the problem is so large that we don't know where to begin, so we all do what we can." John stood up and walked to the large window that provided a great view of the black hills in the distance. "Look around, Bryce—this area was set aside as a reservation because no one else wanted it. There isn't anything around. The Black Hills are sacred to us, but most of the land was taken away because it contained gold. Our beliefs and generation upon generation of history didn't matter. Instead, they gave us this land because they didn't want it. There isn't much water except when it rains in the spring. The lakes that there are often dry up during the heat of the summer. The few streams that don't are used to the best of our ability, but without resources, there isn't much hope." The frustration in John's voice came through loud and clear. "The tribe has thought of turning to casino gambling like so many others have, but the land we have is out of the way. We tried to buy some land closer to Rapid City, but another tribe already has a casino there, and it doesn't make sense for there to be two, so we couldn't get a license."

"So how do people here survive?" Bryce asked. He'd already seen part of it, but he needed to know the entire picture.

"Some on government welfare. I'm sure that's where Little Wamblee's mother gets what little money she has. I know she works when she can, but there isn't much here, and with the kids, she doesn't have the ability to do what others have done—mainly what my dad does, work in the North Dakota oil and gas fields." John shook his head and continued looking out the window. "I wish he didn't have to do that, but it's the only way he, Mom, and the rest of the family can survive."

"Your dad is amazing," Bryce said. "After everything and all the time away, he still laughs and looks happy."

"He's making good money, and I know Mom is keeping tabs on every cent so he won't have to do this forever," John said. "But others don't have that luxury." John continued staring out the window and their conversation trailed off.

"Dinner is almost ready," Ichante said, hurrying excitedly into the room. "I did the cooking," she announced proudly, and John turned away from the window. Rushing across the room, he scooped her up. She squealed and laughed as he swung her around and into a huge hug. Mato came in to see what the ruckus was, and Bryce scooped him up to the same laughter. After what he and John had been talking about, they both probably needed to hear laughter and happiness—Bryce knew he certainly did.

"Let's go see what you made," John said as he carried Ichante into the kitchen.

"Daddy, Jerry called Grammy and Paw-Paw, and they are going to go with us to the water park tomorrow," Mato told John, and Bryce swung him around, to raucous laughter.

"Do you think your grandma and grandpa are going to go down the large water slide?" Bryce asked as he tickled Mato.

"No, but I am," he said, giggling.

"You are, are you?" Bryce teased, throwing Mato over his shoulder and carrying him into the kitchen.

"Yes." Mato laughed. "And so are you," he added.

"We'll see about that," Bryce said as he set Mato back on his feet. "I think I'll stick to the kiddie pools."

"Naw," Mato said as he pulled Bryce toward the table. "You're not a chicken."

"Is your grandpa a chicken?" Bryce teased.

"No, but he and grandma are old," Mato retorted.

"Don't let Grammy hear you say that," John warned as they all got the table ready for dinner. The laughter and joking extended through dinner, with all of them talking, telling jokes—mostly bad ones—and the kids having the time of their lives. Bryce couldn't remember the last time he'd laughed so much and had such a good time.

"What's got you so quiet?" John asked Bryce when the meal was over and the kids had followed Jerry to the other room.

"I don't know. We were laughing and talking all through dinner, and I was just thinking that I bet Paytah probably hasn't had a meal like that in a very long time."

John snorted slightly and then shook his head before turning away. Bryce thought he heard him mutter, "You got it bad," but he could have been wrong.

CHAPTER
FOUR

"WE'RE going to the water park!" Mato yelled through the cabin at dang near the crack of dawn. Bryce rolled over and groaned loudly. He knew the kids were excited, but the sun was barely up, and he certainly wasn't ready to get out of bed. He'd closed his eyes again when he heard both John and Jerry shushing the kids and getting them settled down. Of course, that only lasted for so long. Eventually his door opened and Mato rushed in and jumped on the bed.

"It's time to get up." Mato told him, and Bryce wondered which of his so-called friends had put Mato up to this.

"Mato, let Bryce get up and get dressed," John said from behind him, and he had his answer. Sometimes John was a big kid himself when he got excited about something.

"I'll be up in a few minutes," Bryce promised Mato, and he left the room, John closing the door behind them. Bryce got up and put on his robe before checking, and surprise, surprise, the bathroom was free. Bryce hurried and got his things together, but still had to race before Ichante got there first.

He cleaned up and quickly showered before dressing, careful to leave some hot water for the next person. Before leaving the bathroom, he made sure to clean up after himself and then hurried to his room. He finished dressing and joined the others in the living room. "My parents will be here at about ten," John said, and Bryce looked at the clock and groaned.

"It's not even eight," Bryce groused. Jerry came in from the kitchen and handed him a cup of coffee. Bryce sipped from the mug and felt the bitter, hot energy work its way into his veins. "Okay, I'm better now," Bryce said with a smile as he continued sipping. "Why did we have to get up this early?"

Jerry shook his head as he sat on the sofa. "We tried, but the kids have been up for hours already. They're so excited. We've been here working for three days, and I think they're getting a bit stir-crazy just playing games." Jerry lifted his mug.

"What are we having for breakfast?" Bryce asked.

Jerry peered over his mug at John, and Bryce wondered what they were up to. "I think the kids want doughnuts." Jerry sipped, and Bryce knew he was trying to keep from laughing.

"They do, huh?" Bryce asked, shifting his gaze to John, who tossed him the keys to the van and hid his eyes behind his own mug. Bryce caught the keys and stared at the two of them before finishing his coffee. Then he stood up. He placed his mug in the sink and headed to the door. As he pulled it open, he heard Jerry and John snicker. Bryce leaned so only they could see him, flipping both of them the bird. They laughed as Bryce shut the door.

He hurried to the van. After getting inside, he started the engine and headed down the foliage tunnel toward the road. Of course, this time he didn't get lost and reached the store in no time. He walked through the door, then stopped when he saw Paytah sitting behind the counter, working on his computer. "Are you doing okay? Any problems?"

Paytah looked up and glared at Bryce, but said nothing before returning to his work.

"I suppose I deserved that," Bryce said, leaning against the counter. Damn, why was it so hard to say he was sorry? "I shouldn't have taken my frustration out on you yesterday, and I'm sorry I called into question the way you fight for or care about the people here." Paytah stopped keying and turned to him. "I know you do everything you can to help everyone here." Bryce swallowed hard, waiting to see how Paytah would react, but he simply stared at him.

"You hurt me," Paytah said, his eyes blazing with something Bryce couldn't read. He knew it wasn't anger, but he couldn't figure it out.

"I didn't mean to," Bryce said. "I was upset about what happened earlier in the day and I took it out on you. I shouldn't have. I accused you of not helping, but I've been thinking and I can't come up with any answers either."

"Some questions don't have answers, no matter how much we might want them," Paytah said, and his expression softened. "Is that all you came in for?"

"Well," Bryce began, not sure what else to say. "Is your brother okay? He looked in pretty rough shape yesterday."

"Yes," Paytah answered curtly, glancing back to his computer screen. Bryce was tempted to get his doughnuts and leave, but he finally understood the look in Paytah's eyes—loneliness, deep and profound.

"Does that happen often?" Bryce asked, trying to sound sympathetic.

Paytah looked once again at the monitor, and Bryce figured he'd turn away and go back to work without answering. "More than it should," Paytah answered. "He drinks too much." Paytah looked around the empty store. "Many people do. They have nothing, so they drink to forget or to simply pass the time. No liquor is sold on the reservation, so they travel to get it. Either that or they distill it themselves." The sadness in Paytah's eyes hit Bryce hard. "There is nothing here. Jobs are scarce, so people take their monthly government checks and spend them trying to forget."

"That's what John told me, and I'm trying to understand."

"I don't know if you can. I was born here, and hunger, poverty, alcoholism, and even…." Paytah stopped and swallowed. For a second, the fear in his eyes was almost palpable. "I've been around this all my life and it isn't likely to change." Paytah turned away this time.

"I know you're probably right," Bryce said.

"No 'probably' about it," Paytah muttered before swiveling his chair toward Bryce. "What I don't understand is why you care. You're here for a few weeks and then you go home to your comfortable house in a nice neighborhood. You'll be back a few times to spend a few days teaching a class or two and then leave again. You don't have to live here and see the pain and hunger day after day. You don't have to live with children not getting enough to eat and stealing from their brothers in order to eat." Paytah was about ready to explode, Bryce could feel it.

"Do you think that just because I don't live here that I don't care about what's happening here? That Jerry doesn't? That's why he's trying to do something." Bryce looked at the computer screen. "The kids in the tribe can now be a part of the outside world. They can see that there's more than just what happens around them." Bryce took a deep breath. "Yes, I know they can't eat the computers, but hopefully that equipment will allow them to learn more, get a better education, and they can make something of themselves."

Paytah chuckled. "Eat the computers," he said, rolling his eyes slightly, then his expression turned serious again. "You do good work. You help people here. I don't mean to sound like I'm complaining, because I'm not. You're helping to teach people to fish and that is good."

Now Bryce chuckled. "That's what Jerry says too. He and John have gotten the donated pieces of equipment, refurbished them, and over the past few years, gotten enough for the school kids as well as other people in the tribe," Bryce said proudly, because he'd helped with those efforts... and so had Percy, but Bryce pushed that thought away.

"I know, you helped me too, remember?" Paytah said, and Bryce nodded. He did remember the time he'd spent close to Paytah, and he remembered helping him with his computer and the way his hair felt when it brushed against his arm. Bryce had sudden wicked thoughts surrounding Paytah's hair and just what he'd like to do with those long, silky strands. Instead, Bryce nodded and tried to return his mind to why he'd come. He had come here for something other than to talk to Paytah, but dang if he could remember.

"Oh, yeah, I need a dozen doughnuts. We and the Black Ravens are taking the kids to the water park in Rapid City. They're going a little stir-crazy at the cabin."

Paytah bagged up the doughnuts for him, and Bryce passed over a ten. Paytah was handing him the change when the door opened. "Morning, Paytah," a bright-faced woman said as she strode over to where they were standing and then went around the counter, shooing Paytah away. "It's Thursday, remember?" she said, and Paytah nodded. Bryce thought he was going to growl at her, but he walked around to Bryce's side of the counter. "I have things here. Don't worry. Go home and rest or something."

"Alowa, I'm fine," Paytah said but she ignored him.

Bryce figured that now was a good time to leave, so he grabbed his bag and headed to the door. He expected a fight from Paytah, but he followed him outside. Bryce walked to the van and got inside, watching through the windshield as Paytah stood in front of the store, looking this way and that like he wasn't quite sure what to do with himself. Bryce started the van and was about to put it in gear when he banged his hand on the wheel. "I know I'm going to regret this," he said out loud before turning off the engine and getting out of the van again. "Paytah, you'd be welcome to come and spend the day with us. We're going to the water park, and then we'll get dinner somewhere before coming back. We won't be too late because of the kids, but it should be fun."

Paytah looked like he was considering it.

"Go on and have some fun," Alowa said through the open door, closing it behind her. She eyed Paytah through the glass.

"It should be fun," Bryce offered, and Paytah nodded. "I'll wait while you get your things," Bryce said, and Paytah walked to the small house next door. Bryce knew he was definitely going to regret this, but he still couldn't keep his eyes off Paytah's backside, his gaze following him as he moved with a surprising grace.

"It's about time he did something other than sit in this store. I'm Alowa," the woman said as she walked up to the van.

"I'm Bryce," he said as he studied the attractive woman more closely. "I'm here with Akecheta Black Raven."

"I know. The rumor mill works at lightning speed here," Alowa said with a smile. "Thank you for offering to take him with you. I work in the store one day a week, and most of the time he sits around at home doing nothing. I'm supposed to give him a day off, but he rarely does anything." The door to Paytah's house closed with a bang, and Bryce shifted his gaze, watching as Paytah moved closer. When he turned back to Alowa, she had a knowing look on her face, and Bryce instantly schooled his expression. "Have fun, ya grump," Alowa told Paytah, nudging his shoulder, and Paytah grunted softly before getting into the van. She went back into the store. Bryce got in as well, starting the engine and the blessed air-conditioning before beginning the drive back to the cabin.

Paytah was no conversationalist, and that showed on the ride to the cabin. He sat in the passenger seat without saying a word.

"I'm not transporting you to your death or something," Bryce said.

"Sorry," Paytah said, but then he went quiet again. "Alowa has the hearing of a wolf and she can be really pushy."

"You're going to have a good time. The kids will have fun, and as hot as it's going to be, it will be nice to cool off." Bryce felt the prospect of some excitement starting to catch on with him. "I will warn you. The kids have been up since some ungodly hour, and they're wired." Bryce thought about the doughnuts resting on the console. He probably should have specified the ones without sugar, but it was too late now.

"They're good kids," Paytah said. "They are always well-behaved when they come in the store. Akecheta takes good care of them."

"He and Jerry love those kids to death," Bryce said, slowing down cautiously to take a nearly blind corner.

"They do not suffer because they are being raised by two men?" Paytah asked. Bryce glanced over at him, but he didn't see any judgment in Paytah's expression, only curiosity.

"No. Children respond to love, and those two are loved. John and Jerry fought very hard to get those children. You may have heard part of the story." Paytah nodded. "John adopted the children a while ago, and now they don't have any more issues with child services."

"Do they have any… problems because they're a gay couple?" Paytah hesitated as he asked his question.

"Yes, sometimes. It goes with the territory, I guess. But we have good friends, and most of the time, our families come to understand. Not always, but most of the time." Bryce continued driving down the narrow road. "My mother was supportive, but it still took her a while to get used to the idea. Jerry and John had a neighbor who tried to cause trouble, but he ended up being the one in trouble when the police came knocking on his door for making false accusations."

After another quiet minute or two, Bryce asked, "Do people on the reservation know about you?" He thought Paytah was going to choke. Paytah sputtered and then began to cough. Once Paytah got ahold of himself, Bryce began to chuckle slightly.

"Am I…." Paytah gasped, and then coughed again, appearing a little nervous.

"No," Bryce answered, anticipating the rest of Paytah's question. "No one would know to look at you. I got this feeling in my stomach when I met you, and my gut is rarely wrong." Bryce's chuckles slipped away as Paytah settled in the seat again. "I don't think other people in the tribe know unless you've told them. John didn't, but I think your friend Alowa knows, or at least suspects."

Paytah groaned loudly. "That woman has a huge mouth and talks all the time. My business will be all over the tribe before I get back."

"I don't think so. From the expression on her face, she's probably known for a while," Bryce said.

"You told her?" Paytah sounded almost panicked.

"Of course not, but she saw me watching you, and I know she knew," Bryce admitted, desperate to keep Paytah from panicking. The normally still man settled down some, but still fidgeted in his seat. Bryce breathed a sigh of relief when he turned into the long driveway.

"You were watching me?" Paytah asked as they passed through the tunnel of green.

"Duh," Bryce responded as he parked at the cabin. The kids ran out to meet him and pulled open the door.

"You got the doughnuts?" Mato asked, his excitement lasting until he saw Paytah. It was like a switch had turned him off.

"Yes, I have them," Bryce said, lifting out the bag and handing it to Mato, who walked quickly back toward the cabin, looking over his shoulder every few seconds until he disappeared inside. "Come on in. You can leave your things in here," Bryce said to Paytah before closing his door and leading the way inside.

John met them at the door, and he and Paytah clasped hand to wrist in a greeting Bryce had seen a few times before, then John motioned for Paytah to enter. The kids waited in the kitchen, already eating, while Jerry got out plates for the rest of them. "This is a surprise," Jerry said as he got an extra plate. "Would you like some coffee?"

"Yes, please," Paytah answered, and Jerry got him a mug and filled it from the pot. He also filled Bryce's mug for him.

"John's mother and father will be here in about half an hour. They are going to follow us in their car and they want the kids to ride with them," Jerry told them. "Glad you could join us, Paytah, it should be a lot of fun." Jerry smiled and filled his mug before placing the pot back on the coffeemaker. Bryce glanced at Paytah and then at his friends. He hadn't figured they would be upset that he'd asked Paytah, and they seemed to take it in stride.

"You two finish your doughnuts and then say thank you to Uncle Bryce before you get your things together to go swimming. I'll be in to check you have everything in a few minutes," John said, and Mato shoved the last of his doughnut into his mouth, chewing like a huge chipmunk. "Take it easy," John told him, and Mato drank from his glass of milk, then chewed awhile before swallowing.

"Thank you, Uncle Bryce," Mato said.

"Paytah made them," Bryce said, and, grinning, Mato looked up at the stoic man.

"Thank you, they were good," Mato added quickly before hurrying out of the room at a near run. Ichante finished her breakfast and milk and then she too was gone. The sound of their light bickering as they got ready drifted into the kitchen.

John ate his doughnut and then grabbed another one. "I better make sure they get all their things," John said before taking a bite of his second doughnut. "Glad you're coming with us," he added to Paytah before following the kids.

"I need to get my things together too," Bryce said, finishing his breakfast before rushing to his room. He'd brought a small bag with him and he filled it with what he thought he'd need. He was just finishing when the kids' yelling came through his door and Bryce knew their grandparents had arrived. Bryce got the last of his things together and joined the others. Of course, everyone had to eat before they left, but with the coaxing of grandchildren, it was surprising how quickly the older generation could move.

Soon, somehow, they had everyone and everything in the two vehicles. John started the van and got it turned around and then drove down the drive with the other car behind.

"How's business at the store?" John asked once they reached the main road north off the reservation.

"The usual. It doesn't change much," Paytah answered.

"I suppose you have to stay pretty close most of the time," Jerry said, and Paytah agreed, but didn't say much more. "Have you been to the park before?"

"No. I don't get off the reservation much except to pick up supplies and merchandise. I was only able to come today because Alowa is watching the store."

"I haven't seen her in a while. How is she doing?" John asked. "She and I were in the same class."

"She's fine. Pushy as ever," Paytah said, and Bryce had to keep himself from laughing. But he wasn't going to complain. She might have been pushy, but she was the reason Paytah had agreed to come, so he reminded himself to bring her something back. After all, Bryce had the sneaking suspicion that the highlight of the day wasn't going to be the water slides, but the sight of Paytah without a shirt on.

"She is that," John said with a small laugh. "But she was always a great person and fun to be around." John sped up when they reached the highway and continued heading north. "I thought if we had time on the way home, we could stop at Crazy Horse. The kids keep asking to see it again."

That was fine with Bryce, and Paytah nodded as well, but Jerry shook his head.

"They close at five during the week. We'll have to take the kids another day. I know they want to see it, but after we get done at the park, we'll need dinner, and on the way home they'll both probably fall asleep anyway. We can probably go on Saturday, stop there, maybe take the kids to the caves and see the buffalo herd."

Bryce smiled because all that stuff sounded like fun to him.

"Have you seen Crazy Horse lately?" Bryce asked Paytah, who shook his head.

"My dad used to take us to see it once a year. He said it was something we all should be proud of," Paytah said. "I haven't seen it since he died." The conversation in the car quieted after that. Bryce rode and watched the scenery out the window. The highway made travel faster, and in under an hour John pulled the van into the parking lot of the water park. John's parents parked next to them, and the kids were out of the car almost before it stopped.

They all got their things, and Bryce thought John and Jerry looked like pack mules as they carried everything while Mato and Ichante ran ahead, occasionally stopping to peer through the fence into the happy water wonderland beyond. "Can we go in now?" they said in unison.

"Yes," John said as Jerry paid the admission, and they went inside. Bryce went up the window and paid for him and Paytah. He got a stern look in return.

"I invited you to come," Bryce said and turned away, signing the credit card slip, and then they went inside.

The entire place was one screaming child after another, presided over by a huge water slide and filled with pool after pool with all sorts of fun stuff to do. "I found a quieter place over here," Jerry said as he met them and guided them under an awning, where the grandparents were already reclining on loungers. "John took the kids to change."

Bryce grabbed his bag and motioned Paytah toward the changing rooms. He picked up his stuff as well, and they made their way through the throngs of running, playing kids. The changing rooms were private, and Bryce got into his bathing suit, then slipped a T-shirt on. He dug out his flip-flops and placed them on his feet before folding his clothes and placing everything in his bag. He rolled up his towel and looped it over his shoulders before heading back out.

Bryce waited outside the door to the changing area, watching as people came in and out. He felt a bit like a roadway median for a few seconds, and then Paytah came out of the changing room and Bryce forgot about everything else. Bryce had imagined, especially last night, what Paytah would look like out of the baggy clothes he tended to wear, and during the drive, he'd watched and wondered what Paytah would look like in only a bathing suit, but the reality was so much better than what he'd imagined. He wasn't cut or anything, but he was lean, with smooth, flawless, reddish-brown skin and muscles that flowed under his skin rather than bulging. He'd gathered his flowing hair into a ponytail and….

"Is everything all right?" Paytah asked, looking down at himself. "You were staring."

Bryce nodded slowly. "Everything is fine," he said. "You look just fine." Bryce thought he saw Paytah color under his darker skin. He tore his eyes away from Paytah and cleared his throat. "Let's put our things by the chairs," Bryce suggested.

John's parents agreed to watch their stuff. They didn't seem to be ready to get wet. "We will later," Kiya explained. "Right now, we're relaxing." She looked at her husband with a soft smile, and he gently took her hand.

"Uncle Bryce," the kids called as they ran up, dripping water everywhere. "Come with us on the big slide," Mato said, pointing to the top of a wooden tower with stairs. "Please," Mato added, taking his hand.

"Are you big enough?" Bryce asked.

"I can go on the twisty one," he clarified. Bryce glanced at Paytah, who had an indulgent look on his face. Bryce followed Mato, and Paytah got in line behind him, with Ichante quickly joining them. The line went halfway down the stairs, and they found the correct one and waited. Water dripped from the steps above them, but no one seemed to care. It was already hot and getting hotter, so the water felt good.

"Are you an Indian chief?" the kid behind them asked Paytah. He must have been about six years old, and his eyes were as wide as saucers. Paytah didn't seem to know how to answer the kid.

"No, he's not a chief—he's a warrior," Bryce said, and Paytah became very serious, and the little kid stepped back. Then Paytah smiled, and the kid relaxed and smiled back. The line moved, and they began climbing the stairs. The little kid behind them kept watching Paytah and smiling at him whenever Paytah turned around.

Slowly, they climbed higher and higher, the park laid out below them like a water-filled map complete with lakes, a river, islands, boats, and rafts. Bryce wasn't so sure how much he liked this, but he'd promised the kids, so he tried his best not to look down.

"Don't like heights?" Paytah whispered from behind him, and Bryce nodded.

"I'll be okay," he said and continued to look up to where they were going instead of down. They finally reached the top. Bryce looked around, closed his eyes, and clutched Paytah's arm. "Give me a minute."

"Uncle Bryce, look, there's Grammy and Paw-Paw," Ichante called, waving down at her grandparents, who waved back.

"If you want to go down, it's okay," Paytah said, and Bryce shook his head, forcing his attention to getting Mato into the slide. When his turn came, Mato cheered and disappeared into the slide. He emerged at the bottom, jumping out into the water. Ichante was next, and she slid down as well. Then it was Bryce's turn. He got into position and waited until the man told him to go. Bryce closed his eyes and launched himself into the tube.

After a few seconds, his fear subsided and he started having fun. Bryce twisted and turned, the water zooming him downward, and he quickly found that if he arched his back, he went faster, which added to the fun. At the end of the ride, he zoomed out of the tube into a pool of water.

"Let's do it again," the kids said as he stepped out of the pool. Bryce wasn't ready for that yet. Paytah came down next, splashing into the pool. Bryce couldn't stop a smile when Paytah stood up, water cascading down his skin. Damn, it had been a long time since he'd seen anyone hotter than Paytah. "Let's do it again."

"Go see if John or Jerry wants to go down with you," Bryce said, and the kids took off. Thank goodness for parents. "I think I saw something quieter back here," Bryce said, and Paytah led the way. They got in line for the Lazy River, and after picking up rafts, they joined the other adults, who were floating down a curving loop of slow-moving water. Paytah held onto Bryce's raft and they floated together.

"This is nice," Paytah said, and Bryce hummed his agreement, relaxing in the refreshing water. They floated in silence for a while, which didn't surprise Bryce. Paytah seemed to be a man of few words. "Did you have a boyfriend before?"

Bryce lifted his head, almost startled that Paytah had asked him a question. "Yes. His name was Percy. We were together for almost three years and were going to get married, but he died in an accident." Bryce waited for the waves of sadness that always came when he talked about Percy, but nothing happened. "He was a nurse and had gone to New York for some special training. There was an accident at the airport and he was hit by a luggage truck. The driver was drunk on the job. Have you had anyone?"

"Once," Paytah said. "A long time ago, but we were kids." Paytah fell silent again, and Bryce hoped he would continue, but he didn't.

"What happened?" Bryce asked as they passed under one of the light waterfalls.

"We were kids. He was nice and we spent a lot of time together. Eventually we started messing around. I thought there was more to what we were doing than he did, and when we were almost caught once, he backed away. His father was on the council, and after about a year, he went to college and I was left on the reservation." Paytah scoffed lightly. "Once he left, he never came back for other than short visits. He stopped in the store a few times, but acted like nothing happened between us. Last I heard he got married." Paytah shrugged and lay back in his float.

"The spineless bastard," Bryce said softly. "I knew a guy like that when I was in school, too. I think we all meet the same guy at one time or other. Mine is a minister, married, with two kids. I saw him once at one of the bars in Sioux Falls. He saw me, and I made sure he knew I recognized him. After that, he took off, but I wouldn't be surprised to find him hanging around rest area bathrooms or something." Bryce lowered his voice when some kids paddled closer and then went past them, laughing and having a good time. "After that I dated a number of guys, none of them for very long, until I met Percy. He was special," Bryce said, breathing evenly through his mouth.

"It must be hard to lose someone like that," Paytah said.

"It was." Bryce paddled slightly to move away from the wall. "My mother was diagnosed with cancer a short time after Percy's death, so I had plenty to worry about. She's doing okay now, but we both know it's a matter of time. She's in remission, but no one can say how long it will last. Hopefully quite a while, but you never know." Bryce moved toward the edge of the river, positioning them toward the exit. This was too slow and it was giving him way too much time to think and talk about things that would be better talked about while everyone around them wasn't having fun. They got out of the current and headed up the exit, then stacked their floats with the others.

They made their way to one of the larger pools with pads floating on the surface and ropes strung over it. Bryce was trying to figure the best way across when Paytah darted over the floats like he was walking on water. The kids in the pool watched as Paytah did it again. "How'd you do that?" a boy asked with a touch of awe.

"Speed and balance," Paytah said with a smile. Bryce tried it multiple times and fell in the water after two steps. Some of the kids tried as well, but the only one who ever made it across was Paytah. "I'm going to go down the fast slides," Paytah told him after a while, and Bryce nodded. There was no way he was getting back to the top of that platform, so he found Jerry, John, and the kids playing together near where the grandparents watched.

There was an empty lounger in the shade next to Kiya, and Bryce sat down, instantly cooling once he was out of the sun. "You better put on sunblock," Kiya warned, and Bryce fished it out of his bag and slathered it on himself.

"I'm going to change," John's dad said, and his mother handed him the bag.

"I take it you like Paytah," Kiya said once they were alone, or as alone as they were going to get. "He's a nice young man. Had a hard life, though."

"He is nice in an intense way," Bryce agreed, getting a laugh in return

"That's one way to put it," she said with a smile that lasted for a few seconds.

"John told me that he used to be different—happier," Bryce said, and Kiya nodded her agreement. "He said he always figured something happened to him, but he doesn't know what it is," Bryce said, and from the dark look in her eyes, Bryce figured she either knew or had a pretty good idea.

"There were rumors some time ago, but that's all I know," she said as she sat up and adjusted the back of her lounger. "So I don't really know what happened, but... it isn't my story to tell even if I knew for sure. For what it's worth, I agree with John. I believe something did happen, but what it was, I—" She seemed to be searching for the words. "I can't really say, because at the time it was a lot of people taking a few facts and filling in the blanks." She was clearly uncomfortable with the entire subject. "You should ask him." Bryce knew it wouldn't do any good to press, so he finished putting on the sunscreen and then lay back on the lounger, closing his eyes for a few minutes.

"Paytah's about to go down the big slide," Mato said from next to him. Bryce opened his eyes and sat up, shifting so he could see the top of the platform. It was definitely Paytah. Bryce would know those wide shoulders and bearing anywhere now—they were etched on his brain. Bryce stood up and waited as Paytah got into position and then sluiced down the slide. He reached the pool at the bottom in a matter of seconds, sending a wall of water ahead of him as he came to a stop. "I wanna do that," Mato said, "but I'm not big enough."

"You will be," his grandfather said from behind Mato before scooping him off his feet. The youngster giggled and laughed as his grandfather carried him away before jumping into the nearest pool with him.

"Those are lucky kids," Paytah said softly as he walked up, and Bryce shook off the thought that all kids should have that.

They played in the water for another hour, and then Jerry gathered the kids and everyone headed to the snack bar for a small lunch to tide them over until a nicer dinner. John made the kids sit still for a while and then he cut them loose in the park.

"Shall we swim for a while?" Bryce asked Paytah, and they headed for one of the larger pools unadorned with play items. They dove in the deeper end and swam around for a while until the water began to roll around them, the waves becoming larger and larger. They were joined for a while by other people intent on enjoying the waves. Once the timer ran out and the water settled, they found themselves largely alone again. "Do you do many things other than run the store?" Bryce asked. "I mean, I know you don't get out much, but do you have any hobbies?"

"Not so much lately, but when my dad was alive, I used to work with wood. I'd hunt for branches and bits of log that I would carve into small animals. I even made a few pipes and things, but since Dad died, I haven't done much of it. There isn't the time, and I don't feel much like it any longer." Paytah seemed to look beyond the immediate area, like he was looking back through time. "Chay and I used to do a lot of things together when Dad was still around, but once he died, Chay began pulling away, and I had to take over more and more of the duties of the store." Paytah kicked his legs in the water and then settled back against the side of the pool. "I didn't realize at first that Chay had pulled away because he was drinking, but it soon became apparent."

"How bad is it?" Bryce asked.

"He's an alcoholic, without a doubt. He can't seem to make it through a single day without drinking and regularly empties a bottle with the intent of getting drunk." Paytah rested his head against the side of the pool. He looked weary and tired. "I don't know what to do. I know I should try to do something, but it never does any good. Last year he nearly got himself killed when he ran his car off the road. He promised that he was going to give up drinking, and for a few weeks he was the brother I remembered, but it didn't last. I should have known it couldn't. So I really don't have time for hobbies or much of anything other than somehow making enough in the store to keep myself and Chay fed. I only give him enough to buy food, but he always seems to have enough money to buy alcohol. I really don't know where he gets it and I don't think I want to. Someday I know someone is going to come in the store and tell me he's dead." Paytah pushed himself away from the side of the pool, gliding through the water, and Bryce stared at him, wondering how he could take something like that so lightly.

Bryce realized that Paytah probably wasn't taking it lightly, but he just couldn't do anything about it. Deciding that Paytah had probably told him things he rarely spoke about, Bryce smiled and pushed off the side, following Paytah across the pool.

They stayed at the water park for a few more hours and then gathered all their stuff and the kids to get ready to leave. Bryce and Paytah helped Jerry and John pack everything in the van, and once everyone was dry and in the cars, they headed out. It was a little early for dinner, so Jerry drove to the mall and they wandered around for a while. Bryce had promised his mother that he'd bring her something back, so he stopped in one of the gift shops and looked around. Paytah followed him in. After a while, Bryce found Paytah standing in front of a display of tacky totem poles and baskets. They were made in China and looked cheap and as fake as they actually were. "I hate things like this," Paytah said. "My people have a noble history and culture, and people manufacture this crap to sell."

"I know," Bryce said, gently removing the brightly colored peace pipe with fake feathers from Paytah's hand and putting it back on the shelf. "John said there was a place where I could buy some handcrafts there were real, but I haven't been there yet."

Paytah chuckled, turning away from the cheap souvenirs. "You've driven past it every time you came to the store. I'll show you when we get back to the reservation. It's the missionary place. They sell some nice artist-made items, but they're too expensive for most people on the reservation, so mostly they sit there."

Bryce looked around the store again as the ghost of an idea began to form. "Can I help you?" a clerk asked as she approached them.

"No, thank you," Bryce said, heading for the exit. He wanted to get out of this place almost as badly as he figured Paytah did. "Are there many artists on the reservation?" Bryce asked as they hurried away from the tackiness as if it might follow them down the mall if they went too slowly.

"Some. In the past ten years or so, some people have returned to the reservation for the quiet to work. A few sell their work in places like New York or Houston. Why?" Paytah asked, his curiosity obviously piqued.

"I have what might be the start of an idea and I need some advice," Bryce said absently, his mind already turning. "One of those artists might be good to talk to. Could you help me?"

"I'll ask when I see one of them," Paytah said, and Bryce nodded, still mulling things over. Bryce saw Paytah scowl slightly. "Is this some harebrained idea?"

"No," Bryce answered quickly, his defenses going up. "I don't know what it is, but if it's harebrained, I won't pursue it." Bryce walked faster, his anger propelling him down the mall hallway. Then he stopped and whirled around. "If you don't want to help, then say so."

Paytah continued walking closer at his usual pace. "Sorry," he said cautiously.

"Okay," Bryce said with suspicion.

"We once had a guy who got this idea that we could mine the iron that colors part of Rainbow Gorge. He wanted us to destroy a place that has been sacred to our people for hundreds of years. He said we could make a lot of money, and the council actually considered it." Paytah hissed between his teeth. "We get crap like that all the time, and while I'm suspicious, I shouldn't have judged an idea I haven't heard."

"I would never do anything that would hurt anyone," Bryce said, and Paytah seemed to think for a few seconds before nodding slowly. "And besides, if this works, you'll be involved."

"Me?" Paytah said surprised.

"Yes, you," Bryce said, and the more they talked, the more his idea crystalized in his mind. "Let's go find the others. I think I've had enough of this place," Bryce added as they walked past the tacky souvenir store again. They caught up with the others near the food court, where the kids were asking for smoothies.

"We're going to get dinner," John said calmly, lifting a whimpering Mato into his arms.

"They won't have smoothies," he said, using logic as only a seven-year-old can.

"You're tired and you've done a lot today. Grandpa bought you french fries and ice cream. You had hot dogs and whatever else you got your grandma to buy you. I think you'll live without a smoothie."

"But we can't get them at home," Mato said, lifting his head off John's shoulder.

"Yes, you can," Bryce said. "I make great smoothies. When we get back to the reservation, I'll stop at Paytah's store and get the stuff. Tomorrow I'll make you my extra special smoothies," Bryce promised.

"You're sure?" Mato begged.

"Yes, I'm sure," Bryce said, and that seemed to end the smoothie crisis. "We do have a blender in the cabin, right?"

John shook his head.

Twenty minutes later they left the mall, Bryce carrying a blender. That's what he got for opening his big mouth. "Smoothies tomorrow, right, Uncle Bryce," Mato said as he took the bag, hugging the blender box to him as he walked. At the cars, they stowed everything and got everyone inside and seated before driving to the restaurant. John's parents had chosen it, and Bryce had expected a buffet or family restaurant, but from the look of the place, they were all vastly underdressed. They parked and got out, and Bryce looked at the building, wondering if they were in the right place. Other people arrived who weren't dressed much better than they were, so Bryce followed the rest of their party inside.

The softly lit dining room was surprisingly quiet. "I'm so sorry," the hostess said to John's father as she looked over the reservation book. "If you'd like to wait about half an hour, we'll have a table large enough for your party. Otherwise, we have a table for six right now." She was visibly distressed.

"That's fine. John and I can sit at a separate table," Jerry said, and Bryce saw John nudge him in the side. The hostess looked visibly relieved and led them all through the dining room. Somehow, Bryce wasn't quite sure how, but he and Paytah ended up at their own table a slight distance from the others.

"This is nice," Paytah said quietly after they'd sat down. He also looked a little nervous. Bryce nodded slowly and opened the menu, instantly seeing the source of Paytah's worry. From what he'd seen, the food looked really good, but the prices on the menu were probably much more than Paytah was used to.

"It really is," Bryce said, setting aside his menu. "I'm glad I'm here with you." The day was beginning to feel like a date, and he hoped he wasn't the only one who felt that way. His question was answered when he felt Paytah lightly touch his hand. Bryce smiled and turned his palm up, easily sliding their fingers together.

"They're holding hands," Ichante stage-whispered to John.

"Shhh," John said. "You mind your own business." Ichante quieted down, and Bryce turned his attention back to where Paytah's hand touched his. Bryce had expected Paytah's hands to be sort of rough, but they were as smooth as the rest of him. Bryce closed his eyes when Paytah circled his thumb lightly over Bryce's palm.

"Good evening," the waiter said, and Paytah pulled his hand away and picked up the menu. Bryce turned toward the waiter, expecting shock or something worse, but instead saw a slight, knowing smile. "Would you like something from the bar?"

"Just a diet soda," Paytah said, and Bryce made it two. It didn't surprise him that Paytah didn't drink, and while Bryce might ordinarily have had a beer, he certainly didn't need one. The server left and Bryce chuckled softly. "What's so funny?" Paytah whispered.

"You don't need to be self-conscious," Bryce said.

"But the waiter, he saw us," Paytah whispered back.

"Yeah, and he probably wishes he was the one sitting here, getting to hold your hand," Bryce said softly, and Paytah glanced to where the waiter was already returning with their drinks. "Yes, really," Bryce said, easily reading Paytah's expression. "Just relax."

The waiter brought the drinks for the other table as well as theirs and then began to take orders. Paytah looked over the menu, and Bryce could almost see him figuring the prices. "Don't worry, dinner is on me." Paytah shook his head. "You can pay the next time." Bryce flashed a quick smile, and Paytah looked a bit shocked.

"You want there to be a next time?" Paytah asked. "Next time for what?" Paytah seemed a bit confused, and Bryce held his gaze until Paytah's mouth formed an "O." The conversation from their friends filtered over, and Bryce turned toward the other table, seeing them all looking at them.

"What?" he asked, lifting his eyebrows, and they returned to their own conversation. "We seem to be a source of amusement for everyone else."

"I guess so," Paytah said before glaring at John and his parents. They made a show of looking away, and Paytah turned back to Bryce, flashing him a wicked smile. Instantly Paytah's mask seemed to fall away before Bryce's eyes.

"I knew it," Bryce whispered. "I knew that grumpiness of yours was just an act to get people to leave you alone." Bryce leaned back in his chair.

"It's no act," Paytah said. "I am grumpy and grouchy." He scowled, and Bryce began to chuckle. Now that he'd seen below the surface, the scowl didn't seem so menacing; rather, it was almost comical, like one of those theater masks that exaggerated the emotion to an extreme.

"Not deep down," Bryce countered. Their salads arrived, interrupting their discussion. They ate and sometimes joined in the conversation with the other table.

"What do you mean, 'not deep down'?" Paytah asked after the server had cleared their salad plates. "You act like there's another part of me somewhere that I don't know about. I'm just me."

"There is another part of you," Bryce said. "Just like there's a part of me not everybody sees. We're all like that. Most of us try to put our best foot forward when we meet new people because we want them to like us. You act like a grump, but I don't think it's because you want people to hate you, but because you want them not to get too close."

"Thank you for that analysis," Paytah said rather sharply.

"See?" Bryce figured he would press a little further. "I started to see who you are and you pulled away." He reached across the table, taking Paytah's hand lightly. "You don't have to hide from me. I'm not out to hurt you and I don't want anything from you." Bryce could almost see the denial forming in Paytah's mind, but he didn't say anything. Instead, Paytah narrowed his eyebrows and tried to look intimidating.

Mato chose that second to look over from the other table. "Uncle Bryce, why is Paytah making faces at you?" That did it. Paytah broke into a smile, and Bryce knew for sure that he'd been right.

"He's just playing," Bryce said, and Mato put his fingers in his mouth, pulling his cheeks wide as he stuck out his tongue.

"Stop that," John scolded mildly.

"But I wanna make faces too," Mato said, turning back to the table.

"You can make all the faces you want in the car on the way home," John said, glaring at Bryce, who looked away, trying not to laugh. He definitely needed to remember that little ears pick up everything.

"What makes you think I'm different deep down?" Paytah asked, leaning slightly across the table.

"The way you smile when you don't think anyone's looking," Bryce told him. "John said you used to be different when you were in school, happier, more outgoing…."

"I don't want to talk about it," Paytah said flatly.

What everyone had told Bryce was correct. Something had happened. Bryce's curiosity was definitely piqued, but now was not the time to pursue it. Maybe Paytah would never want to talk about it. "Didn't say you had to. I'm just saying that person is still there, and he's really rather handsome and attractive when he makes an appearance." That got him a smile that Paytah tried to hide, but the smile broke through anyway. "You have dimples," Bryce teased.

"I do not."

"Yes, you do," Bryce said. "You definitely have smile dimples." Bryce wondered for a split second if Paytah had dimples in other places. That thought sent an image racing through his mind. Bryce tried to stop it, but it was too late. He was happy he had his napkin on his lap. Paytah definitely had hip dimples; Bryce had seen them peeking out of his bathing suit, and in his mind, as the imaginary Paytah turned around, there were butt dimples as well.

"Sorry," Bryce said as Ichante's voice from the other table broke through his imagination.

"Are you going to go with us when we see Crazy Horse?" Ichante asked.

"Of course. I've never seen it," he answered. "I'm looking forward to it." Bryce was about to ask if they could see Mount Rushmore as well, but then he remembered that was a sore subject. All the Black Hills were considered sacred by many Native tribes. He'd ask about it later. "Papa Jerry says we're also going to go to a cave and see buffalo." She sounded so excited.

"I heard there's also a place nearby where you can go horseback riding," Bryce said, and Ichante turned to Jerry.

"We'll see," Jerry said. The server refilled their glasses and then left before returning with their meals. He set the impressive plates, both in arrangement and portion size, in front of each of them. The conversation died down as everyone began to eat.

"Are there buffalo on the reservation?" Bryce asked Paytah.

"Not really. The herd is largely at Custer State Park."

"Is there land for buffalo?" he asked.

"Yes," Kiya answered. "The southwest portion of the reservation had buffalo many years ago, but they were largely poached off by hunters. Why?"

"Just curious. I thought it would be cool if you had some, that's all. Your ancestors lived off buffalo, so I thought it would be fitting if there were some on the reservation." Bryce turned his attention to his dinner, and the conversation fell off slightly. Bryce's mind ran a mile a minute and he had to try to stop the thoughts that all buzzed through his head at the same time. He didn't have much luck until he concentrated on Paytah. Then his mind cleared and he focused only on him.

"Do you always do that?" Paytah asked. "You seem to get these ideas all of a sudden."

Bryce shrugged. "Sometimes," he answered after swallowing. "My mind sometimes goes into overdrive and tons of ideas come to me. Most of them are crap and I let them go, but sometimes I have a good one. I mean, it would be cool if there were buffalo on the reservation. Cattle would really suck, but I know there are places where buffalo are raised in a semiwild setting. They live on the range, but they're managed like cattle—tracked, cared for, and eventually used for meat. There was buffalo on the menu, and that wasn't from some guy going out to kill an animal somewhere—it was raised on a sort of farm. I was curious if there was land and if anyone had ever thought of reintroducing them on the reservation and using them as a source of money." Bryce took a bite of his beef before turning toward the other table. "You have land, and while I'm not sure if there's enough water now, there must have been at one time if buffalo were indigenous." Bryce shrugged again, but he saw that John's parents and Paytah were listening. "I don't know if anyone has looked into it, but it might be a way to combine your heritage and the land the tribe owns, and allow the community to make some money at it without destroying the land. You'd be bringing back an animal that once lived there."

John's father set down his fork. "Where would you get the animals?" he asked, and John nodded.

"I read online once that the state park manages their herd and needs to keep it at a certain number," Bryce said. "Petition the state to see if you couldn't arrange to have the overflow. You might also be able to petition the federal government for some animals. There are also farms where they raise them and you might be able to buy some animals, but that would be more difficult." Sometimes his ability to retain useless information came in handy.

John's dad looked around the table, clearly interested. "I don't know if anyone has thought of that, but it might be worth bringing up," he said with a smile, and Bryce returned it before turning his attention to Paytah, who was smiling as well.

"Now *that* was worth it," Bryce said.

"What was?" Paytah asked.

"Seeing you smile," Bryce said, and Paytah turned away. "Don't. I like it when you smile. You're incredibly handsome when you smile." Bryce took Paytah's hand for a few seconds, squeezing it before releasing it so they could eat.

"What other ideas do you have?" John's dad asked, and Bryce shrugged.

"I'll let you know tomorrow," he quipped, and everyone laughed before returning to their meals.

The kids were definitely winding down by the time they were done eating. The server asked if they wanted dessert, but everyone declined. Mato sat on Jerry's lap, half asleep, and Ichante looked about ready to fall asleep in her chair. The adults finished their coffee, and the server brought the check. John's father took it and would brook no argument. "I don't get to spend time with my grandchildren that often," he said, placing his credit card in the holder before the server took it. Thank-yous were said all around from both tables, and once the bill was signed, they got up to leave. The kids were placed in the backseat of their grandparent's car, and Bryce figured they would probably both be asleep minutes after they pulled out of the parking lot. Bryce and Paytah got in the backseat of the van, and he found his eyes closing as they rode back south toward the reservation.

They rode for a while, the roads becoming quieter, traffic thinning until it seemed like it was only them. They entered the reservation and drove to Paytah's, parking outside his house. He got out and said good night, then walked away toward his front door.

"Go on. We'll wait a few minutes," Jerry told him, and Bryce got out of the backseat and hurried to Paytah's closed door. He knocked softly, and when the door opened, Paytah stared at him, obviously puzzled.

"Did I forget something?" Paytah asked.

"Yes, you forgot this," Bryce said. Standing in his tiptoes, he moved closer to Paytah, put an arm around his shoulders and brought their lips together. At first, Paytah didn't move, but after a few seconds, he kissed Bryce back. Paytah tasted of woods and the outdoors, clean and fresh, regardless of how late it was in the day. Bryce broke the kiss, settling back on his feet. "I'll see you soon," he said, and Paytah nodded in the light that came out of the open doorway.

Bryce backed away and then turned to walk back toward the van. He knew they'd most likely had an audience for their kiss, but Bryce didn't care. He barely felt the ground under his feet the entire way back to the van. He pulled open the door and got inside, seeing Paytah still standing in the doorway. Bryce rolled down his window and waved good-bye as John started the engine. Slowly, they backed up, and Bryce continued watching Paytah's doorway until they rounded the corner.

Then Bryce turned around and stared straight ahead, lightly licking his lips in the hopes of capturing some last lingering taste of him.

John and Jerry talked quietly about mundane things, like getting the kids in bed, but Bryce ignored them, turning over that kiss in his mind.

CHAPTER
FIVE

OVER the course of the next few days, Bryce, John, and Jerry worked almost nonstop. The kids were spending a few days at their grandparents, so everything was quiet at the cabin. Their day off at the water park had been great, but they still had work to do, so they spent some time catching up. Bryce managed to finish a website he'd been developing for a client. He set it up for testing and turned it over to the customer for review almost a week early. Jerry was thrilled. Bryce was thrilled as well. "You're on fire," Jerry told him. "I bet I know what's got you so riled up."

Bryce felt himself blush. "It was just a kiss," he said.

"I know, but you haven't stopped thinking about him, have you?" Jerry asked with a wicked smile. "You know, it's okay," he added seriously. "There's nothing wrong with developing feelings for someone else. Percy would want you to move on."

"I know," Bryce said. "But I'm wondering if I'm ready. I still miss Percy a great deal. Am I being fair to Paytah or anyone if I still feel that way?"

"You'll always miss Percy," John said, and Bryce shifted his gaze to him. "You were too happy and too much in love to stop missing him. He was too important to you. Missing him doesn't mean you aren't ready. I guess the question is, what does your heart want? For a long time, you only wanted to mourn Percy, but I think that time has passed and your heart is ready to move on."

Bryce nodded. "I think so, but what if I'm wrong?"

"Your heart will never lead you wrong," John told him, returning to his computer. Bryce turned to Jerry, who nodded his agreement, and then he too went back to work. "Sometimes you think too much," John added from behind his computer, and Bryce tossed one of the old sofa pillows at John, hitting him on the side of the head. John tossed it back, and then they all got back to work.

"John's parents are bringing the kids back this afternoon, so let's get done what we can. Then tomorrow we'll take them to see Crazy Horse, the caves, and buffalo," Jerry encouraged. "There isn't a lot we need to finish, but let's get it done so we can enjoy ourselves." They all quieted down and the room filled with the soft clicking sounds from keyboards. Bryce's mind sank into the code, and within a few hours, he was deep inside the program, the code singing to him. Jerry and John moved around sometimes, but he barely heard them. Everything was simply clicking into place. It was Bryce's stomach that finally intruded.

Blinking a few times, he looked away from his screen and checked on the time. "There's a sandwich on the counter for you," John said. "You were really into what you were doing, and we didn't want to disturb you." All three of them had experienced times like that and they all knew to respect the zone. Bryce stood up, his legs a bit stiff, and slowly headed for the kitchen. He got a soda from the refrigerator and ate his sandwich quickly before returning to work. He had just a few more hours of work and then he'd be done. Bryce knew Jerry would look it over before sending it out, but everything was running smoothly and he didn't want to stop.

Bryce worked the rest of the afternoon and he indeed finished drafting the program. He tested it and then set his laptop aside. He'd already stared at the screen enough, and he definitely needed a change of scenery.

"We're going to take a ride to town. Do you want to ride along?" Jerry asked.

"God, yes," Bryce said, hurrying to his room to get his shoes. Once he had them on, he went out to the van and got in the backseat.

The now familiar ride didn't take long, and once they reached the reservation center, Bryce hurried to the trading post. Paytah was helping a customer with a special order, so Bryce wandered through the small store, picking up a few items he needed. There were others doing their shopping, so Bryce hung back until Paytah was done. "Hey," Bryce said with a smile as he approached the counter.

"Hey, yourself," Paytah said rather gruffly. "You didn't call and haven't been in."

"Sorry," Bryce said softly. "We've been working for days to get some projects completed. I wasn't ignoring you." Bryce leaned slightly over the counter. "I thought about you a lot, actually."

"You did?" Paytah asked cautiously.

"Yeah. I should have come in to see you, but we were under a deadline and the cabin was quiet, so we all wanted to make the most of it," Bryce explained, wishing now he had called. "The kids come back today, and tomorrow we're doing some of the touristy things. I was wondering if you'd like to come with us. Sort of a second date."

Paytah smiled, but it quickly faded. "I don't think I can," Paytah said. "I don't have anyone to watch the store. I'd like to, though." Bryce nodded slowly. He'd known it was a long shot. "I'll have to see," Paytah added before rummaging around behind the counter. "I put it right...." He came up and handed Bryce a business card. "Running Deer is one of the artists on the reservation. He does a number of things, including pottery and some woodcraft. I wasn't sure if you were still interested, but when he came in yesterday, I got his card, and he said to call—any time after five or six is best."

"Thank you," Bryce said, taking the card. He still wasn't sure his idea would work, but the more he thought about it, the more positive he became. The part he wasn't sure about was how he could really get it started. "I can't stay very long now because I rode in with Jerry and John," Bryce said, "but I promise the next time I see you I'll explain my entire idea."

Paytah was about to answer when the door opened. Bryce turned along with Paytah as an older white man swaggered in like he owned the place. "Hi, Peter, how are things going?" he asked. Paytah nodded without taking his eyes off the man. The door opened again, and a boy of about eleven or twelve hurried up behind the man, a look of awe on his young face. "Go on and pick out whatever ice cream you want." The boy couldn't seem to believe his luck, and the man repeated himself with a smile. The kid rushed through the store to the frozen food case. The silver-haired man walked over to the counter and leaned casually against it. Bryce alternated between watching the kid and the man, wondering who he was. His behavior seemed somehow out of place.

"Mark Grantham," the man said, answering Bryce's unasked question.

"Bryce Morton." Bryce put out his hand, and Paytah nudged his back and got his attention. "What brings you into the store?" Bryce asked before turning to Paytah.

"I'll get your things rung up," Paytah said briskly. "I know you have to meet Jerry and John." Bryce had never seen Paytah move so quickly before.

Mark didn't seem to notice at all. "I have a charitable foundation and I work with a number of the boys down at the tribal school. The foundation tries to help give some of the boys at the school experiences they wouldn't otherwise be able to have. Once a year we take a group of kids to Yellowstone for a week, run sports weeks, and things like that. We also help sponsor some of the food programs at the school to help ensure that these kids get enough to eat."

"That's very noble, but difficult during the summer when they're out of school," Bryce said, but Mark wasn't paying attention. The boy who had come in after him brought a wrapped ice cream sandwich to the counter, and Mark lifted him into his arms.

"Peter, would you add that to the tab?" Mark asked as they headed for the door. Bryce couldn't help following Mark with his eyes. There was something, he wished he knew what it was, that made him want to watch. The door closed, and Bryce continued watching through the window until they passed out of sight.

"He seems like a nice...." Bryce trailed off when he saw Paytah staring nails out the window. He nearly stepped back at the combination of rage and terror in Paytah's eyes. It only lasted a second. He was about to ask what was wrong when Paytah's expression became more normal. "What is it? Who is he?"

Paytah shook his head violently. "You should find John and Jerry," Paytah said, bagging up his groceries. "Can I call you if I find someone to watch the store?" Paytah seemed almost distracted, though he was looking directly at Bryce, who nodded and gave him his number. He also got Paytah's.

"Maybe Alowa can come down. I'd really like it if you could come with us, but I'll understand if you can't," Bryce said, taking the groceries. As he was leaving the store, he turned to take another glance at Paytah, but realized Paytah wasn't paying attention. Wherever he was, it was miles away, and by the pained expression on Paytah's face, it wasn't a pleasant place.

"Bryce," Jerry called as they both walked toward the van. "Is everything okay?"

"I don't know." He had the most unsettling feeling, but he wasn't quite sure why. Bryce shook it off. "I got a few things for dinner as well as the stuff for smoothies for the kids." They really seemed to love them.

"Is Paytah going to be able to come with us tomorrow?" John asked as he joined them, unlocking the door. Bryce placed his groceries on the backseat and then climbed inside.

"He doesn't know if he can get someone to watch the store," Bryce answered, settling on the seat as the others got in. "Do you know who Mark Grantham is?"

"Sure," John said excitedly. "He's a former pro football player. Years ago he set up a foundation. They do a lot on the reservation, help at the schools, take some of the kids on educational trips, have picnics a couple times a year for all the kids in the tribe, stuff like that. Mark's the guiding force behind the charity. You see him on the television occasionally chairing this event or that to raise money. He's been a real godsend to a lot of the kids on the reservation. Why?" John sounded like he too was a bit in awe of the man.

"He was in the store buying one of the kids ice cream. We talked briefly, and I wondered who he was," Bryce explained. He was still puzzled by Paytah's reaction, so he kept it to himself. "He seemed sort of bigger than life. Acted it too." Bryce quieted and sat back as John talked most of the way back to the cabin, mostly about Mark Grantham and all the things he'd done for people on the reservation. Did the guy walk on water?

"He must be quite a guy," Bryce said toward what he hoped was the end of the litany of the wonderful things the man had done. John's parents had already arrived, and once they pulled to a stop, the kids ran over. John scooped Mato into his arms, and Jerry did the same with Ichante, and then they traded before leading them all inside.

"Can we have smoothies?" Mato asked, and Bryce began getting everything out, making a batch of strawberry-raspberry-orange smoothies. The kids delivered the glasses to everyone, and then Bryce cleaned up and put everything away.

"You look puzzled," Kiya said when Bryce joined the others.

"I'm fine," Bryce said, but as he sat down, he wondered why he couldn't stop thinking about Mark Grantham, or more importantly, Paytah's reaction to him.

THE kids were excited about tomorrow. Jerry and John finally got them to bed, and the cabin was quiet. Bryce had been hoping for much of the evening that Paytah would call. His phone had rung once and he'd answered it quickly, hoping it was Paytah, but it had been his mother. Not that he'd been disappointed that she'd called; he'd just been hoping it was someone else. Bryce had talked to his mother for a while. She was still doing well, which was a relief. "Are you trying to get me off the phone?" she asked toward the end of their conversation.

"No, I'm not trying to get you off the phone," Bryce answered.

"Yes, he is," John said from behind him. "He's hoping he'll get a call from a boy," John teased as though they were in junior high.

His mother laughed. "I'm glad you're doing well and starting to move on. Is it serious?"

Bryce moved outside so he could talk more privately. "I'm not sure. He's a... different sort of man, quiet and incredibly intense."

"He sounds interesting. Is he someone you met at the reservation?" she asked expectantly.

"Yes. He runs the trading post on the reservation and...." Bryce faltered. "He's very serious and he seems sad. He smiles around me, though. I think something happened to him some time ago and it hurt him pretty badly, and I think it changed him. No one seems to know what it is, and he won't talk about it." Bryce's mother had been a grief counselor for years, so his next question was on target. "I was hoping you might know a way I can get him to talk about it."

"There are no magic words, and if he doesn't want to talk about it, you can't make him—no one can," she told him, and Bryce figured that was going to be her answer.

"John said Paytah was a happy, normal kind of kid until he was about fourteen. Then he became quiet and withdrew from everything. He said Paytah was like a different person all of a sudden. He and John weren't close at that time, but he told me what he saw. I asked his mother about it, and she said there were rumors in the tribe, but she wouldn't talk about it either. Something happened to him. I know it," Bryce said. "There are times when he forgets and smiles, and I see the person shine through from before he was hurt."

He heard her sharp intake of breath. "Dear, I know you want to help, and this Paytah must be pretty special, but what you've told me could be the result of him being who he is."

"No. John said that people have asked him about what happened, and Paytah nearly punched one guy out. Something did happen." Bryce was sure of that.

"Then it's his secret to share," she told him patiently. "And he might share it with you when he trusts you enough. But you'll have to earn his trust and probably his love before he'll open up. And he may not even then. If he's kept his hurt buried this long, he may keep it forever." That's what Bryce was afraid of. "Be patient." Bryce promised he would. "Now, tell me all about the guy who's captured your interest." She sounded happy, and Bryce told her all about Paytah. After they ended their call, he went back inside and joined the others in the quiet cabin.

John and Jerry were curled together on the sofa, talking quietly. Bryce went right to his room to give them some time alone. Setting his phone on the dresser, he decided to get cleaned up. He got his clean clothes and carried them to the bathroom. Being as quiet as he could so he wouldn't wake the kids, Bryce showered and got ready for bed.

Back in his bedroom, he checked his phone and saw he had a message. He called his voice mail, punched in his code, and heard Paytah's voice. He sounded excited. "Alowa said she would watch the store tomorrow," Paytah said. "Please call me if you still want me to go with you." The message continued in silence, like Paytah wanted to say something else but didn't. Then the message ended and clicked off.

Bryce called Paytah's number right away. "Yes, I want you to come," he said excitedly when Paytah answered. "I've been hoping you'd call, but it was getting late and I was about to give up hope that you would be able to." The words tumbled out of Bryce's mouth.

"I'm glad I can come too," Paytah said. "Alowa was as pushy as ever and said I needed to get out more." Bryce made a mental note to thank her the next time he saw her.

"Should we pick you up at the store? At nine?"

"That would be fine," Paytah answered, and their conversation stalled. There were many things Bryce wanted to ask, things he wanted to talk about, but they all seemed off-limits right now. "I'll see you then."

"Okay," Bryce said, and they ended the call. Bryce put his phone on the dresser, and a soft knock sounded before the door opened and John stepped in. "Paytah can come with us after all. Alowa is going to watch the store," Bryce told him. "Please remind me to pick up something for her as a thank-you."

John smiled. "So you're saying that woman's pushiness is coming in handy?"

Bryce chuckled lightly. "Yeah, I think she's pushing him in my direction." Bryce walked around the bed, closer to where John stood. "Do you think I'm being stupid?"

John tilted his head slightly to the side. "How so?"

"Do you think things could work with Paytah and me?"

"It's too early to worry about things like that. Get to know each other and see where things lead. Enjoy it and don't think too much. Paytah's a good guy, you know that, but he's going to need time. If you call the other day a date, that's probably the first one he's had in years, if at all."

"There's so much pain there," Bryce said. "I saw some of it today while I was in the store. It just lasted a second, but it was there and a bit frightening."

"Do you know what caused it?" John asked, stepping further into the room.

Bryce nodded slowly. "I don't think you'll be happy when I tell you, but I think his pain and anger were centered on Mark Grantham."

"Bryce, you have to be imagining things. Mark Grantham is a great guy. He could spend his time in corporate board rooms or with rich family and friends in Rapid City. Instead, he comes here and spends a great deal of time with the kids here on the reservation." John sat on the edge of Bryce's bed. "Besides, if I remember right, he and Paytah were very close when Paytah was growing up. They went all kinds of places together. I remember how jealous I was that Paytah was one of the guys Mark chose to spend time with. I would have liked to have been able to do some of the stuff they did." John turned so Bryce could fully see his expression. "His foundation tries to help the neediest of the kids on the reservation, in particular, and I didn't qualify, but at the time I wished I had."

"Like I said, John, I knew you weren't going to like my answer, but you asked me what I thought and I told you. The expression on Paytah's face made me shiver, and it was directed at this Mark guy," Bryce said.

"Maybe they had a falling out," John suggested, and Bryce let it go. What he'd seen in Paytah's eyes had not been the result of a falling out. He'd seen terror, and the way Paytah had moved to keep Bryce from touching the other man. There was much more to it than that, but Bryce wasn't going to convince John.

"Maybe," he agreed halfheartedly, and John stood up. "I'll see you in the morning," Bryce added.

"Night," John said, leaving the room and then closing the door behind him. Bryce finished getting ready for bed. He listened to the crickets and small animals as they skittered outside his open window. He tried closing his eyes, but every single time he did, Paytah's face flashed into his mind, contorted in pain, with the anger and terror he'd seen permanently glowing in his eyes. Finally, Bryce fell asleep.

When he woke in the morning, the cabin was still quiet. Bryce got up and used the bathroom first. Then he went into the kitchen and started the coffee and preparations for breakfast. It was definitely his turn to cook, and they had the ingredients, so Bryce whipped up pancake batter. The room filled with the scent of cooking, and one by one, the smell lured the others out of bed. Both Mato and Ichante yawned as they shuffled into the kitchen. Bryce waited while they both climbed onto stools and rubbed the sleep out of their eyes. Bryce got them glasses of juice and began cooking. John and Jerry joined them a short while later, and they looked like hell too. "Bad night?" Bryce asked, and both Jerry and John nodded, with Jerry reaching for the coffeepot.

"Yeah," John said once Jerry had poured him his coffee. "My grandmother would say that my dreams were haunted by bad spirits, and I'd have to agree with her." John turned into the living room and sat on the sofa while Jerry sat with the kids, and Bryce began flipping pancakes.

"Can you do it in the air?" Mato asked, and Bryce flipped the completed pancake into the air and then placed it on Mato's plate. The kids smiled, and Bryce began making a pancake for Ichante, flipping it for her before sliding it onto her plate. The kids began to eat and talk, dispelling the residual gloom that lingered from the night before.

Bryce continued making pancakes. Jerry and John joined the kids at the table, and everyone ate. Laughter quickly filled the kitchen, and gradually even Bryce's memory of the dreams he'd had the night before faded. Bryce then made some pancakes for himself and joined the others at the table, eating heartily.

"I'll clean up," Jerry said as he finished eating and took his plate to the sink. Once the kids were done, John had them clean up and get dressed. Bryce helped Jerry and then got his things together for the day.

It didn't take long to get everyone in the van and then they were on their way. They stopped to pick up Paytah, and Jerry didn't let the kids get out of the van. Paytah was waiting and he climbed in, sitting next to Bryce in the far backseat, and off they went.

They pulled into the drive for the Crazy Horse memorial just after ten, and the kids were bouncing by the time they drove into the parking lot. They burst from the van, jumping up and down, pointing toward the unfinished sculpture. "How long before it's done?" Bryce heard Mato ask Jerry as he took Mato's hand.

"Probably not until you're as old as Paw-Paw," Jerry answered. Bryce climbed out of the van and waited for Paytah. After closing the sliding door, Bryce walked with Paytah toward the visitor center.

"It's something," Bryce said, looking at the huge mountain in the distance with its finished face and the top of the outstretched arm really beginning to take shape, along with the basic shape of the horse's head.

"It's come far since I was last here," Paytah said as they climbed the steps to the visitor center and paid their entrance fee.

"There's a guided tour to the base of the mountain in half an hour," Jerry said, and they all paid the few dollars extra so they could get a closer look. Then they climbed the steps to the visitor center.

"Is that what it will look like?" Ichante asked, pointing to the completed marble sculpture that stood to the side.

"Yes, only much bigger," Paytah answered, and he put his arm around her shoulders and walked her to the front of the deck. They seemed to talk for a while, and Bryce wasn't sure he wanted to interrupt them. Eventually he wandered over anyway and heard the two of them speaking in Lakota, with Ichante giggling and Paytah laughing.

God, that was so good to see. Bryce wanted Paytah to laugh like that more often. The usually moody man set Ichante back on her feet, and she wandered to where John, Jerry, and Mato were admiring the model of what the mountain would look like.

"You two were having a good time," Bryce said as Paytah approached.

Paytah nodded slowly without taking his eyes away from the massive sculpture in progress. Bryce had no idea what was going through Paytah's mind at that moment, so he stood quietly next to him. "The last time my dad brought me here, they hadn't finished the face yet. Now that's done, and they're working to finish the arm. I probably won't live to see it done, but even if it's never finished, people will remember."

"They will remember. Your history isn't as lost to the world in general as you think it is," Bryce said softly, and Paytah turned toward Bryce. "When I was a kid, Native Americans were portrayed as drunks, sidekicks, or bad guys in the movies. Now there are movies from the Native perspective that show just how wrong we were. Your people are portrayed as a full, realized people instead of a mere caricature."

"It's not enough," Paytah said.

"Then the only people who can change that is you—the collective you," Bryce said, and Paytah glared at him for a few seconds, but then his expression softened.

"I bet you have some ideas," Paytah said, and Bryce smiled.

"Yes, I do, and I think they might actually work," Bryce said. "I'll tell you all about it when we have some time alone." Bryce turned toward the visitor center, with Paytah following. They joined the others to watch a short video on the history of the project and where the designers expected to go from here. Then they all looked around for a while before leaving to board their open tram to the mountain.

"Good morning," the guide said as they started to board the tram. "It's going to be a great day, and you picked a fun day to visit. We aren't blasting today, so we can go all the way to the mountain this morning." Everyone boarded, and they rode through pine forests to the base of the mountain, looking up the arm toward the face. The guide gave basic facts about the mountain and project before letting everyone off to take pictures.

"Stay with us," Jerry cautioned the kids, and Bryce took Mato's hand while Paytah took Ichante's. They looked around for a few minutes, marveling up at the sculpture that was taking shape.

"At the current rate of work, it's anticipated that work will continue for at least fifty years, maybe longer," the guide said. "The work being done is financed strictly by private donations. Our founder decided that no government money would be taken and therefore there would be no government say or influence on the project. Because of that, the sculpture is taking decades to complete, but it will be true to its original vision."

"There's someone up there," an old lady said, pointing to the arm.

"That's our sculptor. The son or grandson of our founder—it's hard to tell from here. They're already hard at work, and we need to leave so they can continue." The guide herded them all onto the tram and they rode back to the visitor center."

They got off and walked up into the small store area. Bryce was pleased to see it devoid of the usual tourist crap. They wandered around, looking at the displays. The kids talked Jerry into buying a rock. For a dollar, they could buy a rock that had been blasted off the mountain, and the kids wanted one to put in the garden at home. Jerry forked over the buck, and Mato chose a chunk of rock, which John dutifully hauled to the van.

They rode toward Custer State Park, and Jerry paid for the sticker to enter the park, then they slowly drove the road, looking out the windows. For the longest time they saw nothing, and then there they were: a large group of buffalo congregating in and around the road like nothing was happening. They were eating grass and wandering here and there, backing up a stream of cars, and no one really seemed to mind.

"Are those real buffalos?" Mato asked, his face plastered to the window.

"Yes. Those are real buffalos, and they wander all over the park just like the giant herds did a long time ago," John said. Bryce knew that wasn't exactly true. The park did have boundaries, and the herd was kept to a manageable level more by man than by letting nature take its course. But, yes, it was a real buffalo herd. The cars ahead began to move, and then all of a sudden a buffalo turned and ran at one of the cars. The car sped up, and the animal veered off toward one of the calves.

"What happened?" Ichante asked as she leaned to her brother's side to get a better view.

"The car got between a mama and her baby," Bryce said as they slowly inched forward, the road clearing somewhat and the cars moving on as the herd moved off into the grasslands at the side of the road.

"This is cool," Mato said. Bryce reached into his pocket and pulled out his phone, then snapped a few pictures through the glass.

"Yes it is," Paytah echoed as he watched out the window.

"What are you thinking about?" Bryce asked.

"How traditionally our ancestors hunted these animals on horseback with bows and arrows. If you fell off your horse during the hunt, the chances were you would be trampled, but if you were successful, if the tribe was successful, then everyone ate during the winter and there were skins to keep warm and make clothes and shelter," Paytah said. "Nothing was wasted." Bryce swallowed hard. He knew what Paytah was saying.

They continued on, but didn't see any more buffalo. Donkeys wandered up to the car, peering in the windows before moving on. When they reached the end of the drive, Jerry parked the van near a snack-bar area and they got out. The kids got in line for food, and Bryce thought they had the right idea.

"Can we ride horses?" Ichante asked, pointing toward a paddock once they were seated at a picnic table with hot dogs, chips, and water.

John checked his watch. "I don't think we can do the caves and ride horses, so we'll take a vote. Who wants to ride horses?" John asked. Mato and Ichante both raised their hands excitedly. Bryce looked at Paytah, who nodded, so Bryce raised his hand too, and so did

Paytah. "Looks like we'll ride horses," John said, looking a bit disappointed.

"Why don't I wander over and see what times they offer riding," Bryce proposed, and he got up, throwing the trash of his lunch in the can as he went. As he got closer, he saw that the times were posted, with the last ride leaving at four. Bryce returned to the group. "It's twelve thirty now, and the last ride is at four. We could sign up, go to the caves for a tour, and then return to ride the horses."

With that settled, they got the kids moving and spent part of the afternoon deep in the earth. Bryce found the caves fascinating, but for the kids it was a little slow, and they definitely got restless. By the time they were ready to leave, Mato had fallen asleep on John's shoulder, and Ichante was dragging. They rode the elevator back to the surface and then went out into the lobby and gift shop. Bryce did his best to ignore the tacky made-in-China souvenirs until he passed the register on the way out.

"Don't you have anything authentic?" a woman was asking a clerk. "Everything is made in China or the Philippines." The clerk shrugged, and the woman stepped away. Bryce turned to Paytah with a smile.

"What's that for?" Paytah asked as Bryce headed for the exit. Outside, he found a bench and sat down to wait for the others.

"You heard that woman—she was looking for something real, something nice, to take home. Something that didn't cost a fortune, but was real, not tourist crap."

"Yeah," Paytah said.

"So that's my idea. You and the tribe make it," Bryce said.

"Are you saying we weave blankets by hand to sell?" Paytah asked as a woman carried a fake "Indian" blanket out of the store.

"No. I'm saying...." Bryce snuffed softly. "Okay, you saw the tacky peace pipes with plastic feathers? Well, what if you and the tribe were to make real pipes based on authentic designs?" Paytah looked skeptical. "You don't carve them by hand, but you make them in an assembly line process. Say you turn a hundred pipe bowls on a lathe and then make a hundred pipe stems. They would be assembled and decorated by hand in traditional, authentic ways. You do the same for dolls, or any craft item that will work."

"But they'll be expensive," Paytah said.

"More expensive than the crap in the tourist stores, yes, but we'll brand it, say 'Sioux Made' or 'Lakota Made'. Each comes with a certificate stating that the item was made on the reservation by Native Americans and the proceeds go to help projects on the reservation. That's why I wanted to talk to some artists. They could design what you make and keep the items simple, but authentic and usable, or at least potentially usable." Bryce paused to watch Paytah's reaction. "The people on the reservation would be paid, bringing in income, and we could set up a website if it gets going to sell the items on the Internet."

"Wouldn't that be charity?" Paytah asked.

"How so? The tribal members would be working and making things to sell. It would bring money into the tribal economy. The items could be sold in gift shops around the area. I'm not saying we go full steam ahead. We would need to get the tribe's blessing, and then we could test it to see how it worked."

"Wouldn't we be exploiting our heritage?" Paytah asked evenly, and Bryce could tell he'd captured his attention.

"No. It would be celebrating it. The crap in these stores that costs five bucks is exploiting your heritage. It isn't close to the craftsmanship and care that went into making each of the items your people used every day. A knife, a pipe, a doll, children's toys—they were all handmade with care and love. I'm saying you should do the same thing on a slightly bigger scale. Not massive, but large enough that it might employ some of the people on the reservation and return money to the tribe to help the families who need it, like Little Wamblee's." For some reason, he could not get that child out of his mind.

"Okay. Let's say I think this is a good idea and we are able to get the council's support. How do we get it started? I know about selling stuff, but not making stuff. You know about computers."

"My idea is to ask the tribe. Get as many people in the tribe invested in the idea as possible. This isn't mine or yours—it has to be theirs. I bet there's someone who understands production. I bet there are people who retired from factories or places like that. See if they'll be interested in helping. The idea isn't to make *me* money, but to help the tribe so it can help others." Bryce stopped speaking and waited.

Paytah seemed to be thinking things over. "It's a good idea. If we can get something like that going, it would give families work and help the tribe at the same time."

"It's a start. I mean, it isn't going to make anyone rich, but it could help some families and add to the economy on the reservation."

"You're probably right; it could be a start," Paytah said as he looked around. "It seems like there's so little hope there. Many people have given up and stay in misery or are leaving." Paytah shifted his gaze, and Bryce followed it to where Jerry and John were walking toward them with the kids. "Not that I blame John at all."

"Blame me for what?" John asked as they got closer.

"I was just talking about how people leave the reservation to find work," Paytah said. "Bryce has an interesting idea."

"Why am I not surprised?" Jerry asked with a self-satisfied grin. Jerry had taken a chance on both him and John when he'd hired them three years earlier, and he loved it when Bryce and John proved him right.

"We should get moving or we'll be late," John said, and they got back in the van.

An hour later, after signing forms, finding helmets, and getting set up with horses, they started on their trail ride, with one guide in front and another in back. Bryce had a chestnut-brown horse, and right behind him was Paytah on an almost identical model, except Paytah's was definitely bigger. The thought made Bryce blush. They rode through the woods and crossed a small creek. The horses seemed to know exactly where they were going, and Bryce figured they'd probably been taking this route every day for years.

"Can I ask something?" Paytah said from behind him, and Bryce turned. Paytah seemed very contemplative.

"Of course," Bryce answered, turning so he was looking forward again, but he was still listening. They were toward the back of the group, with Jerry, John, and the kids toward the front. Bryce figured that was matchmaker Jerry's doing. Not that it was a bad thing.

"Why do you care so much?" Paytah asked just loud enough for Bryce to hear. "I mean, you aren't a member of the tribe, and in another week or so, you'll go home and back to your own life. If you don't want to, you'll never have to see anyone here again. So why? It isn't because of me, is it?"

"Would it be so bad if it was because of you?" Bryce asked, looking back over his shoulder, and Paytah seemed a little surprised. Bryce turned back around and figured he'd let Paytah chew on that for a while. Sometimes Paytah seemed completely shocked that Bryce could be interested in him. The ride continued, and there were no more questions from behind him. In fact, Paytah didn't talk much at all for the rest of the ride. Bryce enjoyed the quiet as they continued along the path through the wooded area. It was pleasant and incredibly relaxing. All around him people laughed and talked, but at least for a while, Bryce let himself sink a bit into his own mind.

All too soon the ride was over. The kids groaned good-naturedly when they had to get down. Bryce dismounted and an attendant led away his horse. He also turned in his helmet and found himself walking a little stiffly back toward the van. The kids ran ahead, filled with excitement, chattering on about their ride. Jerry unlocked the van, and everyone piled in and soon they were off.

"What did you mean when we were on the trail?" Paytah whispered.

Bryce thought back to their conversation. "What if I was doing this for you? Would that be so bad?" Bryce said, biting his lips to keep from smiling. "I'm not. Well, I'm not only doing it for you."

"Then why?" Paytah asked, and Bryce looked over at the kids and then back to Paytah, who seemed to understand, and they rode quietly back to the reservation. John parked the van outside Paytah's small house. They worked their way out, and Bryce accompanied Paytah to the door. "I had a nice time."

"I did too. Maybe next time it can be just the two of us," Bryce offered, and he received a warm smile in return. Bryce leaned closer, and Paytah met him for a kiss that started soft, but quickly heated. Bryce had to pull away to keep from giving everyone in the van a show. He took a step back, and as Paytah gazed at him, Bryce felt a surge of excitement run through him. God, the things he wanted to do to Paytah, with Paytah, but.... Slowly, Bryce turned away to head back to the van.

"Could you stay for dinner?" Paytah asked. Bryce approached the van, and John lowered the passenger window.

"I'm going to stay with Paytah for dinner," Bryce explained. "He invited me," he added in an excited whisper.

"Sure," John said. "Call us if you need a ride home." John actually winked at him. Bryce rolled his eyes and stepped away. Jerry backed the van out of its spot, and Bryce joined Paytah outside his door. Paytah unlocked the house, and Bryce followed him inside what looked like a time capsule. The furniture, the rugs, the pictures—everything looked like it had come out of the forties.

"The stuff is all a little old," Paytah said a bit dismissively.

"It's amazing," Bryce said, looking all around him. The house had seen a lot of use, but it was obvious that Paytah took care of what he had and maintained the place beautifully. He hadn't changed anything.

"This is how my mother furnished the place, and I haven't had the heart to make a lot of changes. I had to replace the curtains, but I used something close to what Mom had," Paytah said, and Bryce wandered over to a set of rustic-looking shelves lined with gorgeous pottery pieces. "Mom was an artist, and those are some of her pieces. When she died, I kept what she'd saved. She made her own clay from here on the reservation."

"They're the same color as your skin, warm and rich," Bryce said, and Paytah looked away. "You have nothing to be ashamed or frightened of."

"I'm not scared," Paytah countered.

"Sorry, for a second you looked it," Bryce said as he moved closer to where Paytah stood. "I meant it. You have nothing to be ashamed of. You're warm and rich," Bryce whispered, lightly stroking Paytah's smooth cheek.

Paytah stilled Bryce's hand with his own. "I can't," Paytah whispered.

"Can't what? Allow yourself to be happy or cared for?" Bryce asked gently. "You deserve to be cared for and to have someone to be with."

Paytah shook his head and moved away. "I don't."

"Why?" Bryce asked, and Paytah stiffened. "This has something to do with that guy in the store yesterday, doesn't it? That Mark What's-his-name guy?" Bryce moved closer again, this time hugging Paytah until his tight muscles relaxed just a bit. "I'm not going anywhere, and regardless of what you seem to think, you do deserve to be cared for. I don't care what anyone told you or how anyone made you feel, that's a simple fact." God, whoever had hurt this man was going to answer to him. Bryce was going to find out what happened and then rip the nuts off whoever had done this to Paytah. Bryce got angrier by the second until Paytah finally began to hug him back. Then the anger slipped away. "I shouldn't push you, I'm sorry."

"You really care," Paytah said softly enough that Bryce wondered if Paytah was murmuring to himself.

"Of course I do. I don't understand why you would think I wouldn't." There had to be a reason for Paytah's doubt, and Bryce knew now that this Mark guy was at the bottom of it somehow. Yes, he was jumping to conclusions, but the way Paytah stiffened and braced himself every time Bryce mentioned him was a huge giveaway.

"I...," Paytah began.

"Let's have some dinner and talk about something else, something nicer," Bryce suggested, and some of the anxiety slipped from Paytah's posture.

Paytah went into the kitchen, where Bryce joined him, sitting in one of the chairs. "It will be simple," Paytah said, like Bryce expected something fancy.

"Whatever you make will be wonderful," Bryce said, and Paytah looked at him with such doubt that Bryce wanted to scream. *What or who beat Paytah down like this?* The thought had Bryce's anger rising again.

The kitchen filled with the scent of bacon, and then Bryce saw Paytah cutting fresh tomatoes and tearing leaf lettuce. "Do you have a garden?" Bryce asked as the scent of the tomatoes, which had to be fresh, mixed with the bacon.

"Alowa does, and she brings stuff over all the time. Says I eat too much crap," Paytah answered as he continued working. "She fancies herself as some sort of Indian earth mother." It was the first time Bryce had ever heard Paytah refer to anyone as Indian. "She's a situational vegetarian. When other people are around, she professes to be vegetarian, but when no one's looking I've seen a burger disappear in her presence." Paytah laughed, and Bryce joined him, the last of the residual tension disappeared from the room. "I hope BLTs are okay."

"They're my favorite," Bryce said. "After all, everything's better with bacon."

Paytah toasted bread and then began building hefty sandwiches. He also added a slice of turkey to each one, plated them, and then carried the plates to the small plank table. He returned to the kitchen for drinks, and then they both sat down. Paytah began to eat right away, looking down at his plate. At first, Bryce wondered if he was being ignored, and then it occurred to him that Paytah was used to eating alone, so he just ate.

"Did your dad build the house?" Bryce asked, and Paytah looked up from his food, setting his sandwich on his plate.

"My father's brother originally built it. Uncle Black Wolf died shortly after he finished it, and left it to my dad. He made a lot of the furniture too. After that, we moved in and Mom got her hands on the place. She loved old things and did all this. There are only two bedrooms. Mom and Dad had one; Chay and I had the other. There wasn't a lot of room, but it was always home."

"Where does Chay live now?" Bryce asked after swallowing a small bite.

"He has a place in the hills somewhere," Paytah answered through a sigh. "He used to live here, but I couldn't stand his drunkenness, and he wasn't willing to help himself. Eventually he moved out so we wouldn't fight any longer. Now he figures he's free to live however and do whatever he wants."

"Must be hard to want to help and not be able to," Bryce observed, and Paytah nodded slowly as he picked up his sandwich.

"I know now that there's nothing I or anyone can do for him," Paytah said, pausing with the sandwich in his hands. "That was the hardest realization—that he has to want to change. It has to come from inside him, but he isn't interested. I keep hoping that he will be someday, and I'll be there when he is." Paytah resumed eating. "I thought we were going to talk about something happy."

"Okay," Bryce said mischievously. "Let's talk about your hair."

"My hair?" Paytah asked, setting down his sandwich again in surprise.

"Yeah, it's really sexy," Bryce said, and from the expression on his face, Paytah thought he was kidding. "The other day I was helping you at the computer and it brushed against my hand." Bryce suppressed a shiver. "Like I said, really sexy. How long have you been growing it?" He reached over the table and lightly touched Paytah's midnight-black hair.

"The last time I cut it was when my father died," Paytah said, "and I won't cut it now unless something happens to Chay."

Bryce combed his fingers through Paytah's sensuously silky strands. "I hope you never have to cut it." The hair slowly fell away from Bryce's fingers. "I think it's amazingly beautiful." It took Bryce a few moments to look away, and then he slowly began to eat again. "Do you think I should let my hair grow out like yours?"

"No, I like it like it is," Paytah told him, and then he went back to eating, his expression shy. "I never said those things to anyone before. You know, caring-type things."

"There's nothing wrong with saying how you feel." Bryce smiled softly. "It's nice when you do." Paytah looked down at his food, and Bryce knew it was his way of hiding, not letting Bryce see too much.

"I was eleven years old when I first met Mr. Mark. That was what he let me call him. He was this important man, and I was just a poor kid that he took an interest in." Paytah looked like he was far away. "My dad ran the store then, but we didn't have any extra money. Sort of like now, we made enough to get by on and that was about all. Mr. Mark offered to take me on his camping trips. My dad thought I'd done something really good to be asked and he was so proud. Mostly he was impressed by Mr. Mark the same as everyone else was, just like I was." Paytah pushed his plate back, stood up, and began pacing. "He used to buy me things like ice cream and candy, just like he did when he was in the store the other day." Paytah's voice hitched. "Everyone around this place loves him, they think the sun rises and sets on his ass, but it doesn't!"

Bryce felt a lump form in his throat, slightly afraid of what Paytah was going to tell him. He tried to swallow the lump away but it stayed there.

"Mr. Mark had been some big-shot athlete in college, so at one point he started a sports league, sort of an after-school program where we could learn to play sports like basketball and football. And he chose me to be a part of it." Paytah puffed his chest out slightly. "I knew I was special, then. Mr. Mark liked me, and I would do anything for him." Paytah's chest returned to normal and he shifted his gaze to the floor. "Most of the programs took place in the summer, but some happened after school. As I look back on it, I realize what he was doing, but then... we were kids. It was hot, so we took off our shirts and Mr. Mark told us he was going to teach us how to wrestle."

Bryce closed his eyes. He could already see where this was leading, but he said nothing. Paytah had probably never told anyone about this, or if he had, it had been a long time ago, and Bryce didn't want him to stop now. Paytah needed to say what he wanted to say, he needed to tell someone. Bryce was close to tears that Paytah was opening up to him.

"Mr. Mark would take off his shirt and wrestle with us. We'd laugh and climb all over him, and he'd show us the holds, or at least his version of the holds. Now I know what he was doing was getting us used to being touched in ways we shouldn't have been touched." Paytah continued slowly pacing the room. "When I was about twelve, we got to go camping with him. He'd take two or three of us boys on a weekend camping trip. We'd all sleep in the same tent, but one night it got cold, so Mr. Mark had me climb into his sleeping bag. I didn't know at the time that he was naked. I know now that he got off on us being near him." Paytah turned away, and Bryce shivered before getting up. Without a second thought, he put his arms around Paytah.

"You don't have to go on if you don't want to. I'll understand."

Paytah shook his head. "Those camping trips that I'd looked forward to when I was eleven turned into trips to hell by the time I was fourteen. His touching turned into him asking to be touched, which turned to kissing, and then oral sex. Eventually... he said no one would believe me if I told and that he'd hurt my father, so I let him." Paytah placed his hands over his face. "I was fourteen years old the first time he had sex with me, and it continued for almost a year whenever we were alone—camping, after school, in his car. When I turned fifteen, I told my father that I didn't want to be a part of the group anymore. The only way I could think of to get away was to withdraw, and I guess I pulled away from everyone and everything. Mark tried to lure me back, and he even used his influence with the principal to talk to me about rejoining the group. The principal actually tried to help get me back into that man's group so he could have sex with me some more."

"Do you think he knew?" Bryce asked.

Paytah shrugged. "At the time I wasn't sure, but probably not. Now that I think back, he was probably in as much awe of Mark as everyone else seems to be around here and thought he was trying to help." Paytah was shaking, and Bryce held him. He didn't know what else to do. He wasn't about to tell him a bunch of mindless platitudes. "I still dream about it, and I know he's still doing it. I've seen him. He lures the kids in and then preys on them."

"Did you tell anyone what happened to you?" Bryce asked, and Paytah nodded.

"I couldn't tell my dad. I know I should have, but I was so ashamed and afraid he'd hate me. As an adult I know it sounds stupid, but he had very... definite opinions and was very vocal with them. I finally got up the courage to talk with the counselor at school. He'd always been nice to me and seemed to have noticed the change in me.

He'd actually asked if something was wrong. So I made an appointment." Paytah shuddered. "I remember sitting in his office and I told him the whole story, everything. By the time I was done I felt better, figuring at least now someone knew."

"What happened?"

"He looked shocked and horrified at first. Then I told him who was doing these things to me and his whole attitude changed on a dime. He told me what a great guy Mark was and that it couldn't have been him who did this to me. 'Mark would never do that,' he actually said, and then started questioning me as if my dad was the one who was hurting me. I was so horrified and began yelling that it was Mark, but he didn't believe me." Paytah took a deep breath. "I left the counselor's office near tears, but kept myself together and went back to class, trying to forget everything. I don't remember much of the rest of that day, but I made it through and went home."

Bryce's mouth hung open in disbelief. This was the most unbelievable thing he'd ever heard. "Is that counselor still around?"

Paytah shrugged. "I don't know. He could be. He wasn't that old, and working at the school is a good job here on the reservation because the federal government pays most of the costs."

"Son of a bitch," Bryce swore. "He should have listened to you. That was his job." Bryce calmed himself down when he realized Paytah wasn't done. "Is there more?"

Paytah nodded slowly. "The next day I was called down to the principal's office. The counselor was there and so was Mark."

"Jesus Christ," Bryce muttered.

"They all worked to convince me that I'd either imagined the whole thing or that someone else had done these things to me. None of them believed me. Mark had such a grand reputation here that they believed him." Paytah pulled away from Bryce and went back to pacing, faster and more deliberate now. "I didn't know what else to do, so I kept quiet and left the office when they said I could go. All I wanted to do was get out of there." Paytah stopped nearly dead still. "I made it through the rest of the school day, and when I left the building, Mark was waiting for me."

"Jesus Christ," Bryce swore again, more loudly this time. He could feel the tension building in the back of his head and wondered what hell Paytah must be going through.

"He practically kidnapped me into his car, and we sped away. He was yelling and threatening me the entire time. 'No one is ever going to believe you, so you may as well shut your mouth,' he yelled at me. 'You know I can make sure no one comes in your father's store again. I might open another one on the reservation and run you out of business.' He said all this while we were speeding down a gravel road. All I wanted to do was get the hell away from him and never see him again. I honestly thought he might try to kill me, but then I realized he was taking me toward one of the campsites he used—where he took us for sex."

"Oh my God," Bryce gasped and placed his hand over his mouth.

"He slowed down to take one of the corners, so I pushed open the door and jumped out. The car wasn't moving very fast, and I rolled on the ground before taking off as fast as I could cross-country. I knew the reservation pretty good and stayed away from the roads as I made my way home. It took me a long time, but I made it back home and snuck into my room. I didn't want to see anyone. I sort of felt like my life was over." Paytah took a deep breath. "But as days went by, I started to feel better. Mark stayed away, and the few times I saw him, he kept his distance, and that was all I wanted. For a while, he stayed away from the school altogether, and I don't know if that was because he was afraid of me, but I bet the principal and counselor had him keep away to contain the matter. Everything went back to normal, and after I graduated I started seeing Mark around the school again."

"You know what he's doing," Bryce said, and Paytah nodded.

"He's finding other little boys to do what he did to me, I know that. I tried speaking up, but no one believed me," Paytah said.

"I know." Bryce's heart ached for Paytah and he didn't know what to do for him. What was left of their dinners sat on the table, and obviously neither of them was interested in eating any longer. Bryce's stomach didn't seem to be able to make up its mind if it was happy about what he'd already eaten.

"I think you better go," Paytah said. "Jerry and John will be wondering about you."

Bryce pulled out his phone and called Jerry. "Could you pick me up in the morning?" Jerry chuckled. "It's not like that," Bryce said seriously. "I'll call you in the morning and let you know what's happening."

"I take it this is serious," Jerry said.

"Yes," Bryce answered and heard the phone shift.

"Bryce, it's John. Is everything okay?" he asked urgently.

"It will be," he answered. "I'll see you in the morning." Bryce hung up. "Jerry and John won't worry now."

"You're staying?" Paytah asked.

"Yes. I'll sleep on the sofa out here if you want, but I'm not leaving you alone," Bryce told Paytah emphatically.

"I'm not a child," he countered.

"No, you're not. But you've just told and relived one of the most traumatic events of your life and you shouldn't be alone. You aren't alone. I know you've felt that way for a long time, but that isn't the case." Bryce hugged the larger man. "I believe you," Bryce said softly. "Each and every word."

Paytah trembled in Bryce's arms. "You're the only person to tell me that."

"I know," Bryce said. There were so many things he wanted to say, to tell Paytah, but he kept quiet. Now was not the time. Paytah was exhausted and seemed to sway slightly. Gently, Bryce guided Paytah down onto the sofa and then cleared the table, cleaning up as best he could before returning to sit down next to Paytah.

"I'm tired," Paytah said after a long silence, and Bryce got up with him. He followed Paytah to a small bedroom. Paytah walked inside and then stood still, his eyes unfocused and unmoving. Bryce took him by the hand and guided him toward the bed. Carefully, he removed Paytah's shirt and pants, then helped him get into bed. Paytah stared at him, still looking a bit blank. Bryce thought about leaving the room, but instead took off his own shirt and pants and got into bed next to Paytah, holding him close.

"Just go to sleep. I'll be here with you," Bryce said as he stroked Paytah's hair. "You aren't alone, and I believe you." Bryce kept repeating the words until Paytah sighed softly and closed his eyes. Bryce lay awake for a long time, hoping that Paytah would sleep. He did, eventually, and then Bryce finally dozed off from sheer exhaustion.

CHAPTER
SIX

BRYCE woke in the small hours of the morning. He immediately remembered where he was and felt Paytah thrashing in the bed next to him. He settled for a few moments and then began moving again. Bryce lightly stroked Paytah's arm, trying to calm him, but it got worse.

Paytah gasped and sat straight up in the bed, pulling the sheets around his hips. He sucked air loudly, and Bryce saw him look first one way and then the other. "Bryce, is that you?"

"Yes, I'm here," Bryce soothed.

"I thought you were him," Paytah whispered. "For a few seconds I thought I was back with him. But I'm not, am I?"

"No, and you never will be again," Bryce said, sitting up as well. "You're fine and you're safe. He's never going to get to you again. He can't. I'll rip his balls off first." The vehemence of Bryce's response startled even him. "If he looks at you cross-eyed, I'll make sure he walks funny for a very long time, the sick fuck." Bryce forced his anger away. It wasn't going to help Paytah. "Lie back down, it's okay."

Paytah settled back on the bed, but seemed restless. Bryce tugged him close and lightly kissed Paytah's shoulder. Damn, his skin tasted good, and Bryce had to restrain himself.

"What if he's ruined me forever?" Paytah asked. "I told you I did some stuff when I was a kid, and I did. After I thought I'd left Mark behind. It didn't work too well, and I got scared and backed away."

103

"So you weren't ready. That doesn't mean you're ruined or damaged. It just means you need to take it slow and know the person you're with cares for you. Sex isn't what it was with Mark, not really. That was him being greedy and taking what he wanted no matter what you had to give. That's not caring—that's abuse." Bryce quieted and kissed Paytah's shoulder, then he did it again, moving a little closer to Paytah's neck. Bryce felt Paytah stiffen, so he moved away. "Nothing is going to happen that you don't want to happen." Bryce kissed him lightly again. "Do you want me to stop?" Paytah shook his head. "You have to say what you want."

"No. Don't stop," Paytah whispered into the darkness, and this time Bryce kissed him at the base of his neck. He used his tongue to find that little spot, and Paytah groaned softly. Bryce was willing to bet no one had ever done this with him before.

"Not until you tell me," Bryce whispered before licking up Paytah's skin to just behind his ear. "See, you're not broken. You just need someone to take care and show you what making love really is."

"Making"—Paytah swallowed—"love."

Bryce sucked lightly on Paytah's ear, chuckling softly. He lightly stroked his hand over Paytah's smooth chest, something he'd wanted to do since the first time he'd seen him without his shirt. He wanted to ask if anyone had ever done anything to make Paytah feel good, but he didn't want Paytah to associate this with his past in any way. Paytah seemed to be enjoying Bryce's touches, and Bryce wanted Paytah to associate pleasure and caring with his touch rather than the fear and self-loathing that had been his past.

"Yes, Pay, love. That's what it's called when two people who care for one another give themselves to each other. That's what you've been missing all this time." *That's what Mark stole from you,* he wanted to say, but kept quiet, his anger at bay.

Bryce shifted on the bed so he could see Paytah's eyes. Then he slowly leaned closer, giving him a chance to back away. He didn't. Paytah held still, and Bryce kissed him. Just like outside the door, the kiss deepened quickly, and Bryce let Paytah take charge. Bryce figured Paytah would need to feel as though he were in control. He felt Paytah hold him closer, but the kiss didn't deepen further, and Bryce could feel Paytah's reticence. That was okay, as far as he was concerned. Bryce liked being held, and Paytah's doing it felt great.

They continued kissing, and Bryce continued exploring Paytah's skin with the lightest touch he could muster. "I love your hair," Bryce said as he carded his fingers through the long, strands, pulling out the rubber bands Paytah had used to keep it together. "I like it loose and flowing."

"Do you have some kind of kinky hair thing?" Paytah teased, and Bryce clamped his eyes closed.

"Maybe," Bryce said, knowing if Paytah could tease, he must be feeling more comfortable. Bryce wriggled his hips against Paytah's and giggled. "I could sure develop some sort of hair fetish as long as it was your hair." Bryce laughed outright and tugged Paytah even closer. Then he kissed him again, going slowly and carefully, but his own body was working against him. He was achingly hard, but he wasn't going to press anything on Paytah. That was what Mark had done, so he tried to put that out of his mind and simply reveled in the feel of Paytah against him.

Then he realized Paytah was as hard as he was. Bryce didn't want to be too aggressive, but Paytah moved his hips and he heard Paytah's breathing shorten and become more ragged. "That's it, Pay, let it all out." Bryce pressed closer, giving Paytah more friction, and he felt it the second he tumbled over the edge. Paytah held his breath and made little sounds as he came. Bryce held Paytah tight, moving his hips slightly, and soon the ground fell away for him and he came as well.

Bryce lay next to Paytah, breathing deeply, with a wet mess in his shorts. The only consolation was that Paytah was in the same predicament. Bryce began to chuckle slightly and carefully worked his shorts off, using them to clean up. He felt Paytah doing the same thing, and once Paytah settled, Bryce moved close once again. "Is this okay?" Bryce asked.

"Yes," Paytah answered, and Bryce closed his eyes. "I'm not going to break, Bryce. You don't have to tiptoe around me."

"I'm not. I just want the memories we make together to be good ones," Bryce said, "and I don't want to rush you."

"You aren't rushing me," Paytah said as he tugged Bryce to him. "I'll admit it feels a bit strange to share a bed with someone. The last time I shared a bed, it was probably with Chay, when we were kids." Paytah grew quiet, but Bryce could tell he wasn't asleep. "This feels nice."

"It does," Bryce said, and he thought about Percy and smiled. He'd just had sex, well, a sexual encounter, with another man for the first time since Percy, and it was okay. In fact, he thought about Percy for a while and how different Paytah was from him. But he knew Percy would have liked Pay. Yes, they were very different, but deep down they had many things in common—the important things, like honesty and a good heart. Bryce knew that was what had attracted him to Percy, and he saw the same things in Pay. Bryce closed his eyes and tried to go to sleep.

"Why are you calling me Pay?" Paytah's voice rumbled with sleep in the darkness.

"I liked it and I wanted a special name for you," Bryce said, trying to stifle a yawn, but failed. "Something only I would call you."

"Did you have a name like that for Percy?"

"Yes. I called him Sweetums. He hated it at first, but he got used to it. I didn't do it in public, but it was my way of telling him how much I cared for him." Bryce rolled over to face Paytah. "I know it sounds a bit stupid, but it made me feel better to call him that because it was how I felt. He was sweet and very special to me, and I could say all that in just one word." Bryce yawned again and rested his head against Paytah's shoulder. "If you don't like it, I won't use it anymore." Bryce really hoped Paytah was okay with it because he really liked it. Paytah didn't say anything, but he held Bryce closer, and Bryce took that as a yes.

BRYCE fell asleep at some point and woke with sun shining through the bedroom windows. The windows were open, and the cool early-morning breeze wafted into the room. Paytah was still asleep, his face relaxed and oh so beautiful. Afraid to move in case he woke him, Bryce turned his head and smiled as Paytah shifted slightly and continued sleeping. Bryce simply watched him, quiet, relaxed, peaceful.

"What you doing?" Paytah mumbled, opening his dark eyes slightly and then closing them again.

"Watching you," Bryce said. "You feeling okay?"

"Uh-huh," Paytah mumbled, opening his eyes again, keeping them open this time. "Sorry I got all blubbery yesterday."

"You didn't," Bryce said, shifting a bit. "I have something to tell you and then ask you. My mother has worked as a grief counselor for a long time and she has been trying to figure out when she could come out to visit me. If she does, would you be willing to talk to her?" Bryce felt Paytah stiffen and he could almost feel the denial coming. "She could help you. I know you're still hurting, and I hope talking to me helped, but Mom might be able to really help you."

"You said you believed me," Paytah whispered.

"I do. I don't want you to talk to her because I think you're lying. I want you to talk to her because you were telling the truth."

"She can't change it," Paytah said.

"No." Bryce shook his head slowly. He wished he could take all his pain away, but he couldn't. "Mom is the best listener I've ever come across. You know how some kids have parents who don't seem to hear them? I never had that problem. Mom always listened, and then she did her best to help. I'm not saying you have to. It's only an offer, and you don't need to give me an answer now." Bryce lightly touched Paytah's cheeks. "You've carried this around with you for a very long time, and if you're ready, there are people who will believe you and try to help you." Bryce widened his eyes when he realized he'd forgotten the most important thing. "What is it you really want?"

"What kind of question is that? What do I really want?" Paytah's vehemence took Bryce by surprise. Paytah sat up quickly, the covers tumbling away from him. "I want all this to go away. I want to have never met that man so I could have my childhood back and be happy the last years I had my father instead of miserable and afraid of

107

everyone and everything." He turned to Bryce, his eyes blazing. "I want that bastard's dick cut off so he can't hurt any other kid the way he hurt me." Paytah clenched his fists. "I want to hurt that fucker so bad he can't walk again! I want...."

Bryce let Paytah rage and vent some of the hurt that must have been building up for years. When he quieted, his eyes still burned, but the rest of him seemed much calmer. Bryce tried again. "I meant, what do you want for you? I understand wanting to hurt Mark—I personally want to kill him—but what do you want for yourself?"

"I don't know," Paytah answered.

"Do you want to go after him? You're an adult now, not a kid, and you have a powerful voice. Do you want to use it? Do you want help so you can deal with what happened to you and maybe move on?" Bryce touched Paytah's arm. "I know you'd really like all this to go away and I don't blame you, but Mark was in the store and...." Bryce couldn't bring himself to vocalize what he was thinking, and he could tell Paytah thought the same thing, because the fire in his eyes blazed again.

"He's hurting other kids," Paytah said. "Innocent kids with no more recourse than I had." Bryce nodded his agreement, and Paytah took a deep breath and held it, then released it slowly.

"You don't have to decide now. Take your time and think about what you want. This is one time when you have to put yourself first and make sure you know what you want to do." They were in an awkward position on the bed, but Bryce held Paytah as best he could before shifting and moving closer. "I believe you, and I'll help any way I can." Bryce's stomach was flipping all over the place. Paytah's choices weren't pleasant or easy. In the end, Bryce figured Paytah would do the right thing, but that had to be his decision because it was his pain. "I'd do anything to take the pain and hurt away."

"But you can't; no one can," Paytah snapped softly.

"Except you," Bryce countered.

"How?" Paytah asked.

Bryce shrugged. "I don't know. But someone like my mother does."

Paytah sighed and didn't move for a long time, but then he said, "Please call her." Paytah shifted on the bed, and Bryce moved closer, practically sitting on Paytah's lap. He kissed him hard, pressing Paytah gently back against the bedding.

"Let me help you forget," Bryce said, and Paytah nodded. Bryce grinned and pushed away the sheet that had covered them. In the morning light, Bryce let his gaze roam down Paytah's entire body. "You're amazing," Bryce said, and Paytah smiled a bit nervously. "Remember, Pay, all you have to say is stop," Bryce reminded, but he hoped to God he never heard that word from him.

Bryce straddled Pay's legs, resting his balls right over Pay's hard cock. Then he leaned forward and stroked Pay's strong chest and shoulders. He wriggled his hips slightly, and Pay hissed softly. "You're evil," Pay told him, and Bryce smiled.

"That's the whole point. I want to make you feel good. I want you to know that I care," Bryce told him, locking his gaze on Pay's deep-brown, penetrating eyes. If Bryce weren't already naked, he would have felt it, like Pay was probing deep into his soul. Reluctantly, he broke their locked gaze and leaned forward to suck lightly on a caramel-colored nipple. Bryce loved the taste of Pay's skin, and he licked and sucked as Pay thrust his chest forward, moaning deeply.

"Bry," Pay panted softly, and Bryce smiled against Pay's skin. He wasn't quite sure if he was smiling because of the moan or Pay's new nickname for him. He quickly decided it was for both and switched to the other nipple, which he sucked a little harder. Pay moaned again and again, and with each one, Bryce gave him more. When he stopped, Pay groaned deeply. He wanted time to explore Pay from head to toe, but he also wanted to impress as many pleasant sensations on Pay's brain as possible, so Bryce slid down Pay's legs, settling between them. With a wicked grin, he looked into Pay's eyes and then licked up his shaft, watching his reaction. It was blissful. That was the only word that came to mind when he saw that look: sheer bliss.

"Has anyone ever done this?" Bryce asked, and Pay shook his head. "Then you're in for a treat." And so was he. Bryce smiled and then opened his mouth, sucking the thick head of Pay's cock into his mouth. Pay groaned under his breath, and Bryce took that as encouragement. Sliding his lips further, he took all he could of Pay's length down his throat. God, the man was big, and Bryce loved it as he bobbed his head, the thick crown sliding over his tongue, filling his mouth with Pay's unique flavor. Bryce loved this. He was talented when it came to cocksucking, and he loved the small sounds Pay made, the groan when he sucked him deep, and the tiny whine when he slid his lips away.

Pay bucked his hips lightly, and Bryce met each movement with more and more suction, encouraging him to take what he wanted, what he needed. For Pay, sex had been about being used, and Bryce wanted more than anything to show him just how mind-blowing it could be. Bobbing his head faster, Bryce sucked harder as he ran his hands up and down Pay's stomach and over his chest, tweaking his nipples lightly between his fingers whenever he passed over them. Pay's breathing became ragged, coming in shallow pants, and Bryce felt him tense. Pay was close, very close, Bryce could feel it. His own desire urged him on, but caution held him back.

Bryce let Pay slip from his lips and wrapped his fingers tightly around Pay's shaft, stroking fast and hard, watching Pay's expression shift from confusion to wonder to ecstasy as he came. Bryce oversaw it all, taking in the total beauty of Pay in the throes of passion. Once his lover stopped quivering, Bryce released him and climbed up Pay's body. Too far gone to stop, Bryce kissed Pay deep and hard, holding him tight as he moved against him, using Pay's come to smooth the way. "You're so amazing," Bryce gasped between kisses, and within minutes his own release was upon him. Bryce cried out, and Pay held him through the shakes. Bryce rested his head against Pay's shoulder, breathing hard, holding Pay tightly in his arms. "I could stay like this forever with you."

Pay hummed an affirmative sound and returned the hug. Bryce eventually dozed off on top of him.

CHAPTER
SEVEN

BRYCE called John and Jerry once he and Pay got up. They were planning to stop by for doughnuts (Bryce knew that was an excuse), and they agreed to bring his laptop with them. "You don't have to stay with me," Pay said from behind him while he was on the phone.

"Just a minute," Bryce said and moved the phone away. "Do you want me to go? Because I'll understand if you need some time alone." Pay shook his head, his long, loose hair almost shimmering in the light. "Thanks, Jerry," Bryce said into the phone, "I appreciate it." Bryce hung up, and then he and Pay showered and dressed. Bryce wished he'd thought to ask Jerry to bring him some clothes, but he borrowed some from Pay, which he nearly swam in, and they walked over to the store.

Jerry and John showed up with the kids a little while later, and thankfully Jerry had thought to bring him some fresh clothes. Bryce changed in the bathroom. When he came out, the whole group was still huddled around the register, talking.

"Can I talk to you?" John asked, and Bryce nodded before following him outside. "What happened last night?" John asked. Then he clarified, "I don't want details, but I don't think I've seen Paytah laugh like that in a long time." John smirked. "Now I know why Percy was so happy all the time." He jumped back when Bryce took a light swipe at him.

111

"It wasn't like that," Bryce protested. "Well, it was, but I think he was able to get some things off his chest, and I hope he feels better, about some things, anyway."

"Was it what you thought?" John asked skeptically.

"Yes, but it was much worse than I thought," Bryce said without turning to look in the window. "If Pay ever decides to tell you what happened, you have to believe him, no matter what."

John narrowed his eyes. "Are you telling me what I think you're telling me? That Grantham is involved?"

"Yes, but what happened isn't my story to tell." Bryce shivered slightly at the memory of what Pay had told him. "I will tell you this. Somehow we have got to get that man away from the children on the reservation," Bryce hissed. "I don't care what you have to do, but you must get him away from the kids. Please find out if he's still spending time at the schools." John didn't look convinced, so Bryce played his ace. "If I'm right, would you want Mato anywhere near this man?" John went completely still. "I didn't think so." Bryce turned away and schooled his expression before going back inside.

"Uncle Bryce," Mato called as he rushed over, half crashing into Bryce's legs, holding his doughnut so it didn't get smashed. "Is Paytah your boyfriend now?" he asked in the loudest whisper ever. "I hope so, 'cause he makes great doughnuts."

"You scamp," Bryce said, ruffling Mato's hair.

"Well, is he?" Mato pressed before taking a bite.

Bryce glanced at Paytah, who seemed to be as interested in the answer as Mato was. "Yes, but that doesn't mean you get to mooch doughnuts off of him," Bryce said before adding, "next time go for ice cream." Mato giggle-snorted, watching Paytah, who turned stern for about two seconds before smiling, which sent Mato into renewed peals of laughter. "Go on, you giggle monster," Bryce teased, lifting Mato into his arms before tickling him.

"Come on, Paytah has a store to run and we have things to do too," Jerry called, herding everyone out of the store. Bryce caught John's eye.

"We'll talk back at the cabin," John whispered, and Bryce nodded slightly. The crowd left, and the store quieted. Bryce set up his computer at a small table in one corner and went to work. Not that he got a great deal completed. He found he kept looking over at Pay to see what he was doing.

"You're bad for my concentration," Bryce said with a smile and then turned back to his screen when a customer entered the store. Bryce didn't recognize her, but Paytah talked to the woman briefly and then she began to do her shopping.

"That's Little Wamblee's mother," Paytah said, and Bryce watched as she walked around the store. Bryce noticed the stuff she bought and shook his head. No wonder her kids stole to eat. Yes, she bought stuff for the baby, but she also got a carton of cigarettes and a bunch of magazines. Bryce wanted to say something, but held his tongue. After a few minutes, Little Wamblee joined her, carrying what looked like a six- or seven-month-old.

"Can I hold the baby?" Bryce asked, and Little Wamblee looked at his mother before shuffling closer to Bryce. He took the round-faced boy and smiled at him. Judging from his clothes, the baby was in need of a bath, just like Little Wamblee. "You're a big boy, aren't you?" Bryce asked, tickling the baby's belly, and the baby laughed, opening his eyes and mouth wide, showing his two bottom teeth. "What's his name?"

"We call him Frankie," Little Wamblee supplied, looking nervously from the baby to his mother. "He's a good baby."

Bryce tickled Frankie one more time. "And I'm sure you're a good big brother," Bryce told him, and Little Wamblee smiled. "Since you're letting me hold him, you can get an ice cream out of the cooler."

Little Wamblee smiled excitedly and then glanced at his mother for permission. When she nodded, he ran to the freezer, and Bryce walked a little closer to where Frankie's mother was checking out. "He is a wonderful baby," Bryce told her as Frankie reached for his shirt collar. Bryce continued playing with him, and Frankie grabbed one of Bryce's fingers, taking it toward his mouth.

"Be careful, those two teeth are sharp and he's teething. He'll gnaw you to the bone." Frankie's mother reached into her purse and brought out an old toy, which Frankie grabbed and shoved into his little mouth.

"Are you having any luck with the job?" Paytah asked as he continued working.

"They're giving me a few more hours at the pool in Hot Springs because it's summer, and the diner is steady, thank God, but nothing other than that," she answered. "I'm Hanna," she added.

"Bryce," he replied, returning his attention to Frankie.

Bryce lightly bounced the baby in his arms, Frankie now smiling up at him, and Bryce grinned at the baby and made farty noises that made Frankie laugh. The front door opened and Bryce shifted his attention to look and the smile fell from his face. Frankie began to whimper, and Bryce shifted him onto his shoulder, bouncing slightly while he rubbed his back. Grantham smiled at all of them, and Bryce returned a hard glare. He was tempted to hand Frankie back to his mother, stride up to the smug bastard, and smack that fucking fake smile off his face.

"Morning, Peter," Grantham said, and Bryce sneered.

"His name is Paytah, not Peter," Bryce corrected sharply, and Hanna looked at him curiously. Bryce schooled his expression. "Is there something we can help you with?" Bryce asked, wanting to get him the hell out of there as fast as possible.

"We came in for some ice cream and supplies," Grantham said before moving farther into the store. Bryce was about to ask what the supplies were for when the door opened and three young boys, all with dark hair pulled into ponytails, came into the store. "Get a snack if you're hungry while I get the rest of the food," Mark told them, and they all headed for the freezer, talking animatedly about what they wanted.

"It's okay, Bryce," Paytah whispered just loud enough for him to hear.

"Do you have lighter fluid?" Grantham asked, and Little Wamblee raced back to show Grantham where it was. Bryce cringed, glancing at Hanna, who was looking in Grantham's direction like he was the messiah himself. Still carrying the baby, Bryce wandered over to where Grantham was wrestling a bag of charcoal and a hand basket. "I was going to ask for a hand but I see yours are full," Grantham said to Bryce.

"Yeah," he agreed in a clipped tone, glaring at him. "Make sure your mother doesn't need any help," Bryce told Little Wamblee, and the boy rushed back to where she was finishing up her shopping. Bryce wanted to say something, to tell this asshole that he knew what he'd been doing, but he swallowed the words. He didn't have proof beyond what Paytah had told him. "Where are you camping?" Bryce asked, trying to sound normal.

"Out by the canyons," Grantham answered nebulously. "Come on, boys. Take what you want up to the register because we need to get going."

"Have fun," Bryce said. "But not too much fun," he added in a very low tone. Grantham snapped his head to Bryce, who met his gaze hard and sure. *I see you and I know what the hell you've been doing*, Bryce thought, refusing to look away. Finally, Grantham glanced at one of the shelves, suddenly interested in cans of beans.

"I'm not someone to mess with," Grantham said between clenched teeth, his former jock personality coming through full force. "Don't go there." His eyes blazed, and Bryce knew this guy had a temper. Bryce also realized that Pay had probably seen that temper and been on the receiving end of it. No wonder he'd been afraid as a kid and had a hard time getting away. This wasn't just an adult threatening a kid, but a man with power who wasn't afraid to use it.

"Neither am I," Bryce said with equal force, watching as Grantham stepped around him and up to the register. The bully wasn't used to people standing up to him, that was for sure. No wonder the asshole stuck to children. Bryce shuddered at the thought.

"Just bill the foundation," Grantham told Paytah as he rang up the purchases. The boys brought up their treats as well, and Paytah rang everything up. Grantham left the store with the three boys trailing behind, and Little Wamblee looking longingly after them. Bryce rolled his eyes at Pay, who looked concerned, confused, and maybe a touch afraid.

"I applied to that foundation through the school for Little Wamblee to join their after-school activities and things, but they said he's too young," Hanna said.

Bryce thanked heaven for small favors on that count, but couldn't help glancing at Pay, who cringed slightly. Little Wamblee ran over and showed what he'd picked out to Pay, then he opened it and began eating, fast, like it was going to melt in three seconds.

"Your mother was a basket weaver wasn't she?" Pay asked Hanna, who nodded. "Did she teach you?"

"Yes, and I used to weave in my spare time, but that was a while ago, and I haven't done anything since Frankie was born. There are still a few of my pieces in the mission store, but I haven't sold many. Why?" she asked as she handed over the money for her purchases.

"Bryce has an idea that we're looking into, and if it gets off the ground, we'll contact you. It may be an opportunity," Pay said, and she lifted her purchases.

"There aren't many of those around here, so whatever you're thinking, if it helps bring money into this place, it will be a godsend," Hanna said.

Little Wamblee had already finished the ice cream bar and dropped his trash in the can. "Mato and Ichante are in town for another few days. Maybe Little Wamblee could come out to the cabin to play one afternoon," Bryce offered.

"Those are Akecheta Black Raven's kids, right?" she asked. Bryce didn't quibble that he was actually their uncle and nodded. "I think he'd like that." She smiled and then left the store. Bryce handed Frankie back to Little Wamblee, who hefted him into his arms and followed behind his mother to an old car that Bryce figured was only still running by the grace of God.

"What am I going to do?" Pay asked almost as soon as the door closed. "I can't let him get anywhere near that boy. But what if no one believes me?"

Bryce wanted to tell him that they would believe him, but he knew better. Everyone seemed to be enamored of Mark. "Then we'll have to make them believe it, but if that's what you want to do, I think you should try telling your friends first."

"Do you think so?" Pay asked, and Bryce nodded vehemently.

"You need to have support," Bryce answered, and Pay became quiet. Bryce remembered that he needed to call his mother and stepped outside before dialing her number. "Hey, Mom."

"Hello to you too," she said.

"You must be feeling good," he said with a grin. He loved that she was feeling better.

"The doctors gave me the okay to travel, and I thought I'd come for a visit."

"That's what I wanted to talk to you about. You know I'm at the reservation with John and Jerry for another week," he explained.

"I can come when you get home," she clarified. "I don't need to rush there this second."

"That's not it. I told you about Paytah when I called last and… he told me some things, and I was wondering if you could come here. I think he needs to talk to you."

"Isn't there someone there he can speak with?" she asked.

"No, Mom, and I doubt he'd talk to just anyone. He's agreed to talk to you because you're my mother," Bryce said. "It's important."

She remained quiet for a long time. "Did he tell you what happened?"

"Yes, and believe me, it hurt him. And there are other children still in danger." Bryce thought about how he could explain it to her. "Do you remember the patient you had when I was sixteen, and after he opened up you didn't sleep for five days?"

"Yeah," she said.

"It's that important," Bryce said, and he heard his mother gasp softly.

"I'll make arrangements to get there. You'll have to find me a place to stay while I'm there." He could already hear her moving around. "Mom, take it easy, we're all here for another week, and I can probably stay after that and work from here," Bryce explained, but he knew his mother. There was no keeping her back if she thought she could help. She'd been that way when he was a kid, and the loss of energy had been the hardest thing about her being ill.

"I need something to do. Having everyone around here treating me like I'm about to break is driving me crazy," she said, but Bryce knew there was more to it than that. His mother spent a lot of time alone—maybe too much time. She'd always been a very social person, but when she got sick, she'd been confined to either the hospital or home.

"Okay, but be careful and don't overdo it. I'll ask John to send you directions from the highway, and you can call and let me know when to expect you." Bryce's worry ramped up. Maybe this wasn't such a good idea.

"Don't mother-hen me. I'll be just fine. I'm not leaving this very second. I'll get packed and make some arrangements. I'll probably leave sometime tomorrow." She paused, and Bryce heard what sounded like dishes clinking. "I'm looking forward to seeing my wayward son."

"I haven't been that wayward," Bryce protested with a smile he knew she couldn't see. "Things have been hard, but I think they're getting better now, for both of us."

"I'm looking forward to meeting this young man," she said. "Now, I need to get things done, but I'll call you when I leave." They said good-bye and disconnected, and Bryce went back into the store.

"My mother is coming," Bryce told Pay, who appeared a bit nervous. "She's going to love you," Bryce added, "and she's one of the nicest people you'll ever meet. She's also tough as nails and has talked with and helped people who have been through extremely difficult experiences."

"But what if she blames me?" Pay asked.

"Oh, fuck," Bryce muttered to himself. "What he did to you is not your fault. You were a kid, and he used his power to hurt you."

"But he always said I led him on," Pay said softly.

"That was his way of making you feel obliged to him. Mom told me once that's what predators do. They make the people they're hurting think they deserve to be hurt, and that's what Mark did to you. I know that, and Mom will too. She's a smart, caring person, and I know she can help you." Bryce walked around the counter. "Last night you said she couldn't change the past, and she can't, but what she can do is help you realize how Mark hurt you so you don't feel like anything that happened was your fault." From the look on his face, Bryce saw Pay didn't believe him. "Let me ask you this: Would you think Little Wamblee led him on if he was to tell you that Mark had hurt him?"

Pay thought for a few seconds. "No. He's an innocent kid."

"So were you when Mark hurt you," Bryce said emphatically. "And he alone is responsible for his actions."

"But what are we going to do to keep the kids safe?" Pay asked urgently.

"I don't know," Bryce said. "I'm not plugged in to the way things are done here. John is," Bryce offered, "and you are...." Bryce let his suggestion hang in the air.

Pay sighed but didn't say more, and Bryce didn't push. It had been hard for Pay to tell Bryce what happened. It had been painful for Bryce to hear. Telling others was not going to be a picnic, and if Pay decided to keep it to himself, then Bryce would have to find another way, but somehow he was going to close off Mark Grantham's access to the reservation's children. He'd thought about going to the police, but he had no proof. No, involving the police was something Pay would have to do. Bryce returned to his computer and his work, trying hard to keep his mind on his task.

BY THE end of the day, Bryce had racked his brain to come up with some sort of plan, but he was no further along than he had been that morning. He had eventually managed to get some work done, but he'd had a devil of a time concentrating on anything other than Pay and that asshole Grantham.

"I'm going to lock up the store. Are you ready to go?" Pay asked, and Bryce began the shutdown process on his laptop.

"Yes. This will just take a minute," Bryce said, waiting for the power to shut down before closing the lid. He unplugged the computer and shoved it and the cords into his bag. After making sure he had everything, he followed Pay outside.

"I'll drive you back to the cabin," Pay said, and Bryce nodded. He wasn't going to force himself on Pay if he wasn't wanted, so Bryce followed Pay to his car and got inside. They rode in near silence down the darkening roads before pulling into the drive. Bryce got out of the car, expecting Pay to pull away, but he followed him instead.

Pay approached the door apprehensively, and Bryce held it open for him. He wasn't sure what Pay had in mind and he wasn't about to ask.

"Uncle Bryce," Mato said as they entered, hurrying over. Ichante was nowhere to be seen at first, but she came out of the bedroom a few minutes later, carrying one of her dolls. "Did you bring doughnuts?" Mato asked.

"Mato!" John scolded sharply as he approached. "That's rude."

"Sorry," he said softly, hiding behind Bryce.

"Come in and sit down," John told Pay. "Can I get you anything? We're about to start dinner. I hope you can stay." John was already heading to the kitchen. "I have soda and water."

"Water, please," Pay said before slowly lowering himself to the sofa. Bryce sat next to him, and John brought a soda and a bottle of water, setting both on coasters on the coffee table. "There's something I want to talk about," Pay said softly.

"I sort of gathered that," John said. "Let's have dinner, and we'll put the kids to bed," he suggested before returning to the kitchen. He and Jerry cooked a quick dinner, and everyone went to sit at the table. Dinner was a bit subdued. The kids were obviously tired and their usual energy seemed absent. Once they were done eating, John got them ready for bed. Bryce helped clean up, and after the dishes were done, everyone gathered in the living room, Bryce sitting next to Pay on the sofa.

Bryce looked to Pay, who looked back to him. "Pay needs your help," Bryce said, addressing his remarks directly to John, but glancing at Pay, who nodded his agreement. Bryce took a deep breath and began. "I'm not going into details, but Pay did with me last night." Bryce looked at Jerry and John. "Pay took part in the activities of Mark Grantham's foundation when he was a kid. John knows who he is."

"I've met him as well," Jerry said. "Personable, but a bit weird."

"Eccentric," John said, and Bryce ignored it.

"The thing is that he used that contact to get close to Pay, and then used that closeness to his advantage." Bryce moved closer to Pay. "He told me all the terrible things that went on, and I believe him."

"What happened?" John asked.

"Mark Grantham used his position with his foundation to get close to Pay, sexually. It started when he was eleven, and Pay was finally able to get away from him when he was about fifteen." Bryce locked gazes with a disbelieving John. "Pay was fourteen," Bryce said, glancing at Pay for confirmation, "the first time he penetrated him." John went whiter than Bryce. "They had an illegal and coerced sexual relationship until Pay managed to get away from him."

"My God," Jerry said.

"Yeah," Bryce continued. "The thing is, as far as we know, he still has access to the school, and if he's done this to Pay, he's done this to other kids and is likely still doing it." Bryce looked toward the closed door to the kids' room and then back at John. "There's no mistake. What Pay told me last night was traumatic and real. It happened, and to make matters worse, he told the counselor at school back then, who did nothing." Bryce took Pay's hand. "Everyone here seems so enamored of Grantham that they've allowed a predator to remain in their midst, one who is probably still preying on the children."

"It's hard to believe," John said without much conviction.

"Of course it is, but when I was a kid, Mom told me that people who might want to hurt me look like everyone else. In cartoons, the bad guys always look like the bad guys. Even in the movies, we know who the bad guys are because, eventually, they look like the monsters they are. That isn't true in real life, and predators like him count on that." Bryce knew it was going to take more to convince John.

Jerry stood up and walked to where Bryce and Pay were sitting and wrapped Pay in a hug. "I believe you," Bryce heard him say. Jerry released him, straightening back up. "If he comes anywhere near our kids, I'll kill him."

Bryce looked to John, who still looked shocked. "He's… damn it," John said. "I believe you, I do," he added. "He's been important to many people on the reservation for years, and he's supposedly helped so many people. Has he been…," John sputtered. "Damn it."

"It's the trust he's built on the reservation that has allowed him to do what he's been doing. If a few kids make noise, they're shut down because of Grantham's reputation. The kid is just a kid like Pay was, and Grantham's done a lot for people, so they believe him and turn a blind eye."

"The counselor thought I was lying, and he told the principal, who called Mark and told him," Pay said.

"Jesus Christ, these are the people who are supposed to be protecting our children," John swore, and Bryce knew they'd truly broken through. "What do we do?"

Everyone looked at everyone else, but no ideas came. "Paytah could go to the council," John suggested, but Paytah vetoed that, and Bryce couldn't blame him.

"They aren't any more likely to believe it than you were at first," Bryce said, "and there are more of them to convince. No, I don't think…." Bryce swallowed. "What if they have already had reports, like Pay telling the counselor at school?" Bryce turned to John and then to Pay. "John told me when I first met you that he remembered you being a happy, outgoing person. He wondered at the time what happened to change you, and now we know. I asked Kiya about it when we were at the water park, and she said she'd heard vague rumors, but either didn't remember or wasn't going to pass on gossip."

"You asked about me?" Pay questioned.

"Of course. You caught my attention." Bryce leaned closer. "It was really the hair," he added with a wink before returning to the subject. "If Kiya might have heard things, then the council may have heard things, or worse, may have been told things and didn't pursue it because it would mean the help and resources Grantham brought to the tribe would stop."

"So where does that leave us?"

"Nowhere," Pay answered, and Bryce could almost feel him turning inward.

"Not necessarily. My mother is coming," Bryce announced. "Pay has agreed to speak with her, and I suspect she may have some recommendations for us. She's dealt with a lot of situations like this, including helping people with the authorities. She'll know what to do." God, he certainly hoped so.

"Laura is a force to be reckoned with, Paytah. She's one of the most understanding, patient people I have ever met, but she has a spine of steel and she knows the system and how to put it to work," Jerry said before turning to Bryce. "When will she be here?"

"In a couple of days, but she'll need someplace to stay," Bryce said.

"No problem. I'll call Mom," John said. "She'll have room for her, and with Dad leaving in a few days, having a guest will help keep her mind off things. She always gets a bit depressed and lonely when Dad leaves, so this might help."

Bryce yawned, and the others followed right behind him. Jerry and John said good night. "Turn out the lights when you're ready," Jerry said as they left the room, closing their door behind them.

"I should go," Pay said and stood up, walking toward the door. Bryce got up as well and followed him. "I'll see you soon?"

Bryce said nothing, moving close and tugging Pay into a kiss. "How about you stay here with me?"

Pay looked around the cabin. "Are you sure... with everyone else here?"

"Yes, I'm sure. We need to be sort of quiet, so the trapeze is out, but I think we can manage to spend the night sleeping next to one another without screaming our lungs out." Bryce shifted slightly, sucking on one of Pay's ears. "Although it's definitely going to be difficult," Bryce added before taking Pay's hand and leading him through the cabin to his room. Bryce turned out the lights, and then they stepped into his small, dark room. When Bryce closed the door, they were in their own, small world.

The clicking of crickets and other sounds of the night drifted in through the open window as Bryce slowly removed his clothing, letting it fall to the floor. He could see almost nothing, but knew exactly where Pay was at any moment. He could feel his heat, and Bryce was drawn to him even in total darkness. He heard Pay moving, and then the bed squeaked slightly. Bryce moved toward the sound and felt hot skin as he slid his leg against Pay's. Then Pay stroked Bryce's belly and around to his hips.

The bed welcomed them as Bryce pressed Pay back onto the mattress. "You're so hot," Pay whispered, and Bryce shivered at his light touch even in the warmth of the summer night. "When I first saw you I wondered if you might be gay, and then when I sort of knew you were I didn't think you could possibly be single," Pay told him. "You're way too cute to be single."

"I'm not sure I like that. You know being cute is the kiss of death," Bryce said, and he felt Pay roll onto his side, tugging him close.

"Not as far as I'm concerned," Pay said, and Bryce rolled over to face him. He wasn't going to argue and instead kissed Pay deeply, pressing their bodies together, lips to lips, chest to chest, hips to hips. Pay moaned softly, and Bryce pressed closer, moving slightly.

Pay moaned again, and Bryce kissed him hard, silencing him even as he increased the intensity of the sensation. "I want you so badly," Bryce whispered. "I can't wait until I can have you inside me." Pay whimpered, and Bryce felt him thrust harder and faster. "I want to be able to make love to you properly and fully, join with you in love and make everything from before pale in comparison."

Bryce felt his own desire rise at his words. He wanted Pay badly, and for so many more reasons than just hopefully wiping away some of Pay's past experiences. He was falling for Pay, and with every stroke, heartbeat, and touch of Pay's skin on his, Bryce fell a little farther. He wasn't sure if that was a good thing, but it was happening. Pay covered

Bryce's mouth with his, holding him as tight as Bryce held Pay, each silencing the cries from the other that threatened to split the night. Bryce could feel the same urgency and need that welled inside reflected back at him by Pay. In that moment, they were one, and they moved together in a dance that became more and more urgent with each touch and each snap of their hips, Bryce moving past Pay, who then moved past him.

"Can't last," Bryce gritted through his teeth before kissing Pay hard, pouring all his feeling into the touch of their lips and bodies.

"Let it go," Pay whispered, and Bryce clamped his eyes closed, desperately trying to swallow the cry threatening to erupt. He buried his face in Pay's neck, mouth open as he came, his entire body shaking. On the periphery of the thralls of ecstasy, he realized Pay was coming as well. Bryce held Pay tight, and he felt Pay holding him. They clung together to hold their vocal cork in the bottle until the shakes and pressure passed and Bryce was left with the warmth of afterglow flowing through him.

Neither of them made any effort to move. "I like when you hold me," Bryce said without opening his eyes. He was too content and happy right where he was to move a muscle.

"I like it too. I didn't realize how much I needed it," Pay said, and Bryce moved upward slightly before lowering again as Pay took a deep breath. "How much longer are you staying?" Pay asked.

Bryce lifted his head to try to see Pay's eyes, but it was too dark. "We're supposed to leave at the end of the week. We stayed this long because John's dad had time off from the oil fields and John and Jerry wanted a chance for him to spend time with the kids. I can stay another week after that, but then I have clients I need to meet with back in Sioux Falls." The thought of leaving left a hole in his heart. Up till now, he hadn't given it much thought as far as Pay was concerned. He'd been happy and was enjoying Pay's company, but then things had begun moving pretty fast and now... Bryce swallowed hard as he realized he didn't want to leave.

Bryce felt tension building in Pay, his body coiling beneath him. "So all those ideas you had, all those things, they were just talk. You threw them out there, making big plans, and what? You're going to leave?" Pay shifted, and Bryce rolled a little on the bed as Pay stood up. He snatched a few tissues and quickly wiped his skin.

"Where are you going?" Bryce asked. He heard the zip and snap of denim as Pay's legs slid into his jeans.

"What does it matter? You're going to leave," Pay said.

"It matters," Bryce began, reaching for Pay's arm, "because I don't know any more than you do what's going to happen. Yes, I have to leave because my work is there. We've been able to work from here, but it's been difficult for all of us to get done what we need to." Pay pulled away, and Bryce got out of bed. "I don't know where things are heading between us, but I want to find out." Pay turned around, and Bryce sighed. "Things have happened rather quickly between us." Pay pulled away again. "I'm not saying that's bad, just that we don't need to rush. Yes, I have to go, but I'll definitely be back." Bryce took Paytah by the hand, and relief washed over him when he felt Pay let him tug him back onto the bed.

"What if you go back and you meet someone else?" Pay asked as he settled on the bed again, his denim pants scratching Bryce's legs. "There are going to be lots of guys interested in you." Pay placed his head on Bryce's shoulder. "I can't compete with them."

Bryce stilled as he realized just what he was being told. All those years living with his mother had taught him a few things. "It doesn't matter who's interested in me, because I'm not interested in them," Bryce reassured Pay, lightly stroking his hair as he read between the lines. "Besides, we have work to do, artisans to speak with, and people with traditional craft skills to find." Pay nodded but didn't say anything more. "Come back to bed," Bryce said, and Pay finally moved, removing his pants and then settling in the exact same spot. His mind in high gear, Bryce resumed stroking Pay's hair.

"Your heart's racing," Pay said softly.

"That's because of you," Bryce lied. Well, it wasn't a lie, exactly, Pay did make his heart race, but right now it was anger that had his heart pounding and his blood racing so fast he thought he could hear it. Pay came across as the strong, silent type, but that silence and stern demeanor hid a fragile soul. Bryce knew Pay had been hurt, but what he hadn't taken into account was the deep insecurity the abuse Pay had suffered had left with him. Pay had just given him a brief glimpse into the depths of that pain, and Bryce's heart ached both for Pay and to make the cause of that pain suffer. "I'm not going anywhere for a while, and I certainly won't leave without saying good-bye and telling you when I'll be back."

Pay lifted his head, and there was just enough moonlight shining through the window for Bryce to see the hope tinged with underlying doubt in Pay's eyes. If that look had come from Mato, it would have been accompanied by a, "You promise?" But Pay's questions remained unsaid even if his eyes asked them as clearly as words.

Bryce continued stroking Pay's hair, and the doubt slowly faded from Pay's expression. Bryce knew he could try to reassure Pay with words all he wanted, but true reassurance would only come from his actions. Eventually, Bryce saw Pay close his eyes, and he lay in the bed, staring at the dark light fixture in the middle of the ceiling. *Mark Grantham, you are going to pay for what you did to Paytah and everyone else you hurt.* Bryce didn't know how or when, which was eminently frustrating and made his vow in his head sound a bit stupid, but somehow he was going to suffer the consequences. Bryce smiled as an image of him as Scarlett O'Hara came to mind, specifically, the scene of her in the field with the sunset behind her. "With God as my witness, I will rip his fucking nuts off!" Bryce knew Scarlett had never said that, but he figured in this case, she just might.

CHAPTER
EIGHT

"HI, MOM," Bryce said as he pulled open her car door. She got out, and Bryce hugged her. She was thinner, but seemed stronger since he'd last seen her, and she returned his hug with some of her old gusto. "I've missed you," he said, "and I'm glad you were able to come. Sorry Dad couldn't make it too."

"So is he. But he sends his love," she said, hugging Bryce again. "Something's wrong," she said once she took a look at him.

"Not really. I'm just a little worried," Bryce said, glossing over things a bit. Pay had been, well, a bit more distant in the past few days. He hadn't stayed away physically, but Bryce could feel some of Pay's old walls starting to be rebuilt.

"Do you want to tell me about it?" she asked as Bryce stepped away from her. "Does it have to do with the reason I'm here?" Bryce sighed softly. "I'll take that as a yes."

"He's pulling away, and while I understand why, I don't like it," Bryce said, but he purposely didn't tell her what he thought. His mother would talk to Pay and make up her own mind. "Come inside and I'll introduce you." Bryce led his mother to the door of the trading post. He'd given her directions there, figuring it would be much easier to find than the cabin or John's parents' house. He was also anxious for her to meet Pay.

Bryce held the door, and she walked inside, looking around. "This is like a step back in time," she said. "It reminds me of the small store near where I grew up." She looked all around until her gaze fell on Paytah. Bryce watched as her eyes widened. Slowly she walked to where Pay stood a bit stiffly behind the counter. "You must be Paytah. I'm Bryce's mother, Laura Morton." She held out her hand and Paytah shook it. "I love your place here," she told Paytah, and he smiled.

"Thank you, ma'am," Pay said formally.

"Please call me Laura," she said with a smile. "So, you're the man who's got my son's heart all aflutter." She actually winked at Paytah, and Bryce saw him smile back at her and then at him. "Not that I blame him." Laura opened her purse and pulled out a tissue, using it to wipe her eyes. Her eyes watered more since her treatments.

"Bryce said you could help me," Pay said softly.

"I will certainly try."

"Then how do we do this?" Pay asked nervously. Bryce wasn't sure if he was anxious to talk to someone or simply wanted to get things over with.

"Do you need to rest after your trip?" Bryce asked. "I can get you to John's parents' and you can talk tomorrow."

"I'm fine, dear," she told Bryce before turning back to Paytah. "I suggest we go someplace quiet and comfortable for you where we can talk," she said. "I'll listen, and you'll tell me whatever you want to. What's said between us stays between us, and that goes even for Bryce. If you wish to tell him what we talk about, that's up to you. But I will divulge nothing unless you give me permission."

"I'll watch the store for you, Pay," Bryce offered, joining Pay behind the counter. "Don't worry. She's my mother. Let her help you." Pay nodded and walked around the counter. Bryce wanted to pull him back and kiss him just to reassure him, but held back. They'd never discussed public displays of affection.

Pay led the way out of the store, and Bryce watched through the window until they disappeared from view. Bryce hadn't really planned on his mother and Pay talking right away, but he was thankful he rarely went anywhere without his laptop. He pulled the computer out of his bag and set it up next to Paytah's at his desk. The trading post was quiet, so Bryce got to work.

The tinkling of the bell on the door broke his concentration, and he checked the clock. He'd already been working an hour. He looked up, expecting to see his mother and Pay, but instead saw Little Wamblee's face peeking over the counter. "Where's Paytah?" he asked in a rush, and Bryce heard a wail from below the counter.

"He's away for a while," Bryce said. "Is something wrong?"

"Frankie won't stop crying, and Mama's at work," he said, biting his lower lip. "I made up his bottle, but he's not hungry and I just changed him." The boy was two seconds from crying too, now.

Bryce hurried around the counter and saw the red-faced baby in Little Wamblee's arms. Bryce lifted Frankie and carefully placed him on his shoulder. The baby curled his little legs under him and let out another wail. "It's okay, Frankie," Bryce said as he walked the baby around the store. "When did he eat last?"

Little Wamblee looked at the clock on the wall. "Two and a half hours ago," he answered nervously.

"It's okay," Bryce said as he continued walking, jiggling the baby slightly. Frankie calmed and stretched out for a few minutes before crying once again, trying to curl his little legs under him. Bryce patted his back and continued walking. He considered going to Pay's to get his mother. He checked Frankie's forehead, but he didn't seem to have a fever. "He's going to be okay," Bryce said to reassure Little Wamblee, even though he had little idea what he was doing. "Does your mother leave you alone with the baby often?"

"No. The babysitter was supposed to come, but she never showed up," Little Wamblee said.

"It's okay," Bryce said, relieved this wasn't a regular occurrence. "It's okay," he repeated for both of them. Bryce had hoped it was trapped gas or something like that, but Frankie was obviously in pain. He was about to go over to Pay's to get his mother when a familiar car pulled up in front and Kiya got out. Bryce had never been so happy to see anyone in his life.

"What's this?" she asked as soon as she entered the store. She took Frankie and cradled him. "It's colic," she said. "He's gotten this before." She walked him and sang to him softly. Frankie calmed, and then everyone in the store made the dirty-diaper face.

"Get a package of diapers, cream, and wipes from the shelf," Bryce told Little Wamblee, and he hurried away. "Oh, God," Bryce said as the smell permeated everything.

"Actually, that's good. It means his little system is taking care of things again," Kiya said as Bryce held his nose. Little Wamblee returned, and off toward the bathroom they went. The room became quiet, with only the occasional cry from the bathroom. Bryce breathed a sigh of relief. He went to the shelf and looked up the price of the things Little Wamblee had taken, then returned to ring them up and pay for them.

Little Wamblee and Kiya returned with a freshly diapered Frankie in her arms. She carried him to the counter. He looked much more contented now, but still not happy or smiley like he'd been with Bryce a few days earlier. "He needs a bottle and a nap," she said before gently handing Frankie to Little Wamblee. "Do you know the number for your mother at work?"

"They don't like it when we call her," Little Wamblee said, but he gave her the number and she dialed. Like Moses parting the Red Sea, Kiya soon had Hanna on the phone. She explained the situation like a pro.

"I'm going to take Little Wamblee and Frankie home with me. They can spend the day, and you can pick them up when you get done with work." She paused to listen. "It's no problem. Don't worry; I'm glad I can help." They talked briefly, and then she hung up. "Do you have a car seat?" she asked Little Wamblee, and he nodded. "Okay. We'll stop by and get it." She took the baby, and Frankie curled onto her shoulder, already looking sleepy and much happier. "Oh, before I forget, I came in to see if your mother made it okay," she told Bryce.

"She's with Pay now. They've been talking quite a while," Bryce said, and she nodded.

"That's good. Call me when your mother leaves so I can make sure everything is ready," she said.

Bryce gave Little Wamblee a bag for the baby supplies, and they left the store, the youngster swinging the bag back and forth as he walked. A few minutes later, other customers came in, and a few of the older men in the tribe stopped by for their coffee. They then sat outside on one of the benches Pay kept in front. The more time Bryce spent at the trading post, the more he realized this place was the center of the community.

"Do you need anything else?" Bryce asked as he poked his head out of the door. The old men shook their heads in unison, and Bryce went back inside. Customers came and went for the next hour, keeping Bryce remarkably busy. "Where's Paytah?" almost every single one asked.

Bryce always provided the same answer. "He's away for a bit. I'm a friend of his and Akecheta Black Raven's." That seemed to satisfy everyone. He got a call from Kiya, saying Frankie had eventually eaten and fallen asleep, with Little Wamblee watching over him.

Finally, after more than two hours, Pay and his mother walked back into the store. Pay was definitely a bit shell-shocked but he also smiled quite a bit and had surprisingly little tension in his posture. "Thank you, Laura," he said, taking her hand. "You helped a lot.'

"I'll be here for a few days. We can talk again," she said before turning to Bryce. "I'm going to get settled. Can you give me directions?"

"Of course. You're staying with Kiya," Bryce told her. They'd met a number of times at John and Jerry's, so Bryce felt sure his mother would be comfortable. He wished she could have stayed at the cabin, but there wasn't enough room. Bryce gave her directions as well as the phone number in case she got lost, but that wasn't likely. His mother had an uncanny sense of direction. "I'll see you for dinner at the cabin. It's not hard to find from Kiya's." He hugged her, and she kissed his cheek before heading out to her car. Bryce followed her with his eyes and out of curiosity walked to the door, where he saw the old men had all stopped what they were doing to watch as his mother got in her car. She'd always been attractive, and Bryce knew she would have seen them watching.

"How did it go?" Bryce asked as he walked back to where Pay was already behind the counter. "Did she help?"

"Yes," Pay said. "She was able to help me understand that what happened to me wasn't my fault."

"I know it wasn't."

Pay sighed. "I always wondered why he chose me. Did I do something to lead him on or something special to capture his attention? Laura said he probably chose me because I was a vulnerable and caring person who wanted to please him." Pay took a deep breath. "I know I was. I wanted him to notice me, and I wanted to make him happy. But that didn't give him the right to do what he did."

"It didn't then and it doesn't now," Bryce said. "You know he's probably abusing other children right now?"

"I know, and that's what hurts most. If I go after him, then everyone will think I'm a liar, when it's him who's fooling everyone," Pay said sadly. "Laura understood that too. She said she'd think on it for me." Pay groaned softly. "I want all this to go away. I have for so long." He sighed again. "Your mother helped me see that it won't no matter how much I want it to unless I make it go away."

"She said that?" Bryce asked.

"Not in so many words, but I'm tired of being afraid of him and what people will think." Pay's gaze met his, full of the fire Bryce usually only saw when they were making love. "He made me afraid of everyone and everything, including life, and I want it to end."

"Then it will," Bryce said.

"That's what Laura said too," Pay told him. "So did anything happen while I was away?"

Bryce told Pay about Little Wamblee and Frankie. "They're at Kiya's, and Hanna will pick them up after she's done with work."

"We have to help them somehow," Pay said.

"I know," Bryce agreed as Pay picked up the phone.

BRYCE rode with Pay back to the cabin. He'd planned to spend what was left of the day working. Pay had called the artist he'd spoken to a few days earlier, and Bryce had spent much of the afternoon with Running Deer, or Dave, as he preferred to be called. Bryce had explained what he had in mind, and Dave had loved the idea and seemed willing to champion it. "You don't want anything for the idea?" Dave had asked.

"No. The only thing I want is for the profits to go to the tribe to help those in need," Bryce had said. "I got the idea when we were out doing things with the kids, and I don't have the skills to start something like that. I'm a computer guy; it's what I love. You and the other artisans on the reservation know about making and selling your craft, I don't. Now, when it comes to websites and online commerce, I can help."

They talked for quite a while. Dave agreed to come up with some product ideas and was obviously excited. "Anything that helps bring business and hope to the reservation is a good thing," Dave said thoughtfully before he left. They exchanged contact information, and Bryce explained that he was returning to Sioux Falls in a few days, but that he expected to be back on a regular basis. He'd noticed the unhappy expression on Pay's face and wished he could change it.

"I hate that you're leaving," Pay said as they rode toward the cabin.

"I know. I don't want to leave either." Bryce liked being there. "But you know I'll never fit in here." As he said the words, it felt like fingers squeezed his heart. "I'll always be an outsider, no matter what I do. This afternoon, the old men sat in their usual place, and when I asked them if they needed anything they shook their heads and looked away."

"They're old and set in their ways," Pay explained as he drove.

"Pay, I watched the store for you today, and almost everyone who came in asked where you were and looked at me like they expected me to make off with everything in the store. I do like it here, and I'm developing feelings for you that I haven't felt since... well, since Percy. But I can't stay here indefinitely, and I don't think I can live here." Bryce wanted to ask Pay to come back with him, but his brother, the store, and his friends were all on the reservation. Pay pulled through the tunnel of foliage and parked next to the van. He turned off the engine, but didn't open his door.

"What do we do?" Pay asked.

Bryce reached across, taking Pay's hand. "I don't know. But I'm not going to walk away from you. I'll set you up with Skype and we'll talk over the computer." Bryce squeezed Pay's fingers lightly. His heart was engaged again, and Bryce wasn't letting go unless Pay wanted him to. "I don't have all the answers, so the best I can give you is we'll have to see." Bryce had intended to come here with Jerry and John, work, hold a few classes, and have a bit of fun. He hadn't imagined that Pay would capture his heart.

"You will be back?" Pay asked softly.

"I promise," Bryce said before leaning in. He kissed Pay lightly and was about to pull away when Pay cupped his head with his hand, deepening the kiss. Pay pressed for entrance, and Bryce parted his lips. He heard a seat belt open and then snap back before Pay leaned over him, pressing Bryce back against the door. Bryce wrapped his arms around Pay's neck and held on as Pay took possession of his mouth. Bryce whimpered as his pants tightened and his dick throbbed. He thought about asking to go back to Pay's for a while, but it was too late. Pay kissed him deeper, his tongue and lips tugging, reaching to Bryce's soul.

Pay pulled away, and Bryce blinked up at him, taking a deep breath. "What was that for?" Bryce asked. "Whatever it was, I'll do it again."

"Just so you remember your promise," Pay answered seriously. Bryce nodded slowly, knowing he'd probably remember that kiss for the rest of his life. Bryce shivered with excitement, eyes wide, brain switched off as he panted in the now warm car. Pay stared back at him as if to emphasize his point.

"I always remember my promises," Bryce mumbled, and then he jumped when someone tapped on the window behind him. *Great, nothing like being caught making out by your mother*, Bryce thought as he slowly opened his door.

"You two having fun?" she asked seriously but quickly smiled. "You know you should probably do that when you don't have two kids watching out their windows." Bryce rolled his eyes, and his mother flashed him one of her scolding looks.

"Good God, Mother, those looks don't work anymore," Bryce said, getting out of the car and then closing the door with more force than was necessary.

"Sure they don't," she retorted, carefully walking around to the front. Bryce waited for Pay and took his hand before following her. They easily caught up, and Bryce held the door.

"Uncle Bryce and Uncle Paytah were kissing," Mato said before sticking out his tongue and closing his eyes in the international sign for "yuck."

"Don't knock it till you've tried it," Bryce's mother said.

"Mato, help your sister set the table," Jerry said with a dish of pasta in his hand. "It's great to see you, Laura. We're both so glad you're doing better." Jerry leaned in for a cheek kiss before heading to the table. "Dinner will be ready in five minutes," Jerry told them. "Kids, finish up with the table and then wash up." Silverware clanged a few times, and then Mato ran to the bathroom ahead of his sister.

"They have such energy," his mother commented, and Bryce took her hand.

"You'll get yours back. It will just take a little more time."

"Oh, don't get me wrong," she said to Bryce. "I'm feeling better than I have in a long time. I just wish I had some of their energy." She set down her purse and went into the kitchen, where Bryce heard her greeting John.

A few minutes later, they all gathered around the table. Bryce looked over the sumptuous Italian feast on the table and thought a bottle of red wine would be perfect, but with both John's and Pay's aversion to alcohol, they had ice tea instead. "So how do you find our little backwater?" John asked Laura a little sourly.

"It's quite nice, but I do see what you mean."

"Bryce has plans to turn it into a hub of commerce," Pay said, bumping Bryce's shoulder.

"We're going to try," Bryce said as the dishes were passed around. Jerry and John helped the kids, and Bryce held the heavy bowls for his mother. He explained his craft idea to her. "Dave thinks he can design a number of wooden items, including pipes and drums. He knows Hanna, Little Wamblee's mother, and he's going to work with her to design some simple baskets. He also said that molds could be made for traditional pots that could be hand-painted with simple traditional decorations. We're also going to see about dolls and other traditional toys."

"You know," Laura said, "I bet you could get a grant to help with the start-up costs. There are a number of organizations and government programs designed around the preservation of Native American crafts." She set down her fork. "You'd have to check into the requirements, but that could provide some of the initial cash. You'd need to develop a business plan, of course."

"I figured that, but don't know the first thing about it," Bryce said.

"You could check that Internet you're always using," she told him with a grin.

Pay nudged him slightly. "If you want this to be something for the tribe, then they need to help. I'll put out feelers to see if anyone can help put that together."

"I think Mom has experience writing requests for grants and things. She's the one who helped get the money for the school ten years ago. She can probably help with the business plan too," John said, and Bryce instantly felt better. He might have come up with the idea, but it needed to be the tribe's project to execute and he was thrilled to see that starting to happen.

"Did you bring doughnuts?" Mato asked.

"You know he doesn't have to bring you doughnuts every time he comes to visit," John scolded, and Mato looked down at his plate.

"Sorry," Mato said softly. "Doughnuts are good," he added in his defense.

"Finish your dinner and you can have a fruit pop," John said, and Mato picked up his fork, mollified for the time being.

"We saw you kissing," Ichante told Bryce with a snicker.

"Finish your dinner," John reminded her gently, and she stabbed a few pieces of pasta.

"Grandpa said we're going to get buffalo," Ichante said before popping the pasta into her mouth.

"That's not what he said, exactly," John corrected. "But it seems Bryce's idea is gaining some traction. Dad called this afternoon to say good-bye and he told me that the council met on Monday and the topic of discussion was your suggestion to return buffalo to the reservation. Dad said they loved the idea and were going to look into the possibility and requirements for starting their own herd. They feel the remaining grasslands and meadows are large enough to support a herd of about five hundred head, and it would be like returning some of our history and heritage to the land." John smiled at him, and so did Pay, who bumped him lightly with his shoulder again. Bryce reached under the table, taking Pay's hand.

The conversation around the table continued. When the kids were done, Jerry gave them each a fruit pop and made them sit at the table to eat them. The adults lingered around the table over decaf coffee until it was time to put the kids to bed.

"We have a problem I'm hoping you can help with," Bryce said, addressing his mother once the door was closed to Mato and Ichante's room and everyone else was seated in the living area.

"I sort of assumed that," she said, and Bryce looked to Pay.

"The man who"—Pay swallowed and Bryce took his hand—"hurt me is still on the reservation running programs for children." Pay looked away, and Bryce squeezed his hand. He felt the urge to take over for him, but he stopped himself. Pay had to do this himself. He had to be the one to ask for help. "If he did what he did to me, then he's doing the same thing to other children."

Bryce's mother was quiet for a few seconds. "Does he volunteer or use the school?"

"He did when I was a kid, and that's what scares me," Pay said.

"You could press charges," Laura said. "There would be an investigation, and other boys might come forward."

"And then they might not," Pay said.

"The tribe thinks the sun rises and sets around this guy. It's going to be hard to convince people, and Pay is going to suffer because of it," Bryce said. The last thing he wanted was Pay hurt again. "I want Grantham to suffer, not Pay," he added vehemently.

"I see," she murmured. "Has anyone requested a review of their background checks? Everyone who volunteers at a school has to have a background check. Usually they're done by the FBI and need to be reissued every few years. I think it's three." She was quiet again. "Okay, so this could work," she said to herself a few minutes later. "How about this? Paytah, you make an anonymous call to the FBI from the reservation giving as much detail as you can without giving yourself away—dates, places, everything you feel you can."

"What does that do?" Bryce asked feeling protective.

"It's using the process to our advantage. Paytah makes a report that's credible, and then we get someone like your mother," she said, looking at John, "to request the records on background checks. The background checks are the law, and they have to have current ones. If your mother threatens to make a big deal out of it, they'll scramble to make sure they have them. Grantham's background check will fail because of Paytah's report, and he will immediately lose access to the school. Furthermore, the FBI will investigate or forward the information to local authorities. They'll have to look into the matter, and who knows what they'll turn up? As part of the investigation, you can come forward."

"I don't want the local authorities involved. They're as bad as everyone else," Pay said nervously.

"Tell the FBI that when you call. Explain that's why you're calling them," Laura suggested. "I know this is hard, but you have to take charge of this and see it through. He needs to be punished for what he did to you, and you have to help stop him from hurting other children, you know that."

Pay nodded slowly. Laura stood up. "Thank you for a lovely dinner," she told John and Jerry before turning to Paytah. "This is a good thing you're doing for all the right reasons. This isn't revenge, but justice, and helping spare other children from going through what you did. No matter what anyone thinks, you're doing what's right." Bryce saw her cup Paytah's cheek. "People may give you grief to begin with, but truth will win out, and you'll know you're doing what's right. Wear that like armor if you need to, but don't doubt yourself. You're a lot stronger than you give yourself credit for." She lightly patted Paytah's shoulder. "You may also find you have a lot more friends and supporters than you thought."

Bryce was so proud of his mother at that moment he thought he would burst, and Pay lifted his gaze to meet hers. When Bryce saw strength and determination in Pay's eyes, he knew calling her had been the absolute right thing to do. Bryce stood up and hugged his mother. "Thank you," he whispered as she hugged him back. Bryce released her and his mother said good night.

"Do you need directions?" John asked.

"No, I'm fine," she said as she walked to the door. "Paytah, would you walk me to my car?" She waited, and Paytah got up from the sofa and then the two of them left the cabin together. Bryce wondered what was up and kept his eye on the door.

Pay returned a short while later with a smile on his face. "She gave me a little pep talk," Pay said but didn't go into any additional detail.

"Do you want to go back to your place?" Bryce asked, and Pay shook his head. "You want to stay here?" Bryce asked, and Pay shook his head again.

"I have some things in my truck, if you'll come with me," Pay said, and Bryce got up, taking Pay's hand. "Good night and thank you for everything," Pay said before stopping in the doorway. "I'm going to make that telephone call first thing in the morning. It's time to put an end to this."

"I'll call my mom," John explained.

"Tell Kiya I appreciate her help," Pay said and then continued outside, and Bryce closed the door behind them.

"Where are we going?"

"I… whenever I was confused or upset, I used to go out to nature. Mark took that away from me, and I want to take it back. I want to spend the night outdoors with you. I want us to be together outside." Pay stopped near the car. Before Bryce could answer, Pay pulled him against his body and kissed him hard. Pay roamed his hands down Bryce's back, then cupped his butt in a signal of exactly what Pay wanted. Bryce hummed his affirmative answer, forgetting completely about the outside part of the proposal as Pay plundered his mouth.

Bryce moaned, but thankfully Pay cut it off with a kiss when he slipped his hands into Bryce's jeans and underwear, cradling his bare butt cheeks. "Is this okay?" Pay asked, and Bryce nodded and whined before Pay kissed him again. Outside, inside, none of that mattered right now. Bryce was so turned on he'd agree to being with Pay on top of an ant hill covered in honey.

Pay broke their kiss, and Bryce moaned softly. "Get in the car. It won't take long to get where we're going."

"I think I'm already halfway there," Bryce said and then burst into a fit of giggles. If he didn't know better, he'd have thought he'd been drinking. Pay's kisses must have short-circuited his brain. Stumbling slightly, Bryce walked around the car and got into the passenger seat.

Pay was obviously excited, bouncing a little in the seat as he started the car and carefully turned it around. The foliage tunnel was ominous, all light disappearing as they passed through. Normally, Bryce's imagination would be working overtime, seeing things in the darkness, but he only had eyes for Pay. "It's not far," Pay said, and Bryce sat back, every muscle in his body strung tight and ready to pounce.

141

Pay kept his word. The drive took less than ten minutes, and Pay turned off the road, the headlights shining off the ground before dropping away to nothing.

"Where are we?" Bryce asked.

"My spot," Pay said. "After my mom died, this was where I came to be alone and think." Pay turned off the engine, but left the lights on. "And when things started to get bad with Mark and I didn't know what I was going to do or how I could get him to stop, I came here. This was where I decided to tell the counselor what was happening to me and where I came after the bastard didn't believe me." Pay opened his door and got out of the car, saying nothing more. Bryce wondered what he was supposed to do.

Pay opened the trunk and rummaged around inside it. Bryce opened his door and carefully got out. He knew the drop off wasn't going to reach up to get him, but he had no intention of getting anywhere near it. Pay slammed the trunk closed and walked back to the front of the car, where he reached through the open window to turn off the lights. "Give it a few minutes and your eyes will adjust," Pay said in the darkness.

Bryce closed his eyes and waited, afraid to move away from the car. Then he opened his eyes and let them adjust, and a whole world opened up to him. The canopy of stars stretched as far as his eyes could see. "Amazing, isn't it?" Pay said from next to him, and Bryce turned.

"Yes," he agreed softly, blown away by all he could see. The landscape around them, hidden in the darkness, made what was visible even more amazing and astounding.

"Come on," Pay said, taking his hand. "Don't move fast." Pay clicked on a flashlight, shining it on the ground and led Bryce away from the car. A shape broke the flat ground, and as they got closer Bryce saw a rustic, three-sided shelter with bark roof and sides. It appeared to be near a small stand of scrub trees, but Bryce couldn't be quite sure in the darkness.

"Did you build this?" Bryce asked as Pay shined the light on the enclosure.

"Yes. They don't usually survive the winter. I build one each year so I can come here to think," Pay said as he set down the bundle in his arms. He handed Bryce the flashlight and spread out blankets. "Come here," Pay said faintly, and Bryce approached. Pay took the flashlight and clicked it off before guiding Bryce onto the bedding. It was surprisingly soft, and Bryce wanted to ask what he was sitting on, but thought better of it. He'd find out in the morning.

"It's beautiful here," Bryce said as Pay joined him.

"Hmmm," Pay said, and then he kissed him, his lips hot, sweet, and demanding. Bryce returned the kiss, letting go of everything around him and giving himself over to Pay, who pressed him back against the bedding. Pay tugged Bryce's shirt out of his pants before pulling it up his torso. Bryce lifted his arms and Pay pulled the shirt off. The cool night air kissed his skin, with just enough chill to raise goose bumps. "Get undressed," Pay whispered, and Bryce pulled off his shoes and opened his pants before shimmying them off his legs. Pay guided him under the blankets and then joined him moments later.

The chill from the air dissipated instantly when Pay's heat surrounded him. "I've never brought anyone else here," Pay said, and Bryce's heart lurched. "Only you. I don't even think Chay knows about this place." Pay kissed him hard, like he had before they left, short-circuiting Bryce's brain before pulling them together.

Pay pressed his smooth skin to Bryce's. Bryce loved that hot smoothness against his skin, Pay's weight pressing on him. Bryce parted his legs, curling them around Pay's, sliding a heel up and down his calf. Bryce returned Pay's hug, taking their kiss deeper and deeper. Pay cupped his head as their lips and tongues dueled. Skin to skin— that was how he loved Pay best. Bryce thrust his hips forward slightly, his cock throbbing in its erotic trap between their bodies.

"I love you," Pay whispered in the darkness, his hot breath tickling over Bryce's lips. Most people only got to hear those words; Bryce got to feel them as well. "I know we haven't known each other that long and I'll understand if it's too soon, but I wanted you to know how I felt." Pay lightly brushed his fingers over Bryce's cheek. "Are you crying?" Pay asked.

143

"No," Bryce lied, badly, and then gave it up. "I didn't think I'd hear those words again after Percy died." Bryce's voice cracked. Instead of trying to talk, he held Pay's face in his hands, guiding their lips together, pouring his own love, relief, gratitude, amazement, and passion into his kiss, not trusting his voice any longer. Pay mirrored everything Bryce kissed to him, their shared passion building. Bryce arched when Pay touched his hip and gasped, openmouthed, into the kiss when Pay lightly pinched first one nipple and then the other.

"I brought things," Pay whispered.

"Thank God," Bryce sighed, feeling Pay search around them. Bryce could only see Pay's shadow against the stars outside. "I want to feel you inside me," Bryce whispered, stroking Pay's thigh. "I want to be with you." The muscles in Pay's leg tightened, and Bryce shifted so he could try to see him better. "What is it?"

"I've never done that. I want to. I want to be with you that way, but...." Pay paused, and Bryce waited for him. "I don't want to hurt you."

Bryce scooted closer to Pay, soothing him back toward their outdoor nest. "You could never hurt me; you never would. What happened to you wasn't love and it was designed to hurt—to put him in control and to give him power over you. That isn't what's happening here." Bryce slid his hand down Pay's arm, finding his closed fist and its contents. "I want you to make love to me, more than anything." Bryce needed to show Pay that physical closeness, being together and joined, was beautiful and nothing like what he'd experienced. "I've done this before. Just remember to use lots of lube." Bryce kissed Pay hard and then rolled over on the blankets. But he didn't hear or feel anything. "Touch me, Pay," Bryce said, and he felt Pay's hand on his back. "Can you feel that?"

"You jumped," Pay said.

"Yes. You excite me. I want to feel you, want you to touch me," Bryce whispered and felt Pay move closer, a second hand joining the first. Pay stroked down his back and over his butt. Bryce moaned softly, pressing back. "That's it," Bryce encouraged, and Pay increased the pressure on his skin. "Use a finger, Pay, get me ready for you."

Bryce shook with anticipatory excitement. He heard a rip that sounded as loud as an earthquake out here in the near silence. Bryce laughed when a cold drop of lube fell on him, but quickly forgot about it when Pay touched him again. "Is this okay?" Pay asked, lightly touching his opening.

"Yes," Bryce whispered urgently, pressing back into the touch. "More, please. More." Pay made tiny circles and then carefully, with agonizing slowness, slid into Bryce's body.

"I'm not hurting you, am I?" Pay asked as Bryce's muscles went wild, gripping Pay's finger hard.

"No," Bryce gasped. "Deeper," he said, and Pay slid his finger further into him. "Curl it slightly." Pay did, and Bryce thought his head was going to explode. Half the nerves in his body fired all at once.

"Is that good?" Pay asked, stopping all movement.

"It's heaven," Bryce said through gritted teeth as he tried to keep some sort of control. "Do it again," he begged, and Pay repeated the motion.

"Yes!" Bryce cried, his voice echoing around them. He squirmed on the blanket and felt Pay press a second finger next to the first. The stretch was marvelous, and he sighed softly as Pay moved inside him. "That's it, get me ready for you." Pay was definitely bigger than two fingers, but Bryce was getting impatient.

Pay scissored the fingers inside him and then slowly pulled them away. Bryce groaned when the connection between them broke. Bryce heard Pay open a condom package and waited for him to roll it on. Then Pay positioned himself between Bryce's splayed legs. More lube was added to Bryce's opening, and then he felt Pay pressing into him. "That's it," Bryce gasped as his body began to open and Pay entered him for the first time.

Bryce opened his mouth wide in a silent gasp as Pay damned near split him wide open. The man was huge, and Bryce heaved in a deep breath as Pay slowly pressed deeper. Bryce reached for Pay, tapping his leg. Pay stilled, and Bryce caught his breath as he willed his muscles to relax and stretch. It took a little time, but his body eventually adjusted, and Bryce pressed back against Pay, signaling him to move.

Pay slid deeper, and Bryce arched his back as Pay's cock slid along the spot inside him. Stretched wide and as full as he could ever remember being, Bryce heaved a small sigh of relief when he felt Pay's hips hug his butt. "Jesus Christ," Bryce swore under his breath and then shivered when Pay's cock throbbed and jumped inside him.

"Is that bad?" Pay asked.

Bryce shook his head and then remembered Pay couldn't see it. "No. Just full, so full." Bryce swallowed and held still. Pay slowly began to move, pulling out and then back in, small, slow movements that drove Bryce wild. He clutched the blankets, meeting each of Pay's movements with his own. "Damn, you feel good," Bryce moaned.

"You're a furnace," Pay said, continuing to move very slowly.

"I'm not going to break," Bryce told Pay. "You don't need to treat me like I'm going to shatter."

"I won't hurt you," Pay said, and Bryce chuckled for two seconds until the sound shifted to a deep, throaty moan.

"You won't," Bryce said, slamming his butt back against Pay, who gasped in surprise. He desperately needed more. "Athletic is good," Bryce said, and Pay picked up the pace. "Yes! That's it!" Bryce said, his cries coming back to him time and time again.

"Okay?" Pay asked.

"Hold it a second," Bryce said. "I want to kiss you." Pay slowly pulled out, and Bryce shifted to his back, lifting his knees to his chest. Then he guided Pay back inside him and tugged him down into a hard kiss. Pay began to move, and Bryce grunted and moaned. "Harder," he encouraged, and Pay responded. "Yes!" Bryce nearly screamed, and his call came back, joining with others that built louder and louder, higher and higher.

Bryce stroked himself, surrounded by a world of sensation. He could see almost nothing, but the world was rich with sound—Pay's breathing, the slap of skin against skin, his own constant moan that Pay kept wringing from him. And the scents—sweat, musk, the bark that surrounded them. All of it combined, adding to the intensity and intimacy of the moment, because nothing mattered outside the shelter. The entire world. Everything Bryce wanted was right there, right then.

He stroked harder and faster as Pay drove into his body. Pressure quickly built inside him. Stroking with one hand, he used the other to pull Pay into a sloppy kiss. Their bodies vibrated and shook with each thrust, and eventually it seemed as though the entire world shook along with them. "Paytah!" Bryce hollered as his climax built. "God, *yes!*" Bryce careened over the cliff of his own pleasure, coming and coming, stars dancing in his eyes as he yelled his lungs out.

Through his haze of pleasure, Bryce heard Pay cry and saw him throw his head back. With a mighty thrust, Pay snapped his hips forward, sending a shock wave through Bryce as Pay throbbed and danced deep inside Bryce's body. Pay stayed where he was, groaning softly for a long time before going completely quiet. Bryce tugged Pay on top of him, his lover's long hair flopping against Bryce's shoulder. Bryce stroked Pay's back as he smiled and held him close. "Was that okay?" Pay asked in a whisper.

"That—" Bryce gasped before swallowing to get rid of his dry mouth. Then he cradled Pay's head, guiding their lips together. "That was completely and totally amazing. There was nothing whatsoever just okay about that." Pay kissed him, and Bryce closed his eyes, reveling in the weight and warmth of his lover.

CHAPTER
NINE

Bryce woke with the sun in his eyes. He turned away, groaning softly as he reached for Pay. His hand fell on empty space, but he wasn't ready to really wake up yet. He and Pay had been up half the night making love, and Bryce felt the residual wonderful soreness in every part of his body. He rolled over with a sigh and cracked his eyes open.

Pay was on the far side of the clearing, already dressed, talking to another man, both of them sitting on the ground. When the other man turned, Bryce saw it was Pay's brother, Chayton. They were talking softly, and Bryce heard their voices on the breeze. He closed his eyes again and tried to sleep, but it wouldn't come. If Pay had been next to him to help keep him warm then maybe, but it wasn't going to happen now. Opening his eyes again, he saw Pay and his brother hug, and it looked like Chayton was crying.

"If only I'd known," Pay said, his words reaching Bryce's ears. "I could have helped you if you'd have told me. We could have helped each other." Bryce saw Chayton look toward him and he closed his eyes again, leaving them in peace.

"Does he know?"

"Yes. Bryce knows what happened to me. He's a good and special man."

"But he's white," Chayton said, and Bryce kept himself from smiling, knowing that wasn't going to fly with Pay. What a difference a few weeks made. "You, the guy who doesn't take twenties or speak to white people is suddenly… screwing one and everything's okay?" The smack of skin on skin almost made Bryce jump.

"Talking about Bryce like that is not, and will never be, okay. Got it?" Pay hissed, and Bryce saw Chayton rub his cheek as he nodded. "You should know better than to judge someone by the color of their skin. We all should. How many times have we been judged for ours? He's got ideas that can help our people here. You heard the council is looking into reintroducing buffalo? That was Bryce's idea. Kiya and Wamblee Black Raven, Akecheta's parents, are championing it, but it was his idea, and he has more, so don't discount him. I love him." Pay paused. "But it's more important than that, because he may turn out to be the best real friend either of us or the tribe has had in a long time."

"You're serious," Chayton said, still rubbing his cheek.

"Yes, I'm serious. I was wrong, and so are you." Pay pointed at Bryce. "He saw I needed some help and he called his mother and got her to drive hundreds of miles because he thought she could help me. She did, and by extension she helped you too." Pay stepped closer to his brother, and Bryce realized it was going to get pretty hard to keep pretending to be asleep very soon. "Because she and Bryce are why we talked today, and why, maybe, if you're man enough, you can crawl out of the bottle you've hidden in for years, grow up, and become a member of this tribe and this family instead of a drain on both."

Bryce began to stretch and move, groaning softly and yawning. He hoped his performance was believable. "You're awake," Pay said to him, and Bryce nodded, but didn't make any effort to actually get up. He wasn't particularly interested in Chayton seeing his bits. Pay turned back to his brother. "It's up to you, man, but I think it's time you lived your life instead of running from it." Chayton glared at Pay for a long time, and Bryce wondered who was going to blink first. Then Chayton lowered his eyes.

"You've done a lot of running yourself," Chayton said.

"Yes, but I think it's time for both of us to stop," Pay said as he walked to where Bryce was lying. "You remember my brother Chay?"

"Yes, how are you?" Bryce asked. "I'd get up but...." Bryce figured there was no need to finish his thought. "I thought he didn't come here," Bryce whispered to Pay.

Chayton howled with laughter from behind Paytah. "I don't. But anyone within miles of you two heard you last night." Chayton continued chuckling. "I'll give you one thing, you got a healthy pair of lungs on you." Chayton walked toward the path out of the clearing. "I'll see you round, bro."

"I'm serious. If you want to talk, Laura is a great listener," Pay said. "And she understands a lot." Chayton paused and then continued walking out of the clearing without saying another word.

"How much did you hear?"

"Enough," Bryce said softly.

"Mark got to Chay too," Pay told him. Bryce had sort of figured something like that must have happened, but the confirmation sent a chill through him. "Isn't anyone safe from that man? Or is it just my family that he'd been intent on ruining?"

"Hey. It's out in the open now. I take it you two talked," Bryce added.

"Yeah, we talked. Thankfully, it seems Coyote somehow got wind of what was happening with Chay, and the two of them were able to stop things from going as far as they did with me, but Mark really messed Chay up."

"Is he gay?" Bryce asked, and Pay shook his head. "I see."

"Yeah. Chay was a teenager interested in girls, and Mark pressured him into things that really hurt him. He said he thought Mark was going to try to rape him when Coyote intervened."

Bryce found his clothes and began getting dressed. "The sad part is that if Chay had gotten help when he was younger, he might not have turned to alcohol." Yet another long-term consequence of Mark's abuse.

"Chay's problems are bigger than that, but I hope he'll get some help," Pay said with a soft sigh. "I'd like to have my brother back, but I don't know if it's possible. The will has to come from him, and I don't know if he has it in himself any longer, but I'm hoping that telling me what happened will open the door for other things."

Bryce finished dressing, then sat back down on the bedding to put on his shoes before getting up again and wandering to where he could see, but without getting too close to the edge. "This is so beautiful," Bryce said as he peered down the canyon to what looked like a thin ribbon of water. "Hard to believe that carved all this," Bryce muttered almost to himself and then stepped back as his legs began to shake slightly.

"When it rains, the creek becomes a torrent," Pay said from behind him as he slipped his arms around Bryce's waist. "I don't want you to go."

"I know," Bryce said, and he felt Pay shake his head.

"I don't want to be alone anymore," Pay whispered. "You opened my eyes and my world to include you and other people. I haven't had that in a long time, and I don't want to go back to being alone." Pay held him closer, and Bryce lightly stroked his arm. "I know you need to go back and I don't mean to make you feel guilty. I just want you here with me."

Bryce snuggled back into Pay's warmth. There wasn't anything Bryce could say that would change the near future. Bryce turned in Pay's embrace, placing his arms around Pay's neck, kissing him gently. "I'm going to miss you too, but I'm not gone yet."

"No," Pay said with definite resignation. "And I have a phone call to make."

BRYCE helped Pay get everything in his trunk, and they rode back to the reservation center. Pay parked outside the store. He sat, hands still on the wheel, without moving for a while. Bryce sat with him quietly and let Pay think. "It's time," Pay finally said. "He took my childhood and part of my life, and it's time I took them back." Pay opened his door and got out. Bryce hung behind watching as Pay strode across the open area to the old pay phone standing near a telephone pole. Bryce saw Pay glance at him. Up till that point, he wasn't sure if Pay wanted to do this alone or not. Bryce got out of the car and stood next to Pay as he fished his wallet out of his pocket and found a scrap of paper. Then Pay inserted the coins in the phone and dialed the number.

Bryce listened, heart in hand, as Pay told the person who answered what he wanted. He was obviously transferred to someone else and then Pay began to talk. He explained why he was calling and then gave details about what he'd endured at the hands of Mark Grantham. Bryce had heard it before, but hearing most of the story a second time tore at his heart. At the point where Pay was about to describe exactly what Mark had done to him, Pay's voice faltered. Bryce took his hand and held it as Pay finished telling his story. Bryce was grateful it was still very early and no one was about. He felt no eyes watching them and saw no one else. "There are other people. I know I'm not the only one," Pay was saying. "No, I really don't want to give my name, not now, but I will aid an investigation." Pay listened to whatever the person on the other side of the line was saying. "The local police will not help. They're all Mark's buddies. That's why I'm calling you," Pay said and then hung up the phone without saying another word.

"You did good, Pay. They'll have to do something now."

"No, they won't. She didn't sound convinced," Pay said.

"It's her job to ask questions and get as much information as she can. And it isn't important if she believed you. The report has been made and they'll trace the call back to the reservation. So now all we can do is wait. Kiya will stir the pot even more today or tomorrow and we'll see what happens. They can't know it was you who made the call, so you're safe."

"Not necessarily," Pay said. "Mark will figure out who called if they begin an investigation. If they give him any details, he'll know, but by then I hope it won't matter so much."

"It doesn't matter now. He can't hurt you any longer, and you were strong enough to put aside your own fears and report what happened." Together they began walking back toward Pay's car.

"I'll take you back to the cabin before I open the store and get to work," Pay said. Bryce was about to open the car door when Pay's brother stepped out of the small road near the store, with Coyote and a boy who looked about seventeen trailing just behind them.

"Did you call?" Chayton asked, and Pay nodded. "Good," he said and held out his hand. "Would you give me the number?"

Bryce caught Chay's eye and then shifted his gaze to the kid, who shuffled his feet and basically looked like he was trying to disappear behind Chayton and Coyote. Now that he was closer, Bryce realized the boy was younger than he thought, probably fourteen or fifteen, with short ragged hair that looked like it had been hacked off with a knife. Bryce glanced at Pay, who looked like he was going to be sick.

The kid tugged on Coyote's shirt, whispering a few words Bryce couldn't hear, and Coyote nodded.

"It's okay, Kangee," Pay said as he moved closer to the boy. "We all understand here." Kangee looked first at Coyote and then at Chayton, both of them nodding slowly. Then he lowered his head and silently began to cry. Bryce could see he was trying to hold it in, but couldn't. "Let's go inside," Pay said, and he turned, striding to the store and then quickly unlocking the door. Everyone followed, and Pay locked the door behind them. "There's nothing to be ashamed of. You didn't do anything wrong."

"He said he'd hurt my grandfather," Kangee said, trying to gain the upper hand in the battle with his emotions and losing. To Bryce's surprise, it was Chayton who gathered Kangee into his arms and hugged him as the wrenching tears came.

"It's okay. He's not going to get to you any longer. No one will. Paytah and I are going to see to that," Chayton said. "I promise."

Bryce wiped his eyes and turned away from them to give Kangee some privacy. "See? You already have supporters and friends. One person, people can try to fight; two, they might discount; but three…." Bryce shook his head. "No way, and there will be more," he whispered.

"That's what I'm afraid of," Pay said as Bryce moved into his arms, comforting Pay as the sound of Kangee's tears filled the room to the very ceiling.

"We're okay here," Coyote said to Pay, and he nodded, leading Bryce out of the store and to his car.

"I'll take you back to the cabin," Pay said quietly.

"Are you sure? I'll stay here with you if you want," Bryce offered.

"No. I need to be alone and have some time to think, and you need to work," Pay said before opening his car door. Bryce wanted to argue, but after everything, maybe they both needed a chance to think for a while. Bryce got in the car, and Pay started the engine before putting the car in gear. They rode in silence to the cabin. Bryce leaned over the seat and gave Pay a light kiss before getting out.

"Will you call if…," Bryce began, and Pay nodded, but Bryce knew he wouldn't call. Bryce was fairly sure this was something Pay felt he needed to deal with on his own. "Will I see you tonight?" Bryce asked.

"It's not supposed to rain," Pay said, and Bryce nodded his understanding.

"I'll wait here until you pick me up," Bryce said and then closed his door and walked around to the front door of the cabin. It was still quiet inside, and Bryce made as little noise as possible as he went to his room and changed clothes, then got his laptop and settled on the sofa to work for a while.

"How did it go last night?" John asked quietly. Bryce looked up from where he'd been immersed in his work.

"Nice," Bryce said, and he felt himself color. "Pay took me to his… outdoor place, and we spent the night under a shelter."

John began to laugh softly. "You've come a long way from the guy who just weeks ago was scared he'd be eaten by bears," he teased.

"Yeah, I guess so. I still don't feel comfortable being outdoors, but Pay was there."

"Exactly," John began as he sat down next to him. "You feel safe with Paytah, and that's how it should be with the person you love." John yawned and then put his bare feet up on the coffee table. "So have you decided what you're going to do about it?" He bumped Bryce's arm. "You know, the whole 'he's here, you're there' thing."

"Don't know. Pay wants me to stay, but…." Bryce paused and set his laptop on the table beside John's legs. "I like it here, but I don't fit in. I know you're going to say that Jerry did, but you've seen the hesitation and sideways glances the same as I have. Jerry is accepted, more like tolerated, by many people because he's with you. When I meet people, I have to tell them I'm a friend of yours and Pay's before they stop looking at me funny. Even then the suspicion stays."

"It would take time, yes, but people would accept you," John said.

"Yes, they might, but then there are the other things. I can't buy a house here because of the land restrictions. It's a reservation and I have to be a member of the tribe or I'd have to buy a house with Pay. I would only be allowed here as long as I was with Pay. If anything happened to that relationship, I'd have to leave. We've only known each other for a few weeks. I love him, John, but… it's too soon to uproot my entire life. I think we need to spend some time together, get to know each other better, date." Bryce motioned with his hands. "I told him I'd come back, and I hope he can come to visit, but I don't think either of us is ready to completely change our lives." Bryce was trying to be realistic even as his heart was telling him something very different.

"I know how you feel, and from a logical perspective, you're probably right. But we can't always live from a logical perspective." John yawned again and tried to cover it. "Look at it from Paytah's perspective. He trusts you, and that's saying a lot. He told you his deepest, most painful secret, and you helped him."

"Shouldn't I have?" Bryce asked defensively.

"Of course you should. But in the same few weeks you've known each other, you've gone from a distrusted stranger to the one person he trusts most. That's saying a lot for anyone, but for Paytah, that's like moving the world. I know you'll be back and you'll do what you say, but for Paytah, it's hard to see that now because he's come to rely on you."

"So what do I do?" Bryce asked. "I don't want to hurt him."

"Just be patient and don't expect him to jump for joy at your decision. Yes, it's probably the right one. Love can hit hard and burn hot but then sputter away, or it can grow over time. You two probably need to find out which you have, but it's most likely hard for Paytah to see that right now," John explained before yawning yet again. "I need coffee."

John got up and went into the kitchen. Soon the scent of fresh coffee filled the room. "By the way, Pay made his call this morning and there are at least two other people," Bryce said, getting up, not willing to mention any names.

"Already," John said, and Bryce nodded.

"Please have your mother do her thing at the school, but I'm not sure how much it's going to be needed. Once this hits, it's going to be huge, and victims are going to come out of the woodwork." He leaned against the counter, waiting for the coffee to finish. "I just wish I could see that son of a bitch's face when all hell breaks loose."

"Me too."

"I'd like to…," Bryce began, but then swallowed his words when Ichante came into the room. "Morning," Bryce said, noticing for the first time what a striking young lady she was becoming. "God, you're growing up so fast," he sighed.

"Tell me about it," John said as he hugged his niece good morning. "Soon she'll be too big for hugs and want to borrow the car."

"Uncle Akecheta," she said, giggling. "I won't ask to borrow the car. I'll ask you to buy me one."

"How old are you? Thirteen going on twenty?" Bryce asked, and Ichante giggled. The little girl was definitely smart and was going to give them all a run for their money when she got older.

"Where's Mr. Paytah?" she asked as John poured her a glass of juice.

"He had to work," Bryce began as Mato barreled into the room, "to make this one's doughnuts." Bryce laughed and hugged Mato to him. These kids, Jerry, and John were family to him just like his mother was. "What are you guys doing today?"

"Going to Paw-Paw's," Ichante said, glaring at her brother. "We're having a Lakota day," she announced. "We're only speaking Lakota once we get to Paw-Paw's," she reiterated to her brother, and

Mato looked about as thrilled as if he'd been told about an impending dental appointment.

"Sit down for breakfast," Jerry said as he joined John. "You can speak all the Lakota you want, but Grammy isn't here yet, so English will have to do." Jerry bumped John, and together they cooked up a spread. Bryce was wondering who was going to eat all this when the door opened and both mothers came in.

"I love a man who can cook," Kiya said before being mobbed by the kids. Bryce kissed his mother hello, and everyone greeted everyone else before heading to the table.

"I was wondering what all the food was for," Bryce said, making sure the two women were on the other side of the table, "then the appetites got here, and mystery solved." Both women glared at him before finally breaking into good-natured smiles. Bryce let his mother catch him.

"Look who's talking. Someone's feeding you well—you're getting a belly," she said, patting Bryce's flat stomach before taking a seat.

"So did Paytah make his phone call?" Kiya asked.

"Yes. It went as well as could be expected, and then we got a surprise. Two more in the same situation showed up." Bryce was speaking generally so the children wouldn't know what they were talking about.

"Do you need me to do my thing?" Kiya asked.

"It couldn't hurt. Get Mark out of the school before things heat up," Bryce said, and she nodded before turning to his mother.

"Feel like raising a little hell?" Kiya asked, and Bryce saw his mother smile.

"I'd love to," she answered, popping a bit of fruit into her mouth. Bryce actually sighed. He couldn't quite decide if getting these two together was a good thing or not.

"Okay, but before you two go into battle, I need some advice," Bryce said, looking specifically at Kiya. "I need something traditional that I can give to Pay, something that will let him know I'm thinking of him when I go. I want it to be special and something that will have meaning for him, for both of us."

"Just give him something from your heart," Laura said.

"Let me think about it," Kiya answered.

"Thank you," Bryce said and went back to his breakfast.

Once they were done eating, Kiya and his mother took the kids, and Bryce went to work. The cabin was quiet, and he got tons accomplished. Jerry and John seemed to get a lot done as well. But while Bryce was productive, he kept part of his attention on the phone, hoping that Pay would call. But unfortunately he didn't.

PAY never did call. Thankfully for Bryce, he stopped by the cabin in the late evening. By that time, Bryce had been going crazy wondering what was going on, but Pay had been quiet at the cabin and on the drive out to the shelter. Bryce hadn't pushed, and Pay hadn't talked, at least not in words, but Pay's thoughts had come through in his almost desperate lovemaking that ended with both of them screaming their releases that echoed and melded over the land before dying away. Bryce realized he was alone and opened his eyes, not that he could see much other than stars on the nearly moonless night. "Pay," he said softly when he heard movement nearby.

"Pay, talk to me," Bryce whispered, hearing light footsteps getting closer.

"Nothing to say," Pay said. "I don't want you to leave, but I know you have to and I know I need you to." Pay hesitated near the shelter entrance, and Bryce figured he was taking off his shoes, but he couldn't see well enough to know. Then Pay joined him under the blankets.

"You want me to leave?" Bryce asked, figuring he must have misheard.

"No, but I think I need you to leave. Not forever." Bryce heard Pay roll over, and then he was pulled close to his lover's warmth. "I've been alone a long time and I like having you with me, knowing you're here, and I could get used to this really fast. And that's the problem."

"I know." Bryce rolled over to face Pay, placing a hand over Pay's heart after he'd settled on the bedding. "I was alone after Percy died, and it can feel overwhelming. But I'll be back, and over time we'll figure something out." He had no idea what that was, but a solution would present itself. "I'm hoping you can come visit me too."

"I'd like that. Alowa would probably push the car the entire way if she thought she could get me to spend some time away from the store," Pay said.

"She cares about you," Bryce said. "Everyone seems to care about you. The few times I've watched the store, whenever someone comes in, they ask where you are, almost every single customer. They wouldn't do that if they didn't care." Bryce brought Pay's lips to his. "So you see, you aren't alone, and even when I'm gone, you won't be alone because the entire tribe is there for you, if you'll let them be." Bryce kissed Pay, nibbling lightly on his lower lip. "That's the beauty of having a tribe, a real tribe, one that supports and accepts you no matter what. You have that, and all you need to do is allow them to support you."

Bryce felt Pay nod slightly. "I've felt apart for so long and sort of like I was fighting them."

"But the fight was within," Bryce supplied.

"Yeah, and as long as I fought myself, Mark won," Pay whispered into the darkness. Bryce wasn't sure if the words were for him or the universe, but he closed his eyes and held Pay closer as sleep finally came.

CHAPTER
TEN

"NOT looking forward to going home tomorrow, are you?" John asked, and Bryce looked up from behind his computer, where he'd been pretending to work. He wasn't getting a thing done and, giving up, shut down the machine.

"Yes and no. It'll be good to get home again and be in my own place."

"But you're going to miss Pay," John supplied.

"Very much, and I don't know what we're going to do."

"Take it one step at a time," John suggested. "As long as you're both willing to make the effort."

"I know, I'm just going to miss him," Bryce explained, and they got quiet.

"Did your mother make it home okay?" Jerry asked as he entered the room.

"Yes. She texted me late last night." Bryce huffed slightly. "She was supposed to take it easy and stop along the way, but she pushed herself and made it home." He wasn't sure if he was happy about that, but at least she was home safe. "Have you started packing?"

"Yeah, you?" Jerry said.

"Uh-huh," Bryce hummed. "So what's on for today?"

"The kids are going to my mom's, and we were wondering if you wanted to go in to be with Paytah." John looked over at Jerry, and Bryce got the message loud and clear. They wanted a bit of alone time.

"That would be great. Is Kiya picking up the kids?"

"Yes. She'll be here soon," John said as Kiya walked in the back door.

"Are they ready?" she asked, placing her purse on the counter.

"They're in the bedroom, playing. I'll get them," John said and left the room.

Kiya rummaged in her purse and pulled out a bundle of cloth, handing it to Bryce. "This is what we talked about," she said, pressing the bundle into his hand. "Also, I just heard that there are investigators on the reservation. They showed up late yesterday and have been quietly questioning people. Of course, in a place like this, little is kept quiet for long."

"Thank you," Bryce said urgently and shifted his attention to John, biting his lower lip nervously. This was a good thing, but it was going to be hard on Pay and those he cared about.

"I'll take you to Paytah," John said. He stood up and kissed his mother. "I'll see you before we leave," John added, and they hurried out to the van after Bryce grabbed his computer bag. Bryce had been expecting this and he'd been waiting for something to happen.

"How do you think Grantham will react when he finds out he's under investigation?" Bryce asked, kicking himself that he hadn't thought about this earlier. "I mean, this kind of abuse is all about control, so what will happen when Grantham realizes he doesn't have control any longer?" Bryce's heart pounded in his chest. His imagination was getting the better of him and he was probably overreacting, but all he could think was what if this guy came after Pay.

John pulled up in front of the store, but it was still closed.

"Thanks, I'm going to head to Pay's," Bryce said.

"I'll wait until you're inside," John said, and Bryce headed around to Pay's small house. A dark sedan was parked outside and Bryce walked beside it, peering inside, but seeing nothing unusual.

Bryce knocked on Pay's door and waited. He was about to leave when Pay opened it. "You're okay?" Bryce asked, and Pay nodded before motioning him inside. Instantly on guard as Bryce came in, two men sat on Pay's sofa. They stood as Bryce approached.

"This is my boyfriend, Bryce Morton," Pay told the men. "These are the agents investigating the report of abuse."

"I'm Agent Williams, and this is Agent Donley," the shorter of the two men said. "We're trying to determine if the reported account is accurate."

"They arrived just a few minutes ago," Pay explained.

"The call we received was made from the pay phone just across the way, and we were wondering if you might have seen who made the call. We're sort of at a loss as to where to start other than speaking to the tribal leaders. But with the proximity of the phone, we thought it logical to begin here."

Bryce locked gazes with Pay and nodded. "Yes," Pay began, "I know who made the call." Pay motioned toward the sofa and sat in one of the chairs while Bryce perched on the arm next to him. "It was me."

The agents began making notes. "Would you tell us what happened?" the agent asked, and Pay began recalling the incidents from his childhood while Bryce held his hand. The detail he relayed was astounding and even more eerily gripping than when Pay had first told him.

"Mr. Stillwater, how old were you when you first met Mr. Grantham?"

"Eleven," Pay answered. "He started playing his touching games when I was about twelve, and things progressed to full sex by the time I was fourteen." Pay related his dealings at the school with the counselor and principal as well.

"I want you to get them, as well. They looked the other way instead of protecting the children in their care," Bryce said. "They probably still are."

The agents checked some notes. "We got requests for background checks on a number of school volunteers recently. They're probably covering their asses."

"Mothers can raise a great deal of hell," Bryce commented and then explained how they'd brought the background checks about. "We weren't sure what would happen or how fast, but we need to get this guy out of the school."

"Are you aware of anyone who might have confronted Mr. Grantham?" Agent Donley asked.

"No," Pay answered, and Bryce squeezed his hand. "Not that I'm aware of."

"Do you know of other victims?" Agent Williams questioned.

Pay turned to Bryce, who answered for him. "We can confirm at least two others. One is an adult and the other is currently... fifteen?" Bryce asked, and Pay answered with a nod.

"One of them is my brother," Pay said levelly. "But I can't speak for him or the boy who came to us."

"We need you to give us their names," Agent Williams said, but Pay shook his head.

"I will ask them to contact you, but that's all I can do. Their stories are theirs to tell, and the decision to come forward will be a hard one, but it's their decision to make, just like it was my decision to call you."

The agents stood up. "Can I ask one more question?" Agent Donley asked. "When you made the original call, why did you remain anonymous?"

"I was afraid of what people would think," Pay answered.

"What's changed?" the agent added.

"I guess I realized I could care less what other people think and more about what I think of myself," Pay explained. "I also came to understand, with Bryce's help, that if I didn't do something, Grantham was going to hurt other kids. Let me change that: he *is* hurting other kids, and that has to stop." Not giving a damn what the agents thought, Bryce leaned closer to Pay as a lump formed in his throat. Pay needed his support. "I stayed quiet and let him hurt me for years, long after I got away from him physically. I pulled away from family and friends because I was ashamed of what happened. I didn't think anyone would believe me because the counselor at school hadn't believed me. I don't want anyone else to hurt like I did." Pay leaned forward. "And I sure as hell don't want Mark Grantham to determine the way I live the rest of my life. So, you investigate, and I'll do my best to get others to come forward." Pay stood up and stepped toward the agents. "I want you to nail Mark's balls to the wall. I never want him anywhere near another kid again. I don't care if he has to live in a prison at the fricking North Pole, just as long as he can't hurt anyone else, ever!"

The agents stood up. Bryce expected skepticism or doubt, but what he saw in both of them was compassion. "We'll do our very best," Agent Williams said. "Please call us if you have any other information you feel you can share."

"I'll ask my brother to call you," Pay said.

"Thank you for all your help," Agent Williams said. "We'll show ourselves out."

Pay watched them go.

"How do you feel?" Bryce asked.

"Surprisingly good," Pay said and then smiled. "I really did something to get rid of Mark for good." Pay sat down and pulled Bryce onto his lap, and Bryce giggled like a schoolgirl until Pay kissed him, and then thoughts of everything else vanished. "I feel alive," Pay said once he broke the kiss, holding Bryce tight.

"Do you want to show me just how alive?" Bryce asked sheepishly.

"I'd love to, but if I don't get over to the store, the old guys are going to think I died or something and they'll come knocking on the door."

Bryce got off Pay's lap and they left the house, heading over to the store together. Sure enough, a few of the men were gathered outside. Pay unlocked the door, and the men wandered inside and made the coffee themselves while Pay began making doughnuts in his small kitchen in the back. Bryce sat at the table in the corner and opened his computer to work for a while.

When Pay carried a tray of fresh doughnuts from the back, the entire store filled with the aroma. The men all bought doughnuts and carried them outside to their bench, where they sat in front of the store with their coffee and food, talking and looking at each other. "Remind me to get off my ass when I want to do nothing but sit all day," Bryce whispered to Pay, who smiled.

"It's what they do," Pay said as if that explained everything. "They're mostly alone and they keep each other company. They'll only be out there until it gets warm and then they'll move on to the tribal center or head home. They do it almost every day."

"I noticed," Bryce said and saved his work before closing the lid on his laptop. "They need something to do."

"What are you cooking up?" Pay asked with a smile.

"Nothing. But if we get the craft company up and running, those guys may be able to help. I bet they remember a lot about your culture and may have ideas of things we can make," Bryce explained, and Pay rolled his eyes. "I know—I'm always thinking."

"It's a good idea," Pay said as he looked out of the window.

"Before I forget and someone else comes in, I have something for you," Bryce said, and he opened one of the pockets of his computer bag and pulled out the cloth Kiya had given him.

The front door banged open, crashing back on its stops. The sound ricocheted off the walls and Bryce nearly dropped what he was holding.

"You stupid little son of a bitch! I'm going to make you pay!" Mark Grantham threatened as the door banged closed behind him. "I had a visit from the FBI this morning and I know this is all your doing." He stalked toward the register, where Pay stood immobile. Hell, Bryce did the same thing, unable to believe anyone would think acting this way or making threats in front of a witness was a good idea. "You redskin piece of shit." Mark glanced for a second at Bryce, and Bryce felt the rage pouring off the other man. "If you think anyone is going to believe you or your little white scrawny piece of ass here, you're sadly mistaken. No one will believe you, and once I'm done, not a single person here will shop in your little store anymore either." Mark reached the counter and leaned over it to get right into Pay's face.

"You know, as a kid," Mark said, his voice soft enough that Bryce could barely hear him, "you were great. I cared for you a great deal, and what we did together was special and you loved every minute of it—the attention, the care. You were my boy. What makes you mad is that you aren't my boy any longer. That's what bothers you and why you made up these filthy lies." For a second there, Bryce had thought Mark was admitting to everything he'd done to Pay, but that was too good to be true. Of course he was going to deny it. A confession would be too easy. "Those kids need me, and I give them something no one else around here can, just like I gave that to you." Pay hadn't moved, and Bryce was beginning to wonder if he was buying this load of crap. "I've helped people here for years. They look at me and see someone who has helped many people on his reservation. I'm rich, strong, and loved. When they look at you, they see quiet, pathetic, and now they'll see a liar."

Bryce seethed with anger, but he wasn't sure if he was angry with Mark or with Pay for just standing there and listening without moving a muscle. How could he just take this? Bryce thought Pay had come a long way in the past few weeks, but maybe that was wishful thinking.

Bryce took a step closer, and Mark turned to him. "Just stay away, pencil neck, you don't want any part of this!" Mark said vehemently between clenched his teeth, bits of spittle flying in Bryce's direction. For a few seconds, Bryce thought he looked a bit like a big dog, and then Mark turned his fury back to Pay. "I should have known you were a useless little liar," Mark said and then backed away slightly, glaring at Pay. "Nothing to say?" Mark asked. "I should have known. You never said much at all. I always thought you might have been stupid, kind of retarded, and maybe I was right. Yeah, the FBI is really going to believe a stupid Indian retard." Mark swung his hand, sending everything on the counter flying, including the displays of gum and candy and the doughnut case, which hit the floor with a crash and the clear plastic shattered, scattering doughnuts and pieces of plastic all over the floor. "Clean that up, and don't think of billing the foundation or me for any of it. I'll just deny the payment."

The door to the store cracked open, and Bryce saw one of the old men peer inside briefly. Then the door closed again, and Mark, who had glanced away at the sound, looked back at Pay. "See? No one gives a damn about you around here, and no one is going to believe a fucking thing you say. So if you want to have any friends left, I suggest you tell the FBI you made a mistake. Maybe then I'll consider forgiving you."

"You forgive *him*?" Bryce said. "After what you did, you useless, self-obsessed, pile of—" Bryce stepped forward, but Pay put out a hand to stop him.

"No, Bryce, I can handle this," Pay said softly, and Bryce wondered how in hell he could be so calm.

"So, you can talk. I was beginning to think you'd lost your voice along with your ability to think," Mark sneered. Pay slowly moved out from behind the counter.

"I can talk, and I've done plenty of it," Pay said levelly. "I talked to the FBI and I talked to Bryce's mother. I also talked to other friends here on the reservation, and now I'm talking to you." Paytah continued to slowly move closer to Mark. "And do you know what I found when I talked to people? I found others you hurt like you hurt me. A kid you tried to manipulate and use just like you did me. I found someone who managed to get away from you the way I wished I'd been able to but couldn't for so long. You can think what you want and call me a liar, but I'm not. You're a pedophile who uses children and rapes them." Pay moved still closer to Mark. "You stole my childhood and you stole my innocence. But worse than that, you stole my peace of mind and part of who I was, but I'm taking it back. I'm taking all of it back." Pay's voice became stronger. "I'm going to save other kids from going through what I did and I'm going to send you to prison. I don't care who believes me here and who doesn't, because that doesn't fucking matter. Bryce believes me, and so do other people, and so will a jury!" Pay continued moving forward, and Mark took a single step back. "You're a bully, a coward, and a criminal."

Pay slowly closed in on Mark, and Bryce wondered what Pay was going to do, but he stayed back and let him work it out. Bryce was ready to pounce and beat the shit out of Mark if necessary, but Pay's stiff posture and the way he clenched and unclenched his fists told him he wasn't going to have to do anything.

"Pay," Bryce said softly, now thinking it might be best if Pay let Mark go, but he ignored him.

"You like having sex with little boys. You get off on it. Well, that's going to stop. Once it gets around what you've been doing, all the people you've hurt are going to come forward. They'll be coming out of the woodwork. Your FBI clearance to volunteer at the school is going to be denied, and I'll make damned sure everyone knows why. I may be quiet and an 'Indian retard', but I set your ass up and no one is going to be able to stand up for you when I'm done. Newspapers are going to want to know what happened, and I'm going to talk loud and clear. Your face will be spread all over the state. Your family is going to be so proud of you," Pay added sarcastically before taking a deep breath. "Now get out of my store and off my reservation."

"I'm not going anywhere!" Mark growled, stepping closer to Pay.

Bryce saw Pay clench his fist, but everything else was a blur. Before Bryce could move, he saw Pay snap his arm out and then heard the crunch of bone. Blood spattered from Mark's nose. Instantly, Mark grabbed his face, blood spilling from between his fingers.

"I said get the hell out, and for fuck's sake, stop bleeding on my floor. Go bleed in the dirt with the rest of the animals." Bryce rushed to open the door, and Pay shoved Mark through it. Mark lost his footing and fell flat on the ground. "Stay away from our kids, you pervert. You may have fucked me when I was fourteen and scared, but you can't push me around now that I'm an adult," Pay said, loudly enough that anyone within earshot, and there appeared to be quite a few people, could hear him.

Pay came back inside and closed the door, breathing like he'd just run a marathon, his eyes burning with energy. But it didn't last, and Bryce saw Pay slump slightly, and the flames in his eyes faded.

"I'm so proud of you," Bryce said, barely able to speak.

"But I hit him," Pay said, and Bryce smiled.

"He deserved it, and so much more," Bryce said, taking Pay's hand. "Go wash his blood off so I can make sure you're okay." Bryce didn't think Pay had broken the skin on his hand, but he wanted to be sure. "Where's the card from the agents?" Pay handed him his wallet and walked toward the bathroom while Bryce made a phone call. Agent

Williams answered. "This is Bryce Morton, I think you should come to the trading post as soon as you can."

"Has something happened?" Agent Williams asked.

"Yes," Bryce said.

"We're on our way," the agent said, and he disconnected the call. Bryce was still holding the bundle wrapped in cloth, and he placed it back in his bag for later. The agents must have been close by because they pulled in front a few minutes later, a cloud of dust following them. They got out of the car as Pay slowly walked back toward the counter.

"I should clean this up," Pay said.

"No, just leave it," Bryce said, turning away from the window.

The agents walked inside and looked over the mess. "What happened?"

"Mark Grantham was here," Bryce said flatly. "He threatened Pay. Didn't confess to what he'd done in so many words, but he threatened Pay, and I guess Pay had had enough because he punched him in the nose and sent him sprawling."

The door opened and two of the old men came inside. "We saw the whole thing," one of the men said, and the other nodded his white-haired head. "Paytah didn't do nothing. Grantham tripped and fell flat on his face. Looked like he maybe broke his nose, though."

The agents looked at one another and then back at Pay without saying a word. "Sounds like reliable witnesses to me. We met with Mr. Grantham this morning and were about to come talk to you again when we got your call. We need corroboration of your story. He, of course, denies everything. We could take him in, but as it is, his lawyer will have him back out as soon as he gets there."

Pay sighed and looked defeated. "Get Chay," Bryce said, and Pay absently pulled his phone out of his pocket and pressed in a number.

"Coyote, it's Paytah. I need Chay, and Kangee if he'll talk," Pay said and then listened. Bryce saw Pay turn pale. "Okay, I'll see you all then." Pay hung up the phone and turned to Bryce. He looked like he was about to cry, and Bryce moved into his arms.

"What happened? Is Chay…?"

"What?" Pay asked. "Oh, God, no," he whispered. "It's Kangee. Coyote said they found him at Rainbow Gorge. He was about to throw himself off the side when they got to him. He's okay, but...." Pay's voice hitched. "They talked him down. Coyote said Chay talked him down," he clarified. "They're on their way. It'll take a while. He's a mess. They're going to drop him at home with his mother."

"Is Kangee the boy you were referring to yesterday?"

"Yes. He's fifteen," Pay said before swallowing hard.

"It's all right," Agent Williams said, and he turned to Agent Donley.

"I'm already on it," the other agent said and pulled out his phone.

"We're going to bring in a counselor. It looks like a lot of people are going to be hurt," Agent Williams said. He asked Pay for more details on what happened with Grantham and took pictures of the mess as well as statements from both of them. Bryce then cleaned up while Pay made more doughnuts and the agents made themselves at home. It appeared that the trading post was going to be Grantham Central for much of the day.

It took awhile, but Chay and Coyote arrived. Bryce stayed out of the agents' way as they talked to Chay. When they were done, Chay looked a bit shell-shocked, but his eyes appeared clear. "I'm sober," Chay told his brother quietly, "have been for days now. You were right. It is time I stopped running and took my life back. I figured if you could do it, then so could I."

"I'm proud of you, bro," Pay said. "It's hard doing what we're doing, but it is the right thing." Bryce turned away and left the two of them to talk. The agents talked together off in the far corner for a while and then they approached Bryce.

"I don't think there's anything more we can do here. Please call us if you need anything," Agent Williams said.

"Are you going to talk to Kangee?" Bryce asked. They didn't answer, but their expressions told Bryce what he needed to know. "I know you'll be as kind and careful as you can with him, but please let him know that what happened wasn't his fault." Bryce looked over and saw Pay still talking with his brother. "Pay said that Mark made him believe for a long time that what happened was his fault. I'm sure he did that to Kangee too."

Agent Williams nodded slowly. "When we talk to him, we'll be gentle, and we'll certainly tell him." Agent Williams turned to leave and then stopped. "That's very common and insidiously mean. It uses the victim's own need to please against them. We'll do our very best to help him any way we can," Agent Williams promised, and Bryce heard the sincerity in his voice. He watched them leave and then wandered to where Pay was talking to his brother. They were both smiling, so he felt it safe to approach.

"Where did they go?" Chay asked.

"They didn't say exactly, but I think they were going to talk to Kangee," Bryce said.

"That's not a good idea," Chay said with concern.

"I don't know. Maybe it's what he needs. Those two have seen a lot and they'll be able to tell him that things aren't his fault. Sometimes we need to hear things from strangers. They also called in a counselor, so they'll be able to get him some help."

"There are more," Chay said. "I don't know who, but there are more, I can feel it." Bryce nodded his agreement.

"I think that maybe it's time for one of you to go to the council. They need to know because they may be able to help other people who haven't come forward yet," Bryce suggested, and the brothers looked at one another. "If you don't want to do it yourselves, then see if Kiya will do it."

"No, I need to tell them," Pay said definitively. "I can't hide behind other people. This is something I have to do."

"Do you want me with you?" Bryce asked.

"No. I'll call the head of the council in a few minutes," Pay said, and Bryce sat back down at the table where his computer was, but he couldn't concentrate. He heard Pay making his phone call and Chay pacing the floor.

Things in the store calmed down for the next few hours. No one came in to threaten Pay, and the agents didn't call or show up with more questions. Pay got back to work, although he was jumpy as hell.

Chayton and Coyote stuck around for a while, but they eventually drifted off as well. Customers came in like usual, and Pay handled them, but it was becoming obvious that rumors were flying around the reservation and that people were stopping in to see if they were true.

Bryce had to hand it to Pay—he didn't pull any punches, and when they asked, he told them the truth. Most were shocked, a few didn't seem to believe it, but when Bryce chimed in that there were multiple victims, they changed their tune very quickly. From the expressions on many people's faces, a lot of kids and grandkids were going to be asked some difficult questions that evening.

"Do you think he'll press charges?" Pay asked sometime late in the afternoon.

"If he does, he's got more guts that I'd give him credit for," Bryce said. "No. I think right now, he's trying to figure a way out of this mess, but there isn't one. He could already be in custody. They have your statement as well as Chay's. But it's Kangee's that's the most damaging because it's the most recent." Bryce stepped over to where Pay was looking out one of the store windows. "If you want my advice, I think you should get ready to close up at your normal time. We'll head to the cabin for dinner and then spend the night together before I have to leave." Bryce hated to leave even more than he had when the day started. He'd promised Jerry he'd go back and there were appointments he couldn't postpone, no matter how badly he wanted to.

"It's supposed to rain," Pay said, forlornly.

"Then we can be together at the cabin or at your house," Bryce said. "Unless you'd rather be alone. I'll understand if you need some time." He hoped that wasn't the case, but he wouldn't blame Pay. With everything that had happened today, he could understand if Pay needed some time to himself to think, but it was their last night together for a while and Bryce really wanted to spend it with Pay.

"I was hoping to take you back to the canyon, but the shelter is not good for rain, especially if there's wind too. I'll come to the cabin with you," Pay said. "But no screaming," he added with a wicked grin.

"The screaming is all your fault and you know it," Bryce said, returning Pay's smile before checking his watch. There was only an hour left till closing, and Bryce spent it trying to work, but he got nothing done at all. His mind refused to settle on anything other than Pay, so he eventually gave up and helped Pay around the store. Whenever the door opened, they both glanced to see who it was. Bryce kept expecting the agents to come back, or even the police if Grantham turned out to be monumentally stupid, but it was just customers doing their shopping. Thank God.

At closing, Pay took care of the money and closed everything up before they left the building, locking the door behind them. As they headed over to Pay's car, Bryce's phone rang and then Pay's rang as well. Bryce answered his first.

"Honey, it's Kiya. The word through the grapevine is that Mark Grantham has been arrested." Bryce glanced at Pay, who was also smiling, and Bryce figured he was getting the word from someone else.

"Have you heard anything about Kangee?" Bryce asked. Kiya seemed to know everything about everyone.

"I talked to his mother a little while ago. She says he's going to be okay and they've talked a lot. She wants Mark's head on a platter, but it seems Kangee was most worried about hurting his mother, and once he knew she loved him no matter what, things settled down. She said she's going to find him some help. I also talked to the council president, and he's going to call a special meeting tomorrow. He was shocked off his ass, but agreed to look into bringing in a counselor to help both the kids and the families. This isn't going to be easy for anyone, the tribe the families, the children who were hurt, but we'll do all we can to help."

"The FBI said they were going to bring in counselors as well," Bryce said.

"Yes. But the council realized this will require long-term healing, and they want someone to help with that," Kiya explained.

"Good," Bryce said as he watched Pay continue to smile. That was what really mattered to him. In two weeks, he'd seen the gruff, almost snarly man he'd first met evolve into someone who actually smiled.

"I understand you're leaving tomorrow with Jerry and John. When will you be back?"

"Two weeks. I'm going to teach a class, and Dave said he'd have some possible product designs for me to look at."

"I know. He's already got me looking into possible grant money to help defray start-up costs, and I found someone who might be able to help put together a business plan. So you'll be busy when you visit."

"I appreciate all the help," Bryce said, and Kiya laughed.

"You're the one that's helped. We caught this bastard because of you, and half the tribe is excited about reintroducing buffalo into the range lands on the reservation. And if this craft company idea pans out, you'll have helped add jobs. So it's we who should be thanking you."

"No. I just had the idea," Bryce said modestly.

Kiya humphed softly, and Bryce thought for sure she was going to call him on his modesty. Thankfully she let it go. "You always have a place here. You're family, just like Jerry." Bryce knew Kiya was being nice, and he thanked her before disconnecting the call. He'd like to think he'd made an impression on the people here and that they would come to accept him, but he knew he'd always be an outsider. Eventually, maybe he'd consider living here with Pay. He'd deal with it to be with him once they'd had the time to build a permanent foundation for their relationship.

"He's in jail," Pay said as soon as Bryce hung up the phone.

"Kiya told me," Bryce explained.

"Coyote told me that now the word is out, three more kids have come forward, as well as another two adults." Pay shook slightly. "I knew there would be more, but these are all people I know. Some are customers I see every few days."

"This is going to ripple through the entire reservation. He hurt a lot of people, and everyone here is going to know someone involved. I hope the tribe comes together over this and really stands by you and everyone else who was hurt." Bryce moved closer to Pay and placed an arm around Pay's waist. "I'm here for you and I always will be." Bryce leaned up and was about to kiss Pay when he saw some of the old men walking toward the bench in front of the store for what he presumed was their evening sit and chat. Not really caring who saw or what they thought, Bryce tugged Pay toward him, taking his lips in a deep kiss. Everyone and everything around them faded as soon as their lips touched. Bryce only cared about Pay, and when his kiss was returned and Pay wrapped his arms around Bryce's waist to tug them closer, nothing else mattered.

"Let's go," Pay said once they broke their kiss. "I don't want to kiss you in front of an audience."

"Okay," Bryce agreed, although the rebellious part of him liked the occasional public display of affection. Pay was his and Bryce wanted everyone to know it. "Let's go have some dinner."

"I need to clean up before I can go anywhere," Pay said as they headed to his place.

"Me too. Do you think a bit of water conservation is in order?" Bryce asked while Pay unlocked the door. He turned around, looking at Bryce like he didn't understand, and then he smiled and nodded.

Bryce set his bag on one of the chairs and followed Pay through to the bathroom. Pay turned on the water before pulling off his clothes. Bryce forgot to get undressed as he watched Pay's deep copper skin appear. "Are you going to join me?" Pay asked.

"Yes. I was just watching," Bryce said before pulling Pay closer. "I love to watch you get naked." Bryce kissed Pay, cupping him lightly in his hand, Pay's cock growing hard at his touch. "What I really like is how I can make you do that," Bryce said, his voice a low rumble as he gripped Pay hard, stroking him.

"Get undressed," Pay said as he thrust his hips. Bryce let go and began removing his clothes, with Pay helping. Obviously, he wasn't moving fast enough. Once Bryce was naked, Pay stepped into the shower, and Bryce followed right behind, his gaze locked on Pay's firm, round, perfect butt.

"You have butt dimples," Bryce said as he traced the sides of Pay's butt cheeks with his fingers before pressing himself to Pay's back, nestling his cock perfectly between Pay's butt cheeks. "I love that you have dimples when you smile...." Bryce began to giggle. "Does that mean your butt is smiling for me?"

"Come here, you goof," Pay said as he turned around and then tugged Bryce close, moving them beneath the water. Bryce's giggles subsided when Pay's skin pressed to his, and he forgot about everything other than his lover. Pay reached for the soap and backed away slightly. He worked up a lather and then began caressing Bryce's skin. "Step back," Pay whispered, and Bryce moved out from under the water. "Turn around," Pay said, and Bryce complied.

Pay began at Bryce's shoulders, soaping and massaging them deeply. Then Pay moved down his back and Bryce sighed, closing his eyes. Anticipating that Pay would continue moving lower, he thrust his butt backward, but Pay continued washing his back, and then he began to sing. Bryce didn't understand the words, but that didn't matter. The tone was deep and low in Pay's throat, and the sounds rumbled through Bryce as they filled the small space.

"What is that?" Bryce asked when Pay paused.

"It's a very old love song," Pay answered and began to sing again. He paused in his washing and then started again, this time, finally, caressing Bryce's butt and upper legs. The song became more intense, and Bryce's cock throbbed from both the melody and the way Pay caressed his skin. Pay rubbed him more intensely, parting his cheeks and lightly sliding his soapy fingers over Bryce's opening and then down, between his legs, reaching through to lightly cup his balls and then back.

"Pay," Bryce whined softly, his legs beginning to shake. Bryce held still, and Pay continued his erotic washing while he sang his love song. Pay tapped his hip, and Bryce turned around, his cock jutting forward. Pay got more soap and started washing him again. Bryce's chest was first, followed by his legs, which were shaking so badly Bryce could barely stand.

When Pay wrapped his fingers around Bryce's cock and slowly began to tug, Bryce placed his hands on Pay's shoulders to steady himself. He closed his eyes and let his head loll back as the soapy slickness sent tingles all through him.

Pay stopped rather abruptly, and Bryce opened his eyes in time for Pay to press against him once more, gently pushing him back under the spray. The soap washed away, and the water sluiced over both of them. Then Bryce got the soap and it was his turn. Stepping back from the water, Bryce slicked his hands with mounds of suds, and then Pay stepped from under the water. Bryce touched his skin, washing his shoulders and chest, paying special attention to Pay's nipples. He'd discovered quite early in his explorations of his lover's body that Pay's nipples were sensitive, so each time he came close, Bryce gave them a little tweak, and Paytah would sigh and a shudder would ripple through him. Bryce loved that he could make Pay react with such a simple touch. It was a visual and aural reminder of what Pay felt for him, and Bryce's own love for the man whose rich copper skin, now covered with soap bubbles, flowed beneath his hands. "I love you, Pay," Bryce whispered, a bit overcome, and Pay took him in his arms, pressing and sliding his soapy skin against Bryce's.

"I love you too," Pay said, and Bryce lifted his gaze. "I know you have to leave. You have a job, and so do I. But I know you'll be back."

"Yes, but I hate to leave you when everything seems like it's going to be so hard on you," Bryce said.

"No. You made so many things so much easier, and I feel freer than I have for as long as I can remember." Pay stroked Bryce's cheeks. "Everything is going to be fine, and you'll be back soon." Pay once again moved them under the water. "I have plenty to keep me busy, thanks to you. Chay seems determined to move on with his life, and there will be many kids who are going to need help, so I think I'm going to try to do what I can. I've been through what they're going through now and I survived, so I need to help them do the same."

"But...," Bryce began.

"I think we both need a bit of time to figure out if what's between us is truly lasting. I think it is, but we need to be sure," Pay told him. Bryce wasn't happy to hear his own words come back to him. Pay turned off the water and reached out of the shower, handing him a towel before getting one for himself. They dried themselves, and Pay left the bathroom to get dressed while Bryce gathered up the clothes he'd worn and put them back on, wishing he'd brought fresh things, but he figured he could change once they got to the cabin.

Once dressed, Bryce met Pay in the living room. "I was going to give you this earlier, but we got interrupted." Bryce dug in his bag and pulled out the cloth bundle. "Kiya told me that she wove this bit of cloth when she was a girl and she wanted me to have it to take with me so I would remember everyone here," Bryce said and slowly opened the bundle until he got to the center. "I asked her to help me come up with something I could give you that would be both traditional and special. So I asked Running Deer to help, and he made this." Bryce opened the cloth, and inside was a small wooden carving of a buffalo. The detail was amazing for something so tiny, and on its back were two small gold loops. Bryce lifted out the buffalo and handed it to Pay.

"This is for me?" Pay said, and Bryce nodded, lifting out the two cords he found hidden in one of the folds of the fabric.

"Let me show you." Bryce gently took the buffalo and carefully pulled the two halves apart, so they each had half of the buffalo. "Each has a small pin to hold it together," Bryce said as he fed a cord through the gold loop and handed it to Pay. "You keep one half and I keep the other," Bryce said, feeding the second cord through his half. "Like I said, I wanted something one of a kind and something special. The buffalo was a symbol of your people. Historically, it meant life to them. Without the buffalo, they would have starved as they roamed the plains." Bryce moved closer to Pay. "Without you, I think my soul would starve." Bryce felt his voice begin to falter, but he held steady. "After I lost Percy, I never thought I would feel for another person what I felt for him, but I do with you." Bryce took the cord with its small buffalo suspended from it and carefully placed it around Pay's neck. Then he took his own and handed it to Pay so he could do the same for him. "I love you, Pay," Bryce said as he held still, waiting until Pay had finished.

"I love you too, Bryce," Pay said as he moved back. Bryce touched his neck, feeling the small buffalo that hung at the base of his throat. "Your gift is beautiful, and whenever I see it, I'll always think of you. I know you have to go for now, but with this, I'll always have you near." Pay, too, touched the carved buffalo at his throat. "This is a beautiful and thoughtful gift. Thank you," Pay added before leaning in closer, moving almost in slow motion until their lips touched in a kiss of profound need and hunger that quickly deepened until Bryce was engulfed in Pay's arms, pressed to his strong body, where he wanted to remain always. But that wasn't possible, at least for now, so Bryce reveled in each touch.

"What do you want?" Bryce asked Pay.

"I want to take you back to the cabin and have dinner with your friends, because you need to finish getting ready to leave. Then I want to take you to bed and spend the night giving you something so that when you do go, you'll have part of me to remember, something special in your heart that will last you until you return," Pay said, and then he kissed Bryce hard. Bryce held Pay's shoulders for balance and returned the kiss with everything he had. Then Pay broke the kiss and stepped back before taking Bryce's hand. "Come on, we need to go or Jerry and Akecheta will wonder what happened to us."

"But...," Bryce sputtered.

"We'll have all night," Pay whispered before leaning in to lick the spot behind Bryce's ear. "And I promise you it'll be worth it." Pay licked his skin, and Bryce shivered. Then Pay led him by the hand out of the house and to his car. Bryce got in, glancing over at Pay with a smile every few seconds as they drove out to the cabin. Finally, when he could keep his hands to himself no longer, he reached across and placed his hand lightly on Pay's leg.

When they arrived, they had a welcoming committee. Mato and Ichante hurried out to greet them, excitedly tugging them both in for dinner, which was raucous, joyful, and in a word, wonderful. Bryce packed once they were done. Jerry and John let the kids stay up later than usual so they would sleep on the trip in the morning, and then at nearly ten, with the kids in bed, Bryce took Pay's hand, and after saying good night to John and Jerry, led him to the bedroom and closed the door.

Pay kept his promise, making love to Bryce for most of the night. They were quiet because they had to be, but that only meant Bryce couldn't cry out—not that he didn't want to, over and over again. Eventually, they both fell asleep, only to wake up early so they could make final preparations to leave. Pay helped them load the van, and then John and Jerry got the kids, situating them in the backseat, where they promptly went back to sleep.

"I'll see you in a few weeks," Pay said, and Bryce nodded before throwing himself into Pay's arms. They hugged, and then Pay kissed him. "It won't be forever."

"No, it won't, but it'll seem like forever." Bryce kissed Pay again before hugging him one last time. "I can feel you everywhere," Bryce whispered, and Pay squeezed him hard. Then he let go, and Bryce walked to the van, got in, and quietly closed the door. John turned the van around and then slowly headed down the foliage tunnel. Bryce turned around and waved to Pay one last time before he disappeared from sight.

THE ride home took hours, but they got back to Sioux Falls in the early afternoon. John dropped him off at his house, and they all helped him unload his things before saying good-bye. Bryce waved to the kids and then turned and walked inside, closing the door behind him. Everything was quiet, so quiet he could hear himself breathe. Too quiet. He'd spent the last two weeks with the kids, John and Jerry, and Pay… God, he missed Pay already.

Moping about it wasn't going to help, so Bryce hauled his bags to the laundry room and began filling the washer with a load of dark clothes, placing almost everything he'd brought back into the baskets to be washed. The few clean clothes that were left he carried upstairs to his bedroom to put away.

Bryce pulled opened his dresser drawers, and a picture of Percy he'd put away caught his eye. Pulling out the framed photograph, he stared into the eyes of the man who was to have been his husband. "I found him, Percy. You told me there was someone else for me, and I found him." Bryce traced Percy's face with his finger. "Thank you," Bryce whispered, and then he placed the picture back in the drawer and slowly closed it.

EPILOGUE

"BRYCE, we're going to be late," Pay called from the living room, and then Bryce heard his footsteps through the house. "You'll probably need a jacket," Pay added from the doorway.

"That's what I figured," Bryce said, leaning his head toward the bed, where his jacket had been laid out, as he fastened the small carved buffalo around his neck. When it was secured, Bryce lowered his hands to look at Pay. They were both in jeans and heavy shirts. Yes, they were heading for a ceremony, but it was going to be outside in April, so everyone had been instructed to dress appropriately. In the vee of Pay's collar, Bryce saw that he, too, was wearing his buffalo. Bryce grabbed his jacket and hurried to the bathroom to make sure he looked okay before joining Pay back in the bedroom.

"You look fine," Pay said before tugging Bryce in for a kiss. "More than fine, you look edible," Pay growled.

Bryce chuckled deeply. "You didn't get enough last night?"

"No. I haven't seen you in two weeks," Pay said. "Wouldn't matter anyway, I can't seem to get enough of you." A year hadn't mattered one bit in that regard.

"Me too," Bryce moaned as Pay sucked lightly on his ear. "But didn't someone say something about being late?" Bryce asked, and Pay growled but stopped his nibbling. "When we get back," Bryce promised, and Pay grabbed his butt in what Bryce interpreted as his promise of things to come.

Bryce picked his jacket up off the bed again and followed Pay out. As he approached Pay's car, he glanced over at the trading post, its lights off and door closed. Because of the ceremony, Pay had closed the store for the morning. Most people would be at the ceremony anyway, so he wouldn't be losing much business. Bryce slid into the passenger seat and belted himself in, waiting for Pay, who wandered over to the store to do a quick check and then got in the driver's seat.

The drive took a while. The ceremony was being held in a more remote area of the reservation that Bryce wasn't familiar with. As they rode, the roads got rougher and less used, but they were by no means alone. A steady stream of cars, trucks, and vans followed the road, and they joined the convoy as it wove through some of the most picturesque scenery Bryce had seen on the reservation. "How far is it?"

"Not much farther," Pay said, concentrating ahead of him. Eventually the area around the road widened, the trees and scrub fell away, and an area of relatively flat grassland spread out before them. The cars in front pulled off and began to park. Pay followed behind them and parked, and then they got out, with Pay leading Bryce toward a group of tents. "The council decided to make this a festival since everyone was going to be here."

Bryce nodded and looked all around as people in traditional clothing walked past, heading toward an authentic stand of teepees off to one side. "This is amazing," Bryce said, glancing at Pay, who smiled. "You didn't say anything about all this."

"I wanted you to be surprised," Pay told him and led him toward one of the tents. Running Deer, also known as Dave, smiled from in front of his display of carvings and pottery.

"Bryce," Dave said happily as they shook hands. "Did you have a good drive out?"

"Yes. The roads were clear and I'm sort of getting used to it," he said, bumping Pay's hip lightly. "So how are things going?" Bryce asked as he looked through the booth. "Your work keeps getting more and more amazing," A carved buffalo, basically a larger version of the tiny one that hung from his neck, caught his eye. Bryce picked it up and carefully handled it, amazed at the detail in the horns, the rough texture around the buffalo's head, even the snorting expression on the animal's face. The sculpture looked as though it was at a full run. "Would you put this aside for me?" Bryce asked.

"Of course," Dave said with a pleased smile.

"I told you," Pay said to Dave, and the two shared a smirk. "I saw that last week and told him you'd want it as soon as you saw it."

"Uncle Bryce!" He turned around and saw Little Wamblee holding Frankie's hand as the two brothers walked toward him. Little Wamblee let go of Frankie's hand, and he toddled toward Bryce, holding his arms out to be picked up. Bryce swung him into his arms to peals of little-boy giggles.

"You're getting so big," Bryce told the toddler, who pointed to a booth where Hanna was sitting.

"Mama," Frankie said as clear as a bell, pointing toward his mother.

"Uncle Bryce, Mama asked us to bring you over," Little Wamblee said, although he wasn't so little anymore. The youngster was growing like a weed. One thing Bryce noticed was that the hollow-eyed child he'd seen that first time Little Wamblee had come into the store had been replaced with a healthy, joyful boy. Both kids were clean, happy, and wore decent clothes.

"Okay," Bryce said, following Little Wamblee to where he indicated. "Morning, Hanna," Bryce said as they approached, and she smiled up at him from her chair, a partially formed basket in her hands. "How are things going?" Hanna had turned out to be a diamond in the rough. Dave and Pay had brought her in to help with the craft business, and she'd turned into a marketing and sales dynamo.

"Great. The grant Kiya helped us get got us started. We've got eight artisans working part time." She indicated examples of pipes, dolls, baskets, bowls, and a few toys on the table. "So far I have twelve stores in the region that have purchased items for the tourist season, and the website you set up for us is generating traffic and steady sales." She grinned at Bryce. "I even got the national park gift shop to carry our things at Mount Rushmore." Her energy and enthusiasm were amazing. "I'm hoping we'll do well this year." The entire time she was talking, Hanna's hands never stopped their work on the basket. It was simple, but the finished products were painted with traditional designs. The actual items were polished, quite impressive, and each item retailed for between thirty and fifty dollars.

"Are you able to stick to our price points?" Bryce asked, picking up the doll from the table. Frankie reached for it, and Bryce had to lift it out of his grasp.

"Yes. It hasn't been easy, but we're doing it," she explained as she finished, looking down at her hands for the first time, completing the rim of the basket and then setting it aside. "The hardest item is the baskets because of the handwork in them, but they're also one of the best sellers on the website."

Bryce watched her start another basket, pulling the precut strips from the bag beside her. "If it doesn't make sense to sell the baskets in the gift shops, make them a website exclusive. That way the cost isn't as big a factor because you're selling them at full retail rather than wholesale, or you can raise the price if you think it won't hurt sales too badly. Think about it."

"I will," she said happily.

"Come see the teepees," Little Wamblee said, and Bryce let himself be tugged along. Pay had disappeared somewhere into the crowd, but he reappeared at Bryce's side as they approached the conical dwellings. Bryce peered inside and was greeted by many of the men inside sitting around a small fire smoking a pipe, the smoke billowing up and out a small opening in the top. He returned their greeting and talked briefly before moving on.

"Bryce, they're about ready to get started," Pay said. Bryce set Frankie on his feet, and Little Wamblee held his hand as they walked together toward their mother.

"I'll see you later," Little Wamblee called, and Frankie turned and waved so vigorously, he nearly fell over.

"They're great kids," Bryce said softly, unable to get over the difference in the entire family.

"Hanna's happy," Pay said. "She's only working the one job and she's been doing amazing work with the craft company." Pay sighed. "I doubt it will turn a profit this year, but they're making and selling product, which is helping to bring money and hope to the reservation." Pay guided him toward where everyone was gathering near a small, temporary platform.

"Welcome all!" the president of the council said into a microphone, thankfully without any screeching or feedback. "Today is a monumental day for our tribe, because today we celebrate our heritage as well as our future. We have booths displaying and selling traditional crafts, and the ladies have made some incredible food." Bryce's stomach rumbled as a gentle breeze blew the aroma over the crowd. He hadn't realized how hungry he was until now. "We have displays and demonstrations of our culture," the president added, pointing to the teepees and other demonstrations. "This afternoon there will be contests based on traditional skills for all ages." Excited murmurs rose from the crowd, and Bryce looked around at the sea of happy faces as he leaned contentedly against Pay.

"Uncle Bryce," Mato whispered as he came up beside him. "Grammy and Paw-Paw want you." Bryce looked at Pay, who said nothing, and they followed Mato around the crowd and off to the side where Bryce saw Kiya and Wamblee standing together.

The president became somber as he stood in front of the microphone. "I know today is a day of celebration, but we must also note the hardships many of us have suffered in the last months."

Bryce knew he was referring to the business with Mark Grantham. Nearly two dozen children and adults had come forward. The trial had yet to be held, and thankfully the press had kept their distance from the reservation. At first, there had been speculation in the national media that Grantham was innocent, but that had quickly dissipated once it became clear how many people were involved. Mark Grantham's support had evaporated after that, and in addition to criminal charges, the tribe was suing his family's foundation on behalf of all those affected. Of course, that could take years, but in some strange, almost perverse way, what had happened brought the tribe together. It unified them against Grantham, but more importantly, it made them come together and create the best from their situation that they were able. Pay had told him that this fair was just one of the results.

"We will help one another and support one another," the president continued. "We are all each other's brothers and sisters, and what doesn't kill us makes us stronger. We are strong, and we will look out for and help those who need it." He became choked up and paused for a few seconds.

"But today," the president said after clearing his throat, "we are here to dedicate the restoration of a piece of our heritage. Kiya and Wamblee Black Raven came to the council with a proposal last fall to restore buffalo to the reservation. It intrigued us all, and last fall, after petitioning the state, and after demonstrating our ability to care for them, the state donated twenty head from their herd in Custer State Park, with the promise of up to an additional twenty head for the next two years. I'm pleased to report that those twenty head are thriving, and two calves were born this spring. The state has approved the delivery of the second twenty head in the next few months." Everyone clapped and cheered. "This means that these buffalo are the first herd to live on this land, our land, in over a century." Everyone applauded and cheered loudly. The council president waited until the sound faded. "Our plans are to let the herd grow and become strong. It will take time, but it will happen. Then we will manage it and use it to help provide an income for the tribe. As I said, this will take time, but it's already starting." The cheers rose again, and Bryce clapped along with everyone else.

"Now, there's one more story to tell before I shut up and let you all get back to the fun. The idea to bring buffalo back to our land did not originate from someone within our tribe. The man who suggested the idea was also instrumental in getting the state to change its policy of culling their herd and instead donated their excess to us. This man has also contributed to the formation of a company here on the reservation to produce and sell traditionally inspired crafts."

Bryce turned to Pay, who was grinning from ear to ear. "Did you know about this?" Bryce whispered, but Pay, the bastard, only grinned.

"This company has already brought jobs to the reservation, and as it grows, we hope more will be created. So without going on forever"— he paused as people clapped and laughed—"I'd like to announce that the herd of buffalo you see in the distance will be officially known as the Bryce Morton Buffalo Herd." Everyone applauded, and Bryce stood rooted on his spot as all eyes shifted from the council president to him.

"Go on," Pay said, and Bryce walked slowly to the platform, stepping up next to the president of the council. Bryce looked out on the gathered crowd, all of them smiling at him, but Bryce's gaze tended to travel to Pay and stay there. He was the only one he really wanted to see.

"Today we dedicate this buffalo herd in your name. It's because of you that it's here," the president said. Bryce shook the tribal president's hand and then prepared to step down. "I'm not quite finished, young man," he said, and Bryce colored and stepped back. "Now, dedicating what we believe to be the only buffalo herd on Native American land to a man who is not a member of a Native American tribe is not acceptable, and in order to be a full tribal member, you must be born into the tribe, but we hope we've done the next best thing. So, Bryce Morton, we officially adopt you as a member of this tribe. Each and every one of the men and women in front of you are now your brothers and sisters. You've already demonstrated the kind of tribal member you'll be, and I'm personally pleased and honored to welcome you to our family."

Bryce thought he was going to cry right there in front of everyone. He turned and shook the council president's hand before walking off the platform and back onto solid ground. "You all knew," Bryce accused when he reached Pay, Kiya, and Wamblee.

"Yes, we knew," Wamblee said with a huge grin. "But you know if it wasn't for all your ideas, none of this would have happened. No, you deserve every bit of it, and as he said, you are part of this extended family." Wamblee extended his hand, and Bryce shook it. Then Kiya gave him a hug, followed by John and Jerry. Then Bryce turned to Pay.

"I think I proved you wrong," Pay said, and Bryce looked at him, completely confused. "Some months ago, you said that you loved it here, but that you felt you'd never been accepted, that you'd always be an outsider. Well, you have to know you aren't an outsider any longer." Pay took his hand and led him away from the crowds to a grassy spot under a small tree. "You aren't an outsider, not any longer."

"No, I guess not."

"So I want to ask you, formally, to come live here with me. I can turn the second bedroom of the house into an office for you where you can work," Pay said, and Bryce grinned. "What's that for?"

"It seems Jerry is one step ahead of you. He told me a few days ago that he found a small building on the reservation that he was planning to turn into a satellite office. He wanted enough room for two people and enough space that he and John can work there when they spend time here. It seems he's opened another branch, and he wants me to run it for him."

Pay stood quiet until what Bryce had told him sank in. "So are you saying what I think you are?"

"I told Jerry that as long as a certain person—" Bryce paused and moved closer to Pay. "—was willing to put up with me for the next thirty or forty years, I'd be happy to accept his offer." Bryce burst into a smile, and Pay hugged Bryce close, lifting him off his feet.

"Yes," Pay said laughing. Then he set Bryce back on his feet and kissed him hard in full view of half the tribe. "I love you." Bryce truly meant to tell Pay how much he meant to him, but his words were cut off by another kiss, and that was fine—talk was overrated anyhow.

ANDREW GREY grew up in western Michigan with a father who loved to tell stories and a mother who loved to read them. Since then he has lived throughout the country and traveled throughout the world. He has a master's degree from the University of Wisconsin-Milwaukee and works in information systems for a large corporation. Andrew's hobbies include collecting antiques, gardening, and leaving his dirty dishes anywhere but in the sink (particularly when writing). He considers himself blessed with an accepting family, fantastic friends, and the world's most supportive and loving partner. Andrew currently lives in beautiful historic Carlisle, Pennsylvania.

Visit Andrew's website at http://www.andrewgreybooks.com and blog at http://andrewgreybooks.livejournal.com/.

E-mail him at andrewgrey@comcast.net.

Also from ANDREW GREY

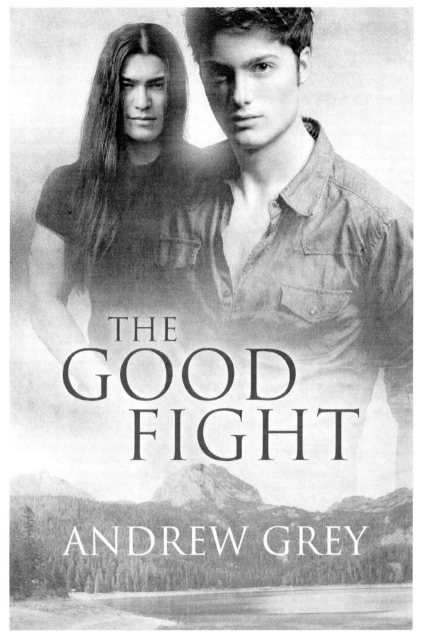

THE
GOOD
FIGHT

ANDREW GREY

http://www.dreamspinnerpress.com

Romance from ANDREW GREY

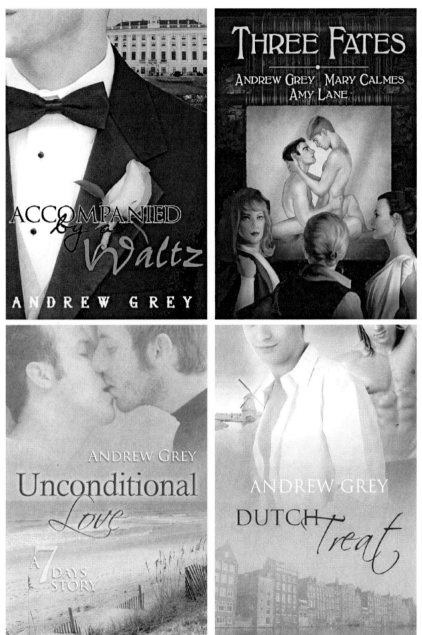

http://www.dreamspinnerpress.com

STORIES FROM THE RANGE

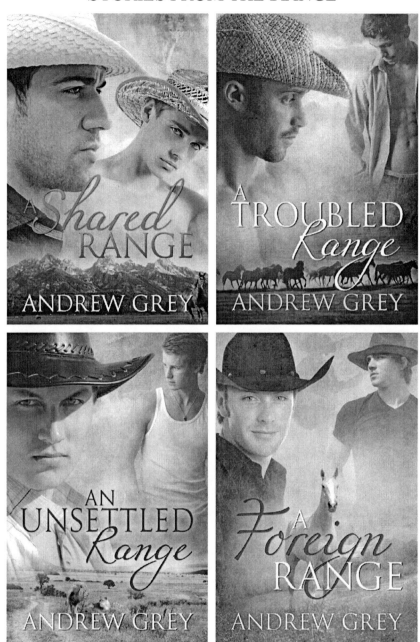

http://www.dreamspinnerpress.com

BOTTLED UP STORIES

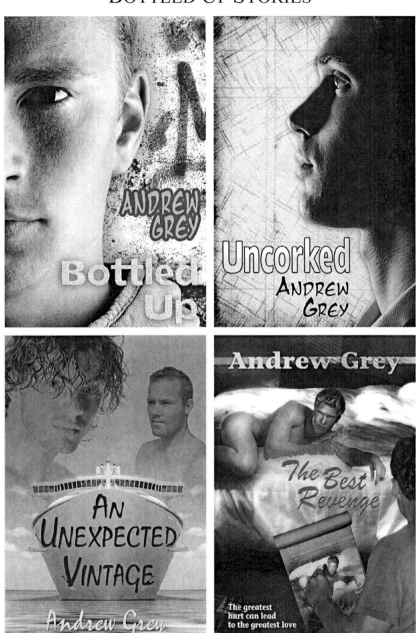

http://www.dreamspinnerpress.com

LOVE MEANS…

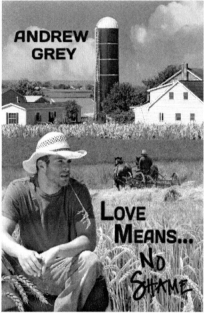

http://www.dreamspinnerpress.com

Now in French, Italian, and Spanish

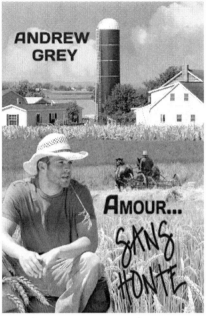

THE ART SERIES

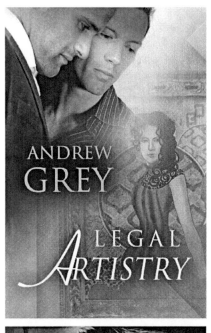

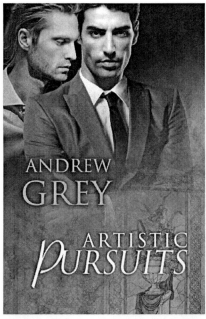

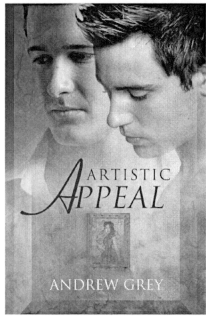

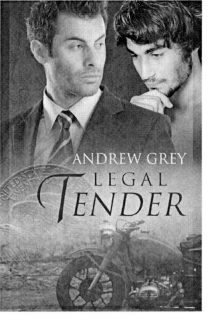

http://www.dreamspinnerpress.com

Also from ANDREW GREY

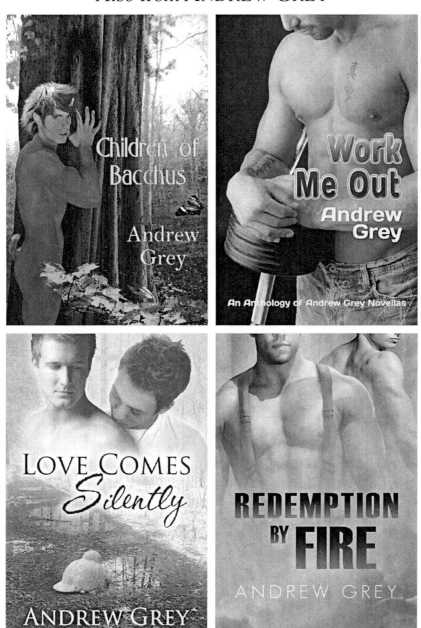

http://www.dreamspinnerpress.com

CPSIA information can be obtained
at www.ICGtesting.com
Printed in the USA
FFOW01n2122070414
4699FF